Returning Your Love

Pippen Creek 1

Lynn Burke

PIPPEN CREEK

Chapter 1

Jamie

Career-ending injury.

Three words no one wanted to hear, especially a rising football star who'd been dreaming since childhood about making it into the NFL.

"Doing okay, kid?"

I cracked an eyelid open.

Dad sat on the chair beside my hospital bed, his eyebrows pinched and lips in a thin line. His wide shoulders were hunched, evidence of his weariness.

Rain slashed against the gray window behind him, the flashes of lightning attempting to brighten the early morning sky that was as dismal as my mood.

"This fucking sucks," I muttered, glancing down at the IV needle stuck into my arm, ready for the meds that would knock me out before going under the knife. A quaint little rest where nothing mattered and I would wake once more to the heaviness clinging to me like a weighted blanket on a hot summer night.

I huffed a sigh and turned my focus on the bright, white

ceiling above me, the scent of bleach and lemon cleaner burning my nose.

Week ten of my rookie season with Houston started with the expectation I would hit one thousand rushing yards while going head-to-head with New England. Shit had been on my side until I got tackled out of nowhere, my body spinning but right foot planted firm in grass and dirt as I went down. The pop in my knee had sounded like a gunshot, leaving me with a combined ACL and meniscal tear—the worst my attending surgeon had ever seen.

So much for being Offensive Rookie of the Year or making it into the Hall of Fame. And I could kiss the rest of my contract worth millions goodbye too.

Desolation stifled, and there would be no easy tossing aside its weight.

A code blue crackled through the speaker right outside my cubicle in pre-surgery, but I couldn't find concern for someone else's pain or grief. Therapy hovered on the horizon along with the physical type because I would spiral into despair if I didn't. I had grit as Dad would say, but this devastation?

Soothing a weary hand over my face and scruffy jaw, I emptied my lungs with a defeated grunt when I should have been hungover from celebrating our tenth win of the season. "My teammates crushed the Pats last night, but I'm really struggling to believe my playing days are officially over, Dad."

He squeezed my forearm, an offering of reassurance I wished could do more to comfort me. "I won't bullshit."

I snorted. Typical Dad telling it like it is. "Thanks for flying down here though. Means a lot."

A brief nod dipped his head, his tired hazel eyes tracking over my face as though he was trying to root out how I dealt with this blow. His missing out on the NFL had been due to knocking up his girlfriend in high school, but he'd never once blamed me. He'd also never pushed his own dreams and expectations on me like some dads did, but his constant support had kept me fighting.

"I can't imagine it was easy getting off work," I said, more thankful than ever to have him as a role model growing up. Lots of kids weren't as lucky.

"I'm the chief. I can do whatever the hell I want," Dad said with a small smirk. "Seriously, though, we're still short on help, but nothing would keep me from being here for you."

"Never considered something like this to bring you halfway across the country."

"We Foresters tend to see the light and not expect the worst." Dad spoke what used to be true. He'd always been a pretty positive guy, but that didn't allow for sugarcoating shit. I'd been that way too until my mom abandoned us. Expecting the worst came second nature now.

Mom—aka Darla—had left us both when I was fourteen. Even worse, Dad hadn't known about the shit she'd been up to behind his back. The fraudulent checks. Maxing credit cards and not paying them. Siphoning money from the fundraisers she'd been in charge of as Pippen Creek's Chief of Police's other half.

She'd been a great wife and mom.

Until she wasn't.

Dad and I had gotten super close after she'd gone, and I felt confident in the one parent in my corner who supported me no matter what.

"What the hell am I gonna do now, Dad?"

"At least you stuck to college and got your degree. I'm sure you'll find work back home."

The sticks of northern New Hampshire was the place I'd escaped from, and I wasn't too excited to head there again. It'd been years since I'd set foot in Pippen Creek and for good reason. The people in my small town hadn't ever been homophobic, but wariness had kept my mouth shut about my sexuality. I hadn't even told my best friend Chaz because queer dudes didn't step foot on a football field, and I'd had big plans since grade school and the talent to achieve them.

I had wanted a new start outside my hometown. To pave a path toward a winning season. Make a name for myself before retiring and figure out how to enjoy life off the gridiron because that was where most of my joy came from. While I'd managed to tick off that first goal of leaving no-man's land, everything else had gotten tipped off a cliff where jagged rocks had shattered my dreams.

Someone pushing a clanging medical cart strode past the curtain that blocked me off from the rest of the patients waiting to be sliced open.

"Coach Bernard has been talking about retiring for over decade." Dad shifted on his hardback chair, rubbing a roughened hand over his gray-speckled beard. "Maybe your return will be the encouragement he needs to visit Arizona like he's been dreaming of for half of forever."

Go back home to coach high school football. Could my life be any more cliche?

I grimaced rather than snorting.

No fucking way my happily ever after would come about like a goddamn Hallmark movie. A marriage had taken place four years ago that ensured my lifelong heartache and loneliness.

"Yeah, we'll see, Dad," I said noncommittally. "Right now, I need to focus on healing. Probably gonna sell my condo down here and move back to Boston though. I at least have a few friends up there."

Hell, not a single Houston teammate had reached out to me since last night's win to see how I was doing. Coach and the head trainer had called for an update, but that was it. Guess no one cared their star running back was gone for good.

Life went on, right?

Dad squeezed my forearm again as my eyes slid closed against reality. "Hang in there, kid. This shit sucks, but you'll come out stronger on the other side."

I appreciated his words of encouragement, but they did fuck-all to make me feel any better.

"Jamie Forester?"

A dude in scrubs and cap over his brown hair rounded the curtain with a smile on his face.

It's go time—I've got this.

My Boston apartment window was cracked open, the cool evening air like a kiss on my bare skin. I sprawled naked as usual on my couch, bored with my unemployment, missing football, and horny as fuck.

As expected, surgery hadn't done jack toward getting me back on the field, but at least I could walk around with a barely noticeable limp and had finally been given the green light for heavier lifting. It'd been a long-as-fuck five months full of agonizing stretching, physical therapy, and sitting with a shrink to keep me from spiraling. Regardless of hours spent with my therapist, I still hadn't figured out what to do with myself because nothing compared to rushing into the end zone.

I'd been celibate for a goddamned year too, and there was no one around I was comfortable enough with to help ease the restlessness brewing in my balls I toyed with.

Since my NFL career had been shot to shit, I at least didn't have to keep my sexuality to myself. I wouldn't call it a silver lining though. No matter how badly I needed to get laid, I couldn't stomach a quickie with a random off Grindr. That shit just wasn't for me. I needed some sort of connection before sharing my body.

Back in college when I'd been in the closet and desperate to get laid, I'd gone to crazy lengths to be able to afford the action I needed. I opened a faceless OnlyFans account, and with my body unmarked by tattoos, no one had known the muscled jock's real name. I'd never done a collaboration and had quadruple-checked to make sure my live backgrounds and pre-recorded videos were clean as a whistle as far as telltale giveaways of where I lived before uploading them for salivating fans.

Jerking off and playing with my hole online had afforded me the financial ability to book with Elite Escorts MM. Not only did they ensure confidentiality, but I was also a paying client, which meant I had time to connect with someone before getting dicked down.

The second I'd laid eyes on the escort Zack, I'd been driven to meet him and eventually have him on top of and beneath me. Even before checking out how he preferred to please customers, I'd set a financial goal so I could book a night to get to know him. OnlyFans had given me that opportunity, and I'd taken advantage of the discreet escort service to ease that deep itch inside me.

I'd gone through those great lengths for a few nights with Zack because he looked like the guy who had owned my heart since childhood. He had the same muscular build, dark hair, and hazel eyes as Chaz, my best friend who'd married the third member of our three musketeers from high school.

Last I'd heard, Chaz and Shelly were still together, happily married, and trying for a baby. Having to watch them first hold hands our sophomore year then start kissing over the summer had been as motivating for me to leave Pippen Creek as the drive to be drafted into the NFL.

My stomach turned over the memories assaulting me, so I shoved them from my mind and got back to my dick that had wilted somewhat. A few strokes over my length while thinking about sinking into a tight hole brought my hard-on back to full life, but jerking off again just wasn't going to cut it this time. Having no other options, I picked my cell up off the cushion beside me with my free hand, the other still playing with my shaft and soft sac.

As an escort, Zack had known exactly how to please. Give and take, he'd been a pretty damn good fit for whenever my need had grown too great and using a dildo on myself for my subscribers hadn't been enough to satisfy my craving to be stuffed full.

And tonight, I wanted Zack to wreck my hole. Hold me down and make me forget the shit of the last five months and my uncertain future since all my plans, my goals, had been torn apart and still bled.

I opened my bookmarks and frowned at finding his webpage on EEMM gone from existence. The dent between my eyebrows dipped deeper the more I searched Elite's site. Zack was no longer listed as one of their escorts.

"Fuck," I grumbled, scrolling through the remaining men on offer. I would have to start from scratch, but if someone caught my eye, I didn't mind putting in the time to connect with them so I could get off without having to use my hand.

And since I'd gotten a portion of my original contract, I could definitely afford the cost of one of Elite's escorts.

None of their Tall, Dark, and Handsome or Dominants reminded me of the man I really wanted. Desperate, I switched over to the Twinks & Twunks category. Maybe I would get lucky.

I snorted as an image of someone from back home filled my screen, same as the first time I'd been scrolling for an Elite. Jimmy Riley was blond, pretty as fuck with big blue eyes, and a strict bottom. Far from my type and definitely not someone I was interested in building a connection with even if he was. Two years older than me, he'd been a mess in high school from what I could remember, always getting into trouble with the law. The guy hadn't ever been able to keep his mouth shut, but Elite Escorts MM were known for their discretion and had NDAs for a reason. I'd taken a chance in hiring a co-worker of his while in college, but Zack could have been Chaz's older brother, and I would give my left nut for one night with my best friend.

Chaz had been into girls from as far back as I could remember, so I hadn't bothered with sharing my feelings and fucking up the best friendship a kid could have.

Still hadn't.

As far as Chaz was aware, I'd been too focused on getting a few Super Bowl rings to bother with a woman while he'd gone and fallen in love with one.

I'd choked back tears when Chaz had pledged to love, honor, and respect Shelly until death parted the high school sweethearts. In my dreams, I'd been the person facing him, our hands clasped tightly between us as we made vows of undying love to each other.

That day had been the toughest of my life, even more traumatic than the popping sound that had ended my NFL career. Nothing could compare to the drawn-out agony of watching the person you loved fall for another and become so goddamn enamored with them that your friendship took an emotional backseat.

It'd been years since Chaz and I had talked but only because I couldn't stand the pain of hearing his voice or seeing text messages about how happy he was in pursuing his own dreams.

All thoughts of getting a good dicking dissolved at the memories of how I'd lost my best friend and the ache in my chest that always accompanied it.

I tossed my cell aside and slouched farther on the couch, head tipped back and eyes closed. I'd have been a few thousand poorer and well on my way toward needing intervention if getting sloshed appealed to me.

According to Dad, Coach Bernard *was* ready and willing to hand over his whistle to me, just like he had figured. Hell, Coach himself had called and begged me to return. He wanted to retire knowing his boys would be looked after, that someone who loved football as much as he did would continue his goal of making something out of our small town's team.

I held no such high hopes. Never had. Rarely did Pippen Creek even have a winning season. Hell, we barely ever had enough kids try out to *make* a team. I'd been the one and only Bobcat to get a college scholarship, and the fact I'd made it to the NFL had given me Hollywood status back home. That was what Dad claimed, anyway. I hadn't been there since Chaz's wedding to see or hear that kind of gossip for myself.

But that might be about to change...

remembering the day we'd last seen Jamie. It had been at our wedding, and I hadn't even gotten a chance to hug him and tell him goodbye before he'd left the reception long before it had ended. He'd taken off like he'd been desperate to escape Pippen Creek and everyone who lived here, leaving my heart split in two. "What makes you think he's still interested in being our friend now?"

"Can't remember hearing about you reaching out to him the last couple of years either," she stated rather than answering. She spun and stalked into the kitchen.

I followed my wife, needing a beer from the fridge before showering. Shelly spoke the truth, but—

"I swear to God, I've never met a more selfish man." She all but spat the words I'd heard countless times in the previous year since I'd purchased the mechanic shop in Pippen Creek. "All you do is work, Chaz. You're never home!"

"Because I'm trying to build a business so we don't need both of our incomes to cover the bills!" I shot back, my blood pressure rising.

It was bad enough I'd been denied a loan from the bank and had to go to my father for financing. Henderson Auto was the only one of its kind downtown, and still I struggled to make ends meet and payments on time. Father always reminded me when I didn't even when Mother suggested he offer his only son some grace.

Like that would happen anytime soon.

"I've only ever wanted one thing from you, Charles Henderson. One!" Shelly turned stormy eyes on me, arms crossed.

"Don't start, Shell," I warned, yanking open the fridge door as my stomach twisted into knots. "Fuck knows we've been trying for *years*!"

"And if you had a normal job that offered insurance, we could figure out whose fault it is that I'm *not* pregnant!"

Fucking hell.

She'd spouted her disapproval of my decision to take over the shop after working there since high school but never to this extent. Dragging my failure to give Shelly her stay-at-home mom dream into this argument? Was she trying to cause a heart attack or make me want to jump off a goddamned bridge?

We'd been happy enough in the beginning. No fire or crazy passion but a calm, shared existence I thought I could be content with for the rest of my life.

Now?

I'd be fine if I winked out of existence, my failings unable to haunt my every waking breath.

I popped the cap off my bottle of beer and chugged until my lungs screamed for oxygen. A spin on my heel sent me toward the bathroom, but no way would I escape reality so easily.

I fucking bombed at everything, whether it was living up to my dad's standards, getting good grades in school, bringing in enough money on my own and paying my bills on time, or keeping my supposed other half happy...

Shelly continued to rant about those vows I'd made to love and honor her, blah, blah, blah. And she called me selfish for working too hard—to *provide* for her, goddamnit! Shelly had always been an outspoken, determined woman dead set on getting what she wanted, and while I'd been attracted to that part of her personality when we'd still been in school, I'd learned the hard way she was as easily pleased as my father. Which was not at all, no matter what I did or how much I tried.

Lately, I'd been questioning if I'd made a mistake in marrying her.

I closed the bathroom door in my wife's face, locking it so she wouldn't follow me in and gripe at me while I showered.

Part of the reason I wasn't quick to come home at night was due to her constant nagging and complaining. The woman drove me to drink, but I wasn't about to become a drunk and add marriage to my list of failures for my dad to remind me of when I was forced to visit my childhood home across town.

I started the shower and hummed to myself while stripping to drown out the grumbling still going on out in the hallway.

Shelly pounded on the door when I chose not to respond.

"Leave me the fuck alone!" I finally raised my voice to her level. "Let me shower, and we'll go to the party, okay?" I kicked off my shoes. "Jesus Christ," I muttered to myself. "What does a man have to do to get some goddamn peace and quiet in his own home?"

"You've got five minutes!" Shelly yelled. "I hate being late!"

I huffed. The only time she did was when it was her period, but even that had changed because disappointment always followed a delayed menstrual cycle. Too much lack of success in getting pregnant had made her give up hope and left me with a limp cock that wasn't interested in donating sperm even if she asked for it.

Which, she hadn't done for months.

Intimacy had shit the bed when I'd found her sitting on the bathroom floor earlier that spring, pregnancy test in hand and tears rolling down her cheeks over yet another negative result. She'd made sure to remind me it was my fault, same as the prior thirty or so other months we hadn't conceived. She hadn't told me when she ovulated since then, and I couldn't be bothered to initiate.

Didn't want to deal with even more guilt over failing her yet again.

Shelly and I seemed doomed, and I didn't know how to make shit better. Nothing I ever did created a positive change, and I was exhausted physically and emotionally.

The shower rid my body of sweat, grease, and grime, but my thoughts still felt shitty, all jammed up by her usual unwelcome home and the truth of why lay ahead of us tonight.

Jamie Forester had returned to Pippen Creek.

My heart sped even as my stomach twisted into a tight knot over secret, selfish thankfulness he'd come back years earlier than expected.

Once upon a time, Jamie, Shelly, and I had been three peas in a pod. Inseparable. The best of friends who did everything together. Hell, Jamie had even tagged along on a lot of Shelly's and my dates in high school. Senior year, he attended prom with us as Shelly's "side dish." We'd gotten teased over it by others in school, and I often wondered after he'd left town how many people had expected us to end up in a poly relationship.

As a secret pansexual, I would have been down for that back then. Jamie, however, was as rednecked, jock-like, man's man as they came. While he'd never shown much interest in girls, Shelly especially, I'd assumed it was due to football being his focus and ticket out of the backwoods of northern New Hampshire.

I never understood why he felt he had to make a name for himself. His dad Sutton, the chief of police in our small town, had a great reputation and was admired. Respected, even by those he had to toss into a cell to sleep off their drunkenness. Jamie's mom showing her true colors as a piece of trash when we were in middle school hadn't stained him. Not sure Jamie saw shit that way though.

I expected he hated being here again, and while I was nervous about his return, I was glad.

Too glad.

Talk about an asshole best friend or whatever we were to each other now. I supposed time would tell, but my lack of patience and conflicting desires had turned my insides into an absolute mess.

Shelly gave me space to quickly get dressed, so I got a few seconds to breathe without interference. I swore her heated glare singed me through the walls separating us though. Her toes tapped loudly on the cracked tile entry-way, her agitation thick in the air.

Marriage had started out easy enough for us. Sure, we butted heads like every other couple in existence, but a lot of issues had snuck in since we'd exchanged vows four years ago. Distance weaseled between us, and if not for her bitching and fighting for more, I'd think she would be ready to move on as I sometimes wished I could.

But I wouldn't quit. Refused to. Fuck that shit, because I couldn't mess up something else for my dad to harp on, and how the hell would my bills get paid without the additional income?

I'd promised Shelly the family she'd always wanted since she had no one but her mother, who was in a long-term care facility, suffering from severe dementia. I'd been lucky enough to convince Shelly we had to wait for marriage to even try. Not saying we didn't have sex back in high school. Just kept my cock under wraps because I'd refused to be a teenage dad. At twenty-four, we still had plenty of time even though her mom didn't, and I thought that more than anything weighed heavy on her mind.

"Let's *go!*" Shelly grumbled from down the hallway, and I ran a hand through my wet hair.

Scruff lined my usually shaven jaw, and purplish bags lay under my eyes, but depression did shit to a man, made him not care a whole hell of a lot about his appearance. Lips pressed tight, I exited our bedroom and heard exactly what I expected the second I rounded the corner.

"You're wearing *that?*"

I ignored Shelly, grabbed my keys again, and headed out the door. She hated my ripped jeans and plain T-shirts with the stretched-out collars, but it was what I felt most relaxed in, and fuck knew I'd need every level of comfort I could for what awaited us downtown.

Shelly muttered nonstop from behind me, but I did my best to pretend she didn't exist. Shitty of me, but I'd had enough of her bull tonight. Needed something to look forward to, goddamnit. Excitement. A rush of adrenaline. Brightness in my dull, depressing existence.

Jamie's smile used to light me up from the inside out, and that gorgeous grin of his made encouraging words about everything being okay unnecessary. His presence had been all I'd needed. Would seeing him again cause my stomach to flutter? Settle the unrest in my head like his proximity had done before he abandoned us for bigger and better things?

Huffing, Shelly buckled up her seatbelt, and I caught a sniff of her flowery perfume—and whiskey.

My brow furrowed as I cast a glare at her. "Seriously, Shell? You started already?"

"Shut up," she muttered, riffling through her purse for who the fuck knew what. Probably that plumping lip gloss that made her lips puff up like a porn star's. Used to get me hard.

Not anymore.

I backed out of our driveway and took off up the road fast enough that the tires chirped.

Teeth clenched, I fought to swallow down words that would only cause another argument, one we'd had countless times in the past couple of months. The newest reason I wasn't super excited to get my wife pregnant was because her disappointment in me had led to her drinking hard liquor almost every night since our last failed attempt. Couldn't trust a woman who was more interested in drowning her sorrows than agreeing to counseling.

She didn't need a therapist, Shelly had stated with a sneer, just that baby I'd been promising her since high school.

Should have kept my mouth shut on seeking help for our marriage *and* setting myself up for yet another failure.

Fuck, I hated that word.

I released a slow, steady exhale, focusing on easing the tension in my shoulders and stomach. Getting my emotions set straight became a priority because I was about to be confronted with the one man I'd been desperate to forget but couldn't no matter how hard I tried.

Memories played in my mind as they often did of all the good times the three of us had together. The laughter. Adventures. Camping out by Pippen Creek Pond, eating s'mores until we were all sick to our stomachs. Skinny-dipping beneath slivers of moon in a star-dotted sky while I hid my lust for Jamie's perfect body. Drinking cheap strawberry wine we'd managed to sneak from the city south of our small town. The three of us piling up inside a two-man tent, snuggling like a litter of kittens before passing out.

Maybe, just *maybe*, Jamie's return would be a good thing.

Then I remembered waking with boners that were more than mere morning wood, pressing against my best friend's leg even though Shelly had been between us when we'd gone to bed. We'd camped out together three nights, and during each of them, I'd unknowingly clung to Jamie in sleep. Thank fuck he hadn't woken up before I'd snuck away before sunrise. I might have left the temptation of him all three mornings, but the draw, the longing for more than friendship with my straight best friend...

Nope. Shut that shit down.

I'd made my bed and had no choice but to lay in it.

Jamie, I expected, had a different woman under him every night after accomplishing his goal of making it into the NFL. Career ending too early by an injury or not, the man could have anyone he wanted and probably had more notches on his bedpost than I did checks marks on my weekly to-do list.

I had no business thinking about him in that way. I was married. Owned a struggling business, which needed my full focus. Had responsibilities far beyond daydreams and fantasies of him returning home and declaring, "I've been gay this whole time and love you more than Shelly ever could."

Yeah, that shit only happened in the movies, and I didn't deserve a happy ride into the sunset after what I'd done, *not* done, and had fantasized over.

"Why are you parking all the way back here?" Shelly muttered yet another complaint.

Leave it to my wife to question every goddamned thing I did.

Ignoring her, I slammed the truck into park at the back of the lot and threw open my door.

She continued to bitch beneath her breath about the long walk to Frenchie's entrance.

Secrets aside, I needed to keep my heart out of whatever type of friendship Jamie and I ended up hopefully rekindling after his absence. No way in hell I could handle more stress in my life.

Chapter 3

Jamie

I was not in the mood to go to Frenchie's and put on a front, acting like I was happy to be home. Also didn't feel up to accepting condolences for lost dreams, seeing pity in people's eyes, or being asked what I would do now that the NFL was no longer in my future.

Because I didn't fucking know, and even attempting to consider a new plan made me depressed as hell.

I'd rather have stayed holed up in my old bedroom at Dad's since being a nudist in his house wasn't an option, and my balls only swung free behind closed doors. Since arriving back here, I'd done nothing but sprawl on my too-small twin bed and feel sorry for myself. I couldn't wait for August and the high school football season's start that would keep me busy and tired enough that my brain would shut down at the end of every day.

But someone had insisted on throwing a welcome home/retirement party—Coach Bernard—because the old guy was proud as fuck of his favorite past player who'd gone on to those bigger and better things. Never mind he couldn't wait to hit the road for the southwest.

I agreed to go to Frenchie's on this muggy July night for his sake rather than to meeting up with old friends or making new ones. While I'd committed to coaching the upcoming season for our tiny high school in the hopes I would find some sense of purpose again, I didn't have plans to stick around long afterward.

Wasn't sure I would be able to.

Life would be miserable enough having to see Chaz and Shelly together. Even worse, their hanging all over each other when I wanted to be the one kissing Chaz's lips and littering his neck with hickies for the world to see.

But what else could I do? I'd chosen to return to Pippen Creek in order to have some sort of football in my life, and I would make the most of it while I could.

I've got this.

Stitching a smile onto my face at my motto ringing in my ears, I pushed into the thankfully air-conditioned and only bar in town. It had recently been bought by a woman named Frenchie and her wife, Iris. According to Dad, they were Mrs. Grumpy and Mrs. Sunshine. One glance through the massive crowd to the bar on my right revealed who was who.

Both appeared to be in their fifties, and while Frenchie had long graying hair and an icy blue gaze, her wife sported a short, spiky blue haircut, smiling brown eyes focused on me. Regardless of their opposite natures, they both hollered out a, "Welcome to Frenchie's!" as the door shut behind me, wrapping my overheated body in coolness.

My arrival drew attention, and my smile faltered as dozens of heads swiveled my way. Sweat beaded on my forehead for a whole different reason.

"The man of the hour!" Coach Bernard hopped up from his stool and pushed past people to be the first to greet me. "Welcome home, son," he said fondly, wrapping me up in his arms. Nostalgia made my eyes sting.

I'd put on some serious muscle weight since high school, so his barrel-chested mass could no longer lift me up off my feet like he used to, but we both chuckled, caught up in the reunion.

"Congrats on finally retiring, old man," I replied with a teasing tone, slapping him on the back.

He laughed loudly, making it clear he'd already been celebrating for a while. Clasping my shoulder, he turned toward the rest of the crowded bar. "Jamie Forester, everyone!"

As if they didn't know who I was.

Forcing my grin to stick in place rather than grimacing, I followed along where he led, allowing my old coach to reintroduce me to every patron in the room, bragging about my stats from the greatest rookie season ever.

Damn, did I wish he spoke truth.

While I appreciated his enthusiasm over what would have been a killer rookie season had I not gotten injured, I wanted to escape the crowd and attention focused on me. Being on the field with thousands of eyes watching me run plays had only ever psyched me up and pushed me to do better.

Now?

I felt like a damned anomaly on stage at some carnival freak show while everyone stared. My skin itched. Pulse thrummed. I kept glancing around like a skittish cat needing a way out even though the people were kind and smiling.

The bar's door pushed inward, but rather than focusing on the means of escape into the darkness beyond, my gaze landed on the redhead who'd once upon a time been like a sister to me.

Shelly Henderson.

And behind her?

Jesus.

All thoughts of football and a bleak future faded to the back of my mind. I swallowed hard, that pulse in my head beginning to pound with every throbbing punch of my heart against my breastbone.

Tall, dark, and handsome. Haunted hazel eyes I wanted on me so I could drown in them like a lovesick puppy. Wide shoulders I lusted to grasp while he pounded into me. Trim hips my legs had always ached to wrap around.

Shelly grasped Chaz's hand, dragging him in behind her when he seemed to hesitate, her head swiveling as though searching for—

Her shriek and shimmy let me know she'd spotted me, but I couldn't tear my focus off her husband's face.

As though feeling my stare, he turned his head my way.

Our gazes snagged hold.

I fucking grinned like a goddamn dork when I'd expected to curl in on myself from the pain of having to see him again.

As though of the same mind, we stalked forward, brushing past people, and at the last second before we crashed into each other, I remembered the woman still clinging to his hand who he'd taken along for the short walk across the bar.

I wrapped my arms around them *both* and hugged them tight.

But my nose angled toward Chaz, and I breathed him in as deep as I could. Even smelling as though he'd recently scrubbed himself with soap, the underlying smell of the mechanic shop he'd worked in since high school clung to him.

And I fucking loved it. Longed to bathe in his scent. Lick him from head to fucking toe—

Shit.

I stepped away before popping a boner, having to do so forcefully, considering how Shelly had attached herself to my side.

"My *God*, Jamie!" She laughed and finally released me to clasp my cheeks. "It's so good to finally have you back home where you belong!" Her breath reeked of whiskey as she brushed a kiss over my cheek, leaving a smear of lip gloss.

"Thanks, Shell. Good to see you too." I rubbed my face across my shoulder real quick to rid myself of the stickiness.

She grabbed hold of Chaz and leaned into him, caressing his arm with her usual possessive attention. I'd have given my left nut to be able to do the same to him.

I wanted to run my fingers through Chaz's damp hair, attempt to tame the black waves he'd never given much effort into controlling. Same as always, he wore grungy jeans and a T-shirt that had seen better days, and while his smile and hazel eyes appeared haggard, he was still hot as fuck.

"Next round's on me!" Coach hollered, and Shelly let out a, "Woohoo!" before releasing Chaz like he had the plague or something. She headed to the bar without sharing another word. No "sorry about your knee," no begging for gossip from the NFL, no prying into my love life like she used to do. She hadn't even asked how I was doing.

Chaz and I were left facing each other in the middle of the packed bar, and I couldn't find it in myself to care his wife had abandoned us for alcohol. I hadn't gotten him to myself since those brief moments before we'd exited a side door near the church stage where he and Shelly would vow to honor and cherish each other until death parted them.

Should have been me.

"Missed you, brother," he said, his voice low and gaze a little unsure, causing my throat to tighten.

"Same."

Fuck it.

I yanked Chaz into my arms and squeezed the living hell out of him. The tension in my guts eased, and I exhaled all of my pent-up agitation at having to people that night. I could have lingered in being pressed against Chaz for hours, but only a few quick seconds passed before he stepped away, clearing his throat. He glanced over at his wife, who held a shot of amber liquid into the air.

She yelled out some nonsense about getting her party on before slamming the drink back. Her laughter and hip bump against the woman beside her I didn't recognize made it clear she still loved getting buzzed, same as when we'd been teens. The girl had abandonment issues thanks to a father who'd fled the scene with another woman and a mother who'd been ill and pretty much unable to parent for close to a decade. Who wouldn't want to drown their sorrows in her shoes?

"How are you doing, Jamie? Because that there's a forced smile if ever I've seen one." Chaz studied me like a bug beneath a microscope.

"Shitty," I answered honestly, once more giving him my full attention, not bothering to keep my lips upturned. His eyebrows dented inward, creating a deep furrow between them. Smudges beneath his eyes suggested he hadn't been sleeping well, and I yearned to spoon the hell out of him and demand he get some rest. "How about you?"

"Same." He spoke low as though trying to hide how he

really felt from everyone chatting around us. Typical of Chaz to put on a false front to appease his asshole father, who wasn't even at Frenchie's.

That need to comfort and help my best friend, same as all through our childhood, rose inside me as it did whenever he seemed to be hurting. "Maybe we can—"

"Chief!" Coach's holler pulled my attention toward the bar's door, which once more stood open.

Dad strode inside, his uniform slightly wrinkled from having worked all day. His best friend Dexter, the captain at our small firehouse, followed behind him, white teeth flashing from his wide grin.

I'd often wondered why the two of them hadn't hooked up. Dad had admitted to being bi when I came out to him in high school, and it was no secret around town that Dexter liked dick. But I assumed crossing best buddy lines didn't always end well, and I expected they both appreciated their friendship too much to fuck around and find out.

If Chaz had even *hinted* at being curious about dick, I would have gladly jumped over that line and pushed to help him "find out" for sure. In secret, of course, because I'd been destined for the NFL, where being anything but straight wasn't exactly smiled upon.

Dad headed our way, and I glanced at Chaz to find him staring at me.

Neither of us said a word, and if I hadn't known better about him liking women, I'd have assumed he was drinking me in as though he'd been as starved for the sight of me as I'd been for him.

Wishful thinking.

Suddenly needy as fuck, I bro-hugged him once more and shoved rising fantasies to the back of my mind, determined to enjoy the parts of him that I could have. To make the most of my time in Pippen Creek before I figured out what to do with the rest of my pitiful life.

"Your dad still have that old tent?" Chaz asked, and I put a foot of space between us, my grin returning, because the immediate future was suddenly fucking bright as hell.

"Not sure, but I'll buy a new one if you're suggesting what it sounds like you are."

"Guys weekend at the pond?" he questioned, and the lack of including his wife hit me low and hard even though things between us wouldn't go anywhere near where I lusted for.

Still, the chance to have him all to myself?

"Fuck yeah, I'm in," I agreed, my grin easy and *real*.

"Jamie—good to see you, kid." Dexter clasped my hand and yanked me in for a quick hug, tearing my attention fully off Chaz. "Sorry shit worked out like it did."

And just like that, the lack of end goals returned, dragging me down like a defensive lineman hellbent on tackling me into the ground.

"Same, man, same," I mumbled, nodding my acceptance of his condolences.

"Chaz!" Shelly called loudly, waving at her husband. "Get your fine ass over here and do a shot with me!"

Chaz grimaced and nodded. "I'll catch you later, Jamie. We'll make plans."

He ambled toward Shelly, who held two shot glasses in her hands.

He'd erased my sense of drifting without purpose for a few minutes, but seeing them in the flesh together caused my heart to ache twice as bad as having an aimless existence.

But goddamn, that ass. Made my mouth water.

"Sutton said you haven't gone on any ride alongs yet,"

Dexter said, pulling my attention away from a man I had no right lusting over. "That used to be your favorite pastime back in middle school when you weren't hanging with those two."

Memories of driving around with Dad in his cruiser after Mom abandoned us trickled through my brain, sending a fond ache through my chest. The sentimental moments just kept hitting hard tonight.

"Dad?" I asked, glancing at him.

He grinned. "You're welcome to join me whenever you want. Can't believe I didn't think to suggest it before now with how bored you've been at home."

"Tomorrow work for you?" I asked, excited to have something to look forward to.

"Swing by the station whenever. Just grab coffee and some scones before you show up."

I nodded, fighting the need to glance over at Chaz again.

"Sutton said you spent a couple of months in Boston before coming home," Dexter said.

"Yeah, but the few friends I have down there are still into clubs and partying." I shrugged. "Not really my thing, so I was bored."

Dexter turned dark eyes on Dad then back to me. "Ever run into the troublemaker Jimmy Riley? Remember him? A little older than you, on the smaller side. Blond. Didn't know how to shut up?"

I choked on my own spit and coughed before finding my voice. "Nope," I croaked.

While my answer wasn't exactly a lie, I wasn't going to out Jimmy and his way of making a living since leaving home. Last thing I needed was someone asking how I knew he was employed by the gay branch of Elite Escorts. Didn't mind so much if people eventually found out I was into men, but having hired an escort for myself?

Yeah, no. Couldn't take the chance of soiling Dad's name or reputation in any way. Mom had done enough of that on her own.

Dad growled a few words beneath his breath, and I glanced between the two men.

"Am I missing something?" I asked.

Dexter snickered and slapped Dad's back. "I think Sutton here has been a little bored since that boy left town."

"I've been enjoying the peace and quiet," Dad corrected his friend, his tone snippy.

"Sure. Sure." Dexter's eyes twinkled, and I wondered what the fuck was going on. "Want a beer?"

"Yeah," Dad agreed, and Dexter left us alone.

"How are you holding up against all this attention?" Dad asked before I could question what the fuck that exchange with his best friend was about.

I shrugged, my focus once more flitting toward the bar as I considered what Dad had asked.

Chaz sipped a beer while Shelly talked animatedly to the woman she'd hip-bumped. Those feelings of being a third wheel and looking in longingly from the outside I'd always experienced as a teenager slid through me just as strongly as they had before I'd left town. "I'm alright." I outright lied.

"Chaz appears exhausted."

I tore my gaze off him before Dad questioned why I stared at my old best friend the way I did. Full of lust and heartache. "You said he bought the mechanic shop, right?"

"Yeah. His dad loaned him the money last year, and he's been working his ass off to prove himself."

Jesus.

Chaz and his dad's relationship had been rocky enough, and Chaz's supposed shortcomings had been pointed out harshly and often ever since as far back as I could remember. At least his mom had treated him decent enough. She wasn't exactly the nurturing type but better than not having a mom at all.

"Why the fuck did he get the money from his dad? You know as well as I do the man is an asshole."

Dad shrugged. "Bank wouldn't give him a loan. No credit or assets for collateral."

"Fuck. He and Shelly okay at least?" I asked, remembering the not-so-positive response Chaz had given when I'd asked how he was doing. Call me an asshole, but I wanted to hear a negative answer from my dad. If their marriage crumbled, I could help Chaz pick up the pieces.

And maybe eventually more if he would ever be open to being loved by a man.

Shame slithered in like a snake, but I shoved that shit to the back of my mind. Couldn't help desiring my best friend as much as I used to want the NFL. Football had been forced into the backfield, leaving Chaz with a wide open path toward the end zone of my full focus.

"Things seem fine on the outside, but I've heard some stuff," Dad said, scanning the room with his ever-watchful gaze.

"Gossip or...?"

He lifted and dropped a shoulder. "Their neighbors say they fight a lot, but I've never gotten an official complaint that has warranted I check in on them."

Shit.

For the next hour, between bouts of catching up with old football players from high school, teachers who'd claimed me as their pet back in the day, and other townsfolk

I'd known my entire life, I studied the couple stuck in the forefront of my mind.

Chaz followed Shelly around like usual, but she definitely wasn't the koala she used to be with him. She gave him narrowed side-eyes that suggested irritation, and once, I caught her lip curling with what looked like disgust when he'd leaned close to talk in her ear.

The fuck was going on between them?

I sipped my lemon water, wondering and wishing she'd dump him or take off like my mom had. Then I felt guilty for thinking about my best friend's broken heart.

That part of him I could never have, no matter how much I still dreamed of making him mine.

Chapter 4

Chaz

Shelly put on a front, pretending to be the happy wife, bragging up how busy the shop was. At least she didn't complain to everyone about me never being home like she did with me. While I'd much rather have been hanging with Jamie, I had to do the same as Shelly—play my part of the content husband who was financially killing it and winning at life.

God forbid anyone believe otherwise, never mind clue my father in on the truth.

Same as any length of time spent in my wife's presence, I wondered over our future and what more I could possibly do to make shit bearable. I doubted we would ever be *good* again, but if we could exist without being miserable, I would be content.

The initial reunion with Jamie had gone much better than I'd expected and dreaded. He'd welcomed me with open arms, and fuck, he'd felt good and solid—comforting—all up in my space. Hadn't wanted to let him loose when he'd hugged me, but I wasn't about to reveal my true feelings for the man.

While shit might be weird between us on occasion, no way to avoid *that* with unrequited love on my part, something inside me settled at having him nearby. Jamie's return was a breath of fresh air finally filling my lungs, invigorating the deadened emotions I'd been dealing with lately. He was that light I so desperately needed to combat the darkness hovering over my head.

I glanced over to find him still with his dad and Dexter, but a couple of other locals had joined them, voices growing louder with the hours passing and alcohol consumed.

But Jamie didn't drink.

I eyed the beer in my hand, which had grown warm. At least I hadn't taken to drowning in alcohol like my wife. She was already lit, laughing shrilly and stumbling around. My parents didn't go to bars, no matter what type of party was being thrown, but I expected Dad would get wind of her behavior and ask me why I couldn't keep her in line. As if I could. Dad's generation might believe a firm hand was okay, but I sure as fuck didn't. I figured I did a damn good job of not placing any demands on my wife except for that small portion of her income to help cover the bills. If only I didn't feel so goddamned clueless and powerless to make shit better behind closed doors.

Jamie suddenly stood beside me, his grin from earlier replaced with a softer one that suggested weariness. "Hey—I'm gonna head out."

"Already?" I asked, trying for a light tone that suggested shit was fine in my corner of the world.

He shrugged. "Not really into peopling tonight."

"I hear ya. So, next weekend? The following?" I asked about that camping trip, more hopeful than I ought to be to have my best friend all to myself without someone bitching in the background or pretending everything was unicorns and rainbows when it sure as hell wasn't.

"The sooner the better." Jamie's voice hinted at needing peace and quiet, something I rarely got these days. His dark blue eyes suggested he struggled not just with the noise in the bar, but the loss of his dreams as well. Made me want to hug him again, but I didn't because I was *glad* he was home.

What a shit best friend I was. Almost as bad of a husband.

"Friday night, then," I said, a thrill shooting through my stomach regardless of my guilt and waking butterflies I hadn't felt in years.

He nodded, his eyes brightening the slightest bit, which soothed that feeling of failure for a brief moment. "Still have the same number?"

"Yeah." I wanted to give him shit for not checking on that fact years ago, but like Shelly had said, I hadn't reached out to him either.

Knowing I loved him more than I ever had Shelly but not being able to choose him had made him leaving Pippen Creek easier to handle.

But now?

I'd rather go back and do shit over, put my heart on the line in case I'd been wrong in my assumption about my best friend's sexuality. Maybe things would have turned out differently. Perhaps even better.

Jamie studied me a few seconds as though searching out the truth of my life the last four years. Couldn't have him believe I was on the same train tracks toward a wreck as I'd been in high school before he'd stepped in and helped me graduate by tutoring the fuck out of me.

I swallowed hard and looked away. "I'll grab stuff for s'mores."

"I'll bring the strawberry wine."

A corner of my lips quirked up. "I'd rather have a six-pack of beer."

"You got it, brother." Jamie grasped my hand tight, lingering long enough my heart skipped a beat.

He left without another word, and it hurt like fuck not to watch him walk away.

I shouldn't be happy that Jamie was back in Pippen Creek so soon, but I couldn't help myself. Would he hate me if he knew I wasn't all that upset over his injury that had forced him to give up his dream? What would he think about my lack of apology? Everyone else offered condolences. Sure, it sucked. I had really wanted Jamie to hit his goals, but I couldn't be sad about his return a decade or two earlier than I'd expected.

Guilt churned in my guts, but my thoughts weren't something Jamie ever needed to know, no matter how close we became again.

I doubted the three of us would pick up where we'd left off, at least. Shelly hadn't shown much interest in him other than the initial greeting she'd offered, so I expected the three musketeers had disbanded.

Thank fuck.

I wasn't above claiming him as my best friend and hoarding him all to myself. He was my *only* friend, really, even though years and distance had separated us. Between work and attempting to keep Shelly happy, I hadn't had much time for socializing over the years, so no one had taken his place.

No one ever could, either.

Would he and I still fit seamlessly even though so many seasons had shifted between us, forcing maturity and responsibilities I hated to acknowledge?

Jamie was been the only reason I hadn't ended up repeating tenth grade and missing out on graduating with him. I'd been on the brink of failing and had been scared shitless Dad would whip my ass when he saw my report card. My best friend had caught me crying after tanking my geometry midterm.

Numbers and I hadn't ever gotten along. Hell, reading and I weren't best friends either. I realized later that I had difficulty learning the way other book-smart kids did, but put me in a place where I could use my hands to figure shit out, and I succeeded.

Jamie saw me through the rest of high school, then I pursued a future in mechanics because cars made sense more than numbers had since tenth grade when I'd started working in the shop.

Dad wasn't too happy with me for not choosing to become an accountant and eventually taking over his office on Main Street, but I would have been nothing but a liability to the family business my grandfather had started. Dad called my attempts at making a living lazy, but with the hours I put in and how exhausted I was every night, dragging my ass home after twelve-hour days, I knew better.

Still stung like a bitch though when he pointed out his disappointment in me. At least it wasn't outright these days but more in a passive-aggressive way that some might over-hear and not catch onto unless they knew our history.

Jamie would recognize my dad's bullshit for what it was. He always had and been right there to hug me when I needed it while Shelly had been too consumed with her own trauma to see mine.

Fuck, what I wouldn't give for another few seconds wrapped up tight in Jamie's arms. The memory of their strength sent shivers down my spine and intensified a yearning I hadn't forgotten over the years.

He'd used a different soap or cologne from the last time I'd seen him, but beneath lay his usual scent, a warmth I'd never been able to name. I wondered if his sweat and musk was the same as when we'd been teens.

My groin actually fucking twitched at the thought, and I closed my eyes against the mass of people packing out Frenchie's. The noise wasn't as easy to shut down, however, and my head started to pound.

Shelly hung on her girlfriend—couldn't remember her name—their laughter loud and annoying as fuck.

"Shell!" I hollered over the voices and music surrounding us.

She didn't hear or rather, probably ignored me.

"Shell!" I yelled, placing my hand against her lower back to get her attention.

Her head spun my way, but it took a while before her eyes focused on my face. "What?" She slurred a reply, more than three sheets to the wind.

I leaned closer, and the scent of booze on her breath made me want to vomit. "Are you about ready to go home? I'm beat and have a headache."

"We just got here!"

More like she'd been spending my hard-earned cash on Frenchie's liquor for close to two hours, but I wasn't going to argue.

"I've had enough and am heading out."

"Have fun!" she shot back, sarcastic as fuck.

"I'm your ride," I reminded her.

She glanced at her friend, who was just as smashed as she was.

"Sorry, bitch," her friend laughed, "but I'm too drunk to drive. You can crash at my place if you want though."

Shelly had stayed with the friend who lived within walking distance of plenty of times.

"Have fun!" I repeated her suggestion without the same tone she'd given me before turning on my heel and making my way toward the exit.

Ubers weren't a thing in Pippen Creek, and I wasn't about to ask around for someone else to drive my drunk wife home. She was an adult and could make her own decisions. Wasn't my job to babysit, especially since attempting to do so would only end with us screaming at each other in public, which neither of us wanted.

Warm silence wrapped around me when the bar's door shut behind me.

"Thank fuck," I muttered and closed my eyes, breathing in the humid night air that hinted of campfires and grilling meat.

July was already half-over, but the night insects still made their music, reminding me of easier days and muggy evenings beneath the stars.

I tipped my gaze upward, scanning in the vastness of the sky above me.

Pippen Creek wasn't a big enough town to illuminate the darkness and erase the millions of pinpricks of light twinkling down on us.

Jamie and I had attempted to count the stars when we'd gone camping on Coach Bernard's land on Pippen Creek Pond he'd given us unlimited access to. We'd been sixteen and buzzed from sucking down strawberry wine. Shelly had already passed out in our tiny tent, and I'd drunk enough not to be overly concerned I sprawled close enough on the ground to my best friend that our shoulders pressed together. It'd been a dream come true but without the tongues and cum down each other's throats I'd lusted for once upon a time.

Still fucking do, I admitted in the silence of my mind.

The following morning, I'd found myself plastered against Jamie and had hightailed it out of the tent. The other two camping trips after that one had been my idea. Because I'd wanted to experience that closeness again even though it made me feel like a perv, taking advantage for just a few seconds of what it was like to have my boner dig into Jamie's hip.

"Fuck." I rubbed a weary hand over my face and slowly exhaled.

I'd instigated another night by the shore of the small lake called a pond a mile northwest of town, but I wasn't some horny kid who couldn't control himself. Hell, my dick had been ignored long enough I wasn't sure the damn thing still worked.

Jamie could suggest skinny-dipping and strip down like he preferred to do, and I doubted the sight of his tanned muscles would heat my blood.

Okay...maybe I was wrong there.

I rearranged my junk that had started to swell from the memories in my mind, and the simple touch through my jeans felt a little too damned good.

Huffing, I hoofed it to my car and locked myself inside. "Not cool," I muttered, pressing against my dick that had decided to stiffen fully during the short walk. "Seriously?" I shot down at my groin, my voice annoyed as fuck even to my own ears.

Shaking my head, I pulled out of the parking lot and drove toward our quiet house.

I didn't want to feed my imagination or my desire for

Jamie, but goddamnit, it'd been months since my body had shown any interest in blowing a load.

Maybe that was what I needed. To bust a nut so I could sleep like the dead and get the real rest I was desperate for.

I might have driven a little faster than Chief Sutton Forester and his officers would have appreciated, but I was suddenly out of control, burdened by need that had to be met.

At least I managed to strip and crawl into bed, lube in hand and tissues beside me before grabbing hold of my throbbing length.

"Ah, fuck!" I jolted at the first stroke, hissing as I dragged my grip back up to tease the swollen head and leaking slit. Breathing heavy, I fucked into my palm and grasping fingers, hips thrusting, dragging my dick up and down through my wet fist.

Jesus, that feels so goddamned good.

I closed my eyes and gave into the fantasy I hated to remember had gotten me off the last couple of times Shelly had said we needed to have sex. It wasn't her pussy I'd imagined shoving my dick into but a tight hole, furled and pink, with muscular globes bouncing from my thrusts. My fingertips would bruise with how hard I held him, desperate to drill deeper, burrow so far into him I would get lost and never have to leave.

Would he grunt from the force of my snapping hips? Arch his back and beg for more? Grasp at the sheets and whimper because I filled him so goddamned good, thrusting in and out of his hole?

"Fuck!"

Cum shot clear up to my chin, and I gasped, spine curling inward as pulses rocked my taint and spunk rushed up my shaft. Milky white ropes spurted in massive quantities over my stomach and pecs, dripping down my sides and puddling in my navel.

Fuck, I'd gone too long without release.

I collapsed back onto the mattress, boneless and heaving for breath like I'd hiked Mt. Washington, my extremities tingling.

But I didn't stop stroking my sensitive shaft.

I still played out the fantasy, imagining Jamie hadn't yet clenched his asshole around my cock, hadn't emptied his own balls onto the bed beneath him. I set about to make fantasy Jamie groan my name while releasing.

Seconds later, I came again with an agonizing sweetness that overshadowed everything else.

Balls and head empty for the first time in too damn long, I finally slept through the night, guilt over what I'd done as silent as the grave.

Chapter 5

Jamie

It ended up taking us an extra week to figure out the details for camping on our old coach's land by the pond. While he'd hightailed it for Arizona, Chaz had a shit ton of jobs he needed to complete before ditching work on Friday afternoon and Saturday. At least Shelly hadn't given either of us shit for escaping for the weekend without her. According to Chaz, she made plans to visit with her new girlfriend Tara, who lived down in Berlin. He'd never met the woman, but according to Shelly, she was her sister from another mother.

I'd gotten to spend a few days hanging with Dad, cruising around town, and had my paperwork finished with the high school for the upcoming football season starting next month. The assistant coach, Dave, had met with me twice, and we'd gone through the playbook, his thoughts on the players returning from the year before, and how badly that season's schedule would beat us up. While I felt somewhat prepared and hopeful we might do better than expected, nervousness made my head work overtime.

Camping offered a break mentally, and I couldn't fucking wait to set everything aside and give my best friend my undivided attention.

Chaz offered to drive back the mile-plus dirt road leading out of town that circled Pippen Creek Pond, aka PCP. He showed up at Dad's a little past three, freshly showered and smiling, with a flush on his face as though he'd been scurrying to get ready.

Humidity hung in the air, stifling and sticky, and we'd both opted for shorts and shirts with the sleeves ripped off, the usual attire from our high school days.

Seeing him climb from his jacked-up truck had my stomach going all sorts of crazy, my palms sweating from more than just the heat.

He looked good.

Delicious from messy hair to old, scuffed sneakers that had seen better days.

"What's up?" I asked, grasping his outstretched hand and yanking him in for a quick bro-hug.

Goddamn, the man smelled lickable. Fuckable.

Chaz squeezed me tight before stepping back quickly without meeting my gaze. "You ready to roll?"

"Yeah." I didn't let his discomfort bother me. It'd been four years of distance between us, and we probably both had a lot of shit to say. Some stuff would need to stay a secret, but it was time to catch up with the one man who'd always felt like home to me. "I picked up some new fishing gear and a tent over at The Outdoor Shop."

"This one bigger than that piece of shit your dad had?"

I chuckled and grabbed the tent bag off the porch where I'd piled my supplies for the weekend. "Yeah. Four-man instead of two."

"No snuggling like kittens, huh?"

We both snickered, but the thought of being entwined with Chaz's body perked my dick up even though I'd emptied my balls an hour earlier in the shower.

"Too fucking hot for that shit," I said, putting the tent into the back of his truck. "If the mosquitoes weren't so damn bad right now, I'd suggest sleeping under the stars where there might be a chance of a breeze."

Chaz placed my dad's small cooler alongside the tent, I tossed in my backpack with a couple changes of clothes, and we set off.

"You're sure Shelly's okay with us leaving her behind like this?"

"Oh yeah. She spends one if not two weekends a month down in the city with Tara getting their hair or nails done before hitting the bars."

"Still a partier, huh?"

He shrugged, every trace of his earlier smile gone. "So tell me what you've been up to—how was it getting a degree and all that shit?"

"Are you really asking how I'm feeling about the loss of my NFL career?"

A quick glance my way showed concern in his hazel eyes, but I was too wrapped up in him to feel depressed at the reminder of why I'd come home.

Fuck, he had the longest, most gorgeous eyelashes women would kill for. Full lips a pale pink I wished I could bruise with my mouth.

Jesus.

I tore my focus off him for the pothole-riddled dirt road ahead where the blacktop ended.

"You don't have to talk about that part if it's still too

painful," he said. "Fill me in on the last four years. It's been a long fucking time."

"Sorry for not keeping in touch."

I expected Chaz to give me shit, but he didn't. "Same, man. I've been a pretty awful friend."

"Dad told me you bought the old auto shop and that you've been crazy busy." I offered him an out and a chance for me to avoid the topic of how bummed I was over the loss of a dream.

"Yeah—I'll use that excuse if you're willing to accept it."

"Life gets in the way, Chaz. No hard feelings, yeah?"

A small, crooked smile lifted one corner of his mouth. "Yeah. Now tell me about all the trouble you enjoyed down at Boston College."

"Isn't much to share to be honest."

"Bullshit," he shot back with laughter. "Jamie Forester, 'Greek god of football' with the navy blue eyes girls used to swoon over, didn't spend four years in the big city without getting into *some* fun situations."

I wondered what Chaz would think about my Only-Fans account and the fact I'd used those earnings to hire a male escort who was a dead ringer of him. Yeah, those two things were definitely not up for discussion. Secret number one of too many to count.

"I was a good boy for the most part," I said, and he laughed. "What? When did I ever cause trouble?"

As the chief's son, I asked a serious question. Dad had put the fear of God in me back when I'd been a hyperactive kid but also taught me to respect my elders and follow the law. Hell, even lying was a huge no-no to me, which meant I tended to avoid subjects that would require I speak truth.

"Remember when you were caught underneath the

football stands with Jimmy Riley and what was his name...
Sam? Silas?"

I couldn't recall the guy's name Jimmy had been on his
knees for, but I hadn't been involved. Just unknowingly
close by until it was too late to hightail it outta there.

"Fuck you, Chaz—I was in the wrong place on the
wrong day. Don't know how many times I've told you that."

Chaz laughed, and fuck, did I love that sound leaving
his lips. His shoulders relaxed, and he seemed more at ease
when he glanced at me. "Coach made sure those two got a
few days off school while you only ended up with a week's
worth of detention."

"And I shouldn't have even had *that*," I complained. "I
wasn't getting my dick sucked, and I also wasn't gagging on
that dude's cock."

"Jesus, Jamie." Chaz shifted, taking a left to head
around the lake's five-mile encompassing road.

My stomach tightened, my grin fading. He must not like
hearing about what gays got up to.

"Ever see Jimmy down in Boston?" Chaz asked.

"No," I answered a little too quickly, but Chaz didn't
seem to catch wind of how his question caused my insides
to go jumpy. "Met a lot of cool guys in college though. Made
a couple friends but never anyone like you, Chaz. No one I
could call brother or hang with twenty-four-seven like we
used to back in the day."

"Why am I happy about that fact?"

I huffed a laugh. "You always were possessive."

"Really?" He shot me a glance before facing forward
just as quickly. "What'd I ever do to make you think something like that?"

"You hated whenever any of the other players on the
field with us wanted to hang out. I remember a few times

the entire team got together when we'd had plans with Shelly, and you'd get all pouty."

"I did not," he muttered, slowing as we took a hairpin turn around one of the lake's coves.

"Did too!" I shot back, laughing. "And that night what was his name—Ralphie—Vaughn Jackson's cousin had talked Shelly into going to Dig-In with him. You were pissed."

"Who wouldn't be when some outsider came into town and attempted to sweep your girlfriend off her feet?"

"You guys weren't even dating that day," I reminded him, still laughing over his put-out expression. "It was the third breakup of our junior year. The final straw, you'd said."

"Yeah, well, I couldn't let her go like you would have done."

"You broke the dude's nose."

"Because he crowded her to kiss her!"

The memory lay fresh in my mind. We'd been outside our town's only diner, Dig-In, along Route 16, watching through the picture window as that Ralphie kid had tried to weasel his way into Shelly's panties.

At that point, she and Chaz hadn't been fucking yet, but he'd been all about being her first and vice versa. Her going out with another guy during one of their little breakups had settled his mind on Shelly.

Sure, he'd gone caveman on the guy, but it'd been my chest that ached like a motherfucker when he and Shelly walked away afterward, hand in hand.

Again.

Each and every time they got back together had renewed my heartache. It'd sucked ass but not nearly as bad as the day they vowed to love each other until they grew old and gray.

Fuck, those memories hurt like hell.

I needed to get my head set on the now before I made shit weird between us, but it was damned near impossible with Chaz an arm's length away. I turned my focus on the open passenger window, allowing fresh air to flood the cab along with a bit of dust kicked up from Chaz's tires. The sight of sparkling water flickered through the trees.

Pippen Creek Pond was one of the few lakes not built-up like those farther south by Bostonians looking for weekend escapes. We were too damned far into the mountains for convenience. Timber filled the area, creating cozy peninsulas and close to a dozen small coves like where we would camp.

Chaz turned the truck onto a narrow pathway leading down to the westernmost side of the lake. Coach hadn't ever built on the land left to him by his granddaddy. He preferred to rough it—somewhat—and that was fine by us. He'd had an electric line brought into the private campsite from the main road, so there was that alongside a concrete, leveled slab he parked his camper on. An old outhouse stood back a ways into the woods, far enough no unpleasant smells reached where we would pitch our tent.

We set to work, our conversation focused mostly on the fun we'd had as kids rather than the shit we both found our current lives wrapped up in.

August was only a few days away, so the sky stayed lit well past the time we'd grilled steaks on an open fire and pulled foil-wrapped potatoes from the embers. It wasn't until after nine that the stars started to pop out overhead.

Coach's land was one of the more private properties on the lake without immediate neighbors in sight. We'd watched a few boats passing the cove's narrow entrance, enjoying the weather along with a couple of jet skis. The lake wasn't open to public launch, which kept the crowds to a bare minimum of local folks.

We did our share of swimming in the warm water and had spent at least an hour fishing off the end of the small dock Coach used to keep his small fishing boat tied to.

Chaz and I continued to catch up on the four years we'd been separated. I avoided the topic of women when he'd asked about notches in my bedpost at college, and he definitely steered our conversation from his and Shelly's relationship. They'd been trying for a baby since day one, and he didn't have to say jack shit for me to realize the four years of "failure" had been tough on him. But, I didn't poke over the word he'd despised for as long as I'd known him. I'd always hated nosey people attempting to get all up in my space, so I let the matter lie. If and when he wanted to discuss the unrest Dad had told me about, he would.

I expected Chaz and I would both need some time to build back up the trust we'd had as kids, even though things seemed easier than I'd first expected. At least we remembered how to joke and laugh together.

The fire crackled in front of us, shooting sparks into the night sky.

We sat alongside each other, sipping cold beers—my first in over a year, his third. The lake spread out in front of us beyond the small cove, a dark blue that kissed the opposite shore lined by pine trees.

The second major heatwave of the summer had settled over us the day before, and the muggy air made my T-shirt cling to my skin.

"I thought I'd escaped this weather when I left Texas," I muttered, setting aside my beer to yank off the shirt I never should have put back on after swimming. Would have gone completely naked if I'd been able to. No fucking way with Chaz being in the vicinity. I'd been chubbing up since sunrise.

Chaz set aside his marshmallow stick, a final s'more in hand. "You must have been happy to leave the south behind. Shit—sorry."

"It's okay." I tossed a piece of twig I'd broken off the stick in my hand. "Didn't have a choice. Makes acceptance of shattered hopes a little easier to swallow."

He hummed around a mouthful of marshmallow, chocolate, and graham cracker.

"It sucked, not gonna lie," I stated quietly, peering at the flickering flames and figuring if I opened up to him, he might do the same with me. "One tackle demolished my dreams."

"That's fucking bullshit. I know how much you wanted that NFL career."

"I went to a therapist for a while. Needed help wrapping my head around the fact my knee was shot along with my well-thought-out plans for my future."

"I'll be honest," Chaz stated quietly, licking his thumb clean of sticky white sweetness.

I stared, my groin tightening at the peek of his tongue along his skin.

"I'm glad you decided to come back here rather than settle someplace else."

Blowing out a heavy breath, I nodded. "I tried Boston for a while, but it just didn't fit. Being home isn't as bad as I expected. At least the excitement of my return died down so I don't have to deal with people stopping me on the sidewalks and asking me a million questions. That was growing old fast."

"You never did like people poking around in your personal shit."

"Nope." I tossed another stick in.

"Can't stand it, either."

"So I shouldn't ask how shitty life is right now for you like you suggested the other week?" Guessed I wasn't above prying since I'd been bothered by the truth he'd given me that night.

Chaz sighed and leaned forward in his lawn chair, elbows on his knees and focus on the fire's flames. "I work too much. That, along with my inability to knock Shelly up, is the biggest complaint I hear on a daily basis." Biggest, meaning he probably got an earful of others.

My brow furrowed. That wife of his had no fucking clue how good she had it. What lengths Chaz would go to in order to make her happy.

Shelly always had been high-maintenance and tough to please. I'd never understood why Chaz had attached himself to someone with the same outlook as his dad's. They were both about image and success, and anything short of the best wasn't enough.

"You bought out a business," I said, feeling the need to defend him. "Of course you're going to be working a lot. Gotta provide and all that shit. Can't imagine it's easy with your father holding the loan too."

"Your dad told you about that?"

"Yeah. Hope he didn't overstep," I said, glancing at Chaz.

"Nah." He continued to stare at the fire, unmoving. "Makes it tougher though, that's for sure. Financially, Shelly and I are just barely squeaking by, and if I'm one day late, he shows up at the shop to remind me payment is past due."

"What an ass." I wanted to punch the fucker's nose. "Is Shelly aware of how bad your relationship with him is?"

"Don't think so."

"You haven't talked to her about it?"

"No. You and my mom are the only two who are aware of that shit."

I shouldn't have felt such satisfaction over knowing him better than the partner he'd chosen for life, that he trusted me above her.

We sat in silence for a few seconds, the night insects creating a soothing background music that did absolute jack shit to lighten the heaviness that had settled over our conversation.

"What's up with the pregnancy thing?" I asked a little wary, not sure Chaz would be up for discussing that particular issue. But, the can had opened, and I needed the truth so I could figure out how to be a comfort to him.

"I'm a failure." He spoke with finality and a whole lot of guilt, revealing exactly as I'd expected.

"The fuck you are," I shot back, once more frowning on his behalf. There was that goddamned word his asshole dad and the man's high standards made Chaz fear. I'd expected Chaz was dyslexic or had issues with numbers, but I'd never asked. I would just step in when he struggled with classes and made sure he got to graduate alongside me like he deserved.

"It's Shelly's biggest gripe, but we don't have enough money or health insurance for me to get my swimmers tested. Not sure it's really me with the problem, but whatever." He shrugged as though him being at fault was expected and not that big of a deal.

But I could tell it was to him. Could see it in how his shoulders slumped and lips downturned. I also knew how he'd striven to prove himself to his father for years on end. In his mind, and according to his father's high standards, Chaz had always fallen short.

Fire kindled inside me, a protective flare that wanted to burn the negativity from his life.

Including his goddamned wife.

I pushed up to my feet, grabbed his empty bottle from alongside his chair, and tossed them with a little too much force into the trash bag I'd hung off the back of his truck behind me.

Yawning, he stood, stretching enough that his T-shirt rode up and bared pale skin.

I refused to let my gaze linger. "Come here." I pulled him in for a hug, squeezing tight but keeping my groin well away from his, even though my dick lay soft against my thigh. Last thing I needed was to brush my flaccid length against him and go instantly rock hard. It was bad enough having his heat and muscle wrapped around me and not being able to do anything about the want deep in my gut that had just as much to do with sheltering him as it did fucking him.

We both lingered, Chaz probably from enjoying the comfort I offered while I totally perved in my brain over my best friend. I soothed my hand down his back, breathing in the scent of his musk that hadn't changed one bit. Still made butterflies go crazy in my stomach and tempted my dick to twitch.

Chaz trembled, and I wondered how badly he fought off tears.

Or was he feeling the sexual energy between us too?

Temptation to shift my lower half into contact with his slid heat through my veins, and I swallowed hard as blood seeped into my cock, giving me a semi.

"Wish I could promise you a baby will happen when the time's right," I offered, trying like fuck to keep my brain on this side of right. Having just found Chaz again, I did not want to fuck around and find out how quickly I would be friendless if he learned how badly I desired him.

"I kinda hope it doesn't."

I stepped back, hanging onto his biceps, completely thrown for a loop by his muttered reply. All thoughts of sinking into his hole were wiped from my mind. *"What?"*

Lips pressed tight, he shook his head. "Nothing."

I allowed Chaz to separate himself from me and, baffled, followed on his heels toward the tent, thankful he hadn't noticed the bulge in my shorts.

Fuck, I wanted to pry, push for an answer as to what he'd meant, but men kept secrets for a reason. Didn't need him digging into my life because I had some as well. But what the fuck?

The puzzle over him no longer hoping to get Shelly pregnant owned my brain, causing my dick to deflate.

Leaving shit alone, I kicked off my sliders I'd put on after swimming and sprawled atop my sleeping bag. We'd set up the tent and our still too-small sleeping area before night had fallen. The manufacturer's idea of a four-man tent really only fit two full-grown guys like us, both of us being over six-feet tall and two-hundred-plus pounds.

The rain cover had been left in the bag since zero chance of showers had shown on the radar, and while there wasn't much of a breeze, having the screen zippered against mosquitoes of the entrance allowed fresh air for breathing.

A few inches separated us that I longed to erase so I could comfort—and more. Preferably without the shorts that felt restrictive as fuck.

Chaz released a shuddered sigh, and in my fantasies, he thought the same.

"You okay?" I asked, my voice low and quiet. Friendly and caring rather than ragged with want.

He didn't respond, and on instinct, I searched in the darkness for his hand. Chaz wrapped his pinkie around mine without hesitation or question at an action neither of us had ever taken before.

We lay in silence for what seemed forever before I finally slept.

Chapter 6

Chaz

I woke up exactly as I had feared.

Wrapped all over Jamie's hard body like a goddamned octopus, clinging to him like he filled my lungs and gave me the desire to live out my teenage wet dreams.

He breathed heavy, head facing my way so his exhales heated my scalp.

Sweat smeared over both of us, but I'd kept my shirt on last night, so there was that. But my dick was rock hard and aching.

Goddamnit.

I clenched my eyes shut and held still as stone for roughly five seconds before telling myself I had to move away before Jamie woke.

Rather than shifting back, my hips tilted forward, rubbing my length lightly against his thigh, seeking that fantasy of friction I lived out inside my head whenever I climbed into the shower and had a moment's privacy to jerk off.

Fuuuck.

My balls drew up tight, taking me to the edge of nutting

in my shorts without a single caress. It'd been too long since someone else had physically inspired me to come. Last time it had happened with another in close proximity had been back in the spring while attempting to make a baby with my wife.

And I'd been thinking about Jamie then too.

Fucking cheater.

While not unfaithful in the flesh, I'd sure as fuck crossed that line in my head. Wasn't fantasizing the same as committing the crime? Maybe not in court but definitely in a woman's mind if she ever found out.

Guilt swamped in like a stinking bog, black and ugly as fuck.

Dick going limp in a flash made rolling away from my best friend easy.

Jamie didn't move as I unzipped the screened opening of our tent and slipped outside into the cooler morning air. Still, no breeze rustled leaves, the reason the heat had stayed trapped inside the tent with us.

I filled my lungs, stretching my neck side-to-side and forcing thoughts of Shelly and how badly I wanted intimacy with Jamie rather than her from my mind. Talk about a rock and a hard place.

But what choice did I have?

I'd vowed—

Shutting down the usual bullshit once more attempting to take over my mind, I set about making coffee. Coach Bernard had an electric box set alongside the cement pad he used to keep his old pop-up camper on. A new trailer was hitched to his truck and followed along southwestward—probably deep into Texas by now.

Jamie and I had lifted the picnic table onto the platform,

so while he continued to sleep, I set to spoiling my best friend rotten. The coffeepot brewed and griddle sizzled on one side with still-chewy bacon, just the way he used to like it, and the other was readied for his favorite cheesy scrambled eggs.

He'd provided last night's dinner, the beer, and the water since Coach didn't have a well on-site, so I'd brought along the makings for breakfast. Lunch, we hoped to fry up some fresh-caught fish, but we didn't have any luck the day before.

"Fuck, that smells amazing."

I grinned, my focus on cracking eggs into a bowl as Jamie shuffled up alongside me as though asleep on his feet. He'd never been a morning person, and it warmed me to find something about him completely unchanged.

He grabbed bacon right off the griddle, cursing as he juggled it.

"Idiot," I mumbled, and he chuckled before scarfing the piece down.

"Mmm," he moaned, the sound deep in his chest.

Teeth clenched against my unsatisfied dick's wish to swell, I whisked the eggs a little too hard.

"Careful," he teased with a low rasp while pouring himself a cup of coffee. "We only have that one dozen."

"Yeah, yeah," I muttered, tossing in a handful of shredded cheese before pouring the mixture onto the bacon-greased griddle.

Jamie sipped and moved in close to look over my shoulder when he easily could have just checked out my work from my side.

Spatula in hand, I tensed as his chest brushed my back, his chin settling onto my shoulder for a brief second.

"Smells good," he murmured, his sleepy, rumbling voice

so goddamn close to my ear that shivers raced over my skin, causing goose bumps to riddle my arms and neck.

Shifting to my left rid me of his touch, and I crouched to pull a container of OJ out of the cooler. "Want to grab some plates and forks? Won't be but another minute for these eggs to finish."

Jamie did as suggested, and we kept silent when sitting to eat. We chowed down like we had as growing teens out in the wild, the fresh air intensifying our appetites. Food completely wiped out, we sat in our lawn chairs with another cup of coffee each while Jamie's brain came back online and we made a plan for the day.

Fishing in the canoe I'd brought along, swimming once the heat of the day got to be too much, then napping in the shade of the huge oak alongside the water's edge.

Sounded like perfection to me, especially considering my company and the lack of a nagging wife up in my business.

Jamie seemed relaxed and totally chill, so he'd definitely been passed out when I'd been on the verge of humping his leg with my morning wood. Either that, or he hadn't minded one bit—

Nope. Couldn't let my mind start wandering along that goddamned path.

Straight, I reminded myself since Jamie hadn't ever once given me reason to believe otherwise, and I didn't need to *know* otherwise because I had a ball and chain.

That shut-eye in the grass while a nice breeze cooled our lake water-covered skin turned out to be the best part of our day. Both sunburned and beat, we sprawled out and dozed, waking only when a boat beeped their horn from the cove's entrance, the people onboard hollering and waving.

Took my bleary eyes a few seconds to blink clear. By then, Jamie had already identified some of the guys who'd been on our football team back in high school, two of whom had caught up with him at the welcome home party. At least they continued on by rather than pulling in for a visit, which probably would have lasted well into the night considering the beer bottles they'd lifted. Their hoots had made it clear they'd been partying it up and didn't have plans to stop anytime soon.

Jamie and I had bullshitted on and off since morning, the comfort and ease between us as it used to be before responsibilities had swamped our lives. An occasional raunchy thought or certain way he moved his muscled body got my saliva glands going, but I was proud of myself for tearing my focus off him rather than drooling and my dick giving up my secret.

We lowered the grill part of the fire pit over glowing embers again and cooked marinated chicken breasts exactly as we'd done the steak the night before. Deciding to splurge a bit, Jamie had opted for pre-made Alfredo he wouldn't usually eat, but with training long over, he didn't mind foregoing macro counting when he felt like it.

More often than not these days, he'd admitted to doing so, patting at imaginary fluff atop perfect abs I'd tried not to lust over when swimming.

I'd moved the conversation on to the upcoming season and his and Coach Dave's plans. Our town wasn't much, but enough kids were bussed into the high school from smaller settlements miles away. Still didn't make for a lot of athletes, but Jamie held onto hope that his experience would bring more to the table for the Pippen Bobcats.

When we finally sat to eat dinner, the sun had sunk behind us, casting a rainbow of colors through the sky.

"Gonna be better sleeping tonight," Jamie said around a mouthful of food.

I nodded, taking note for the first time that the mugginess had faded from the air. "Supposed to drop into the seventies overnight."

"Thank fuck, because wearing shorts to sleep is bad enough when it's cold never mind stifling hot." His complaints over restrictive clothes always made me chuckle. Also had all sorts of shit I had no business thinking about riddling my mind.

We continued scarfing down our food, once again wiping out what we'd made and leaving us both feeling bloated from the pasta.

"Goddamn," Jamie complained, sprawling on the grass again rather than sitting by the fire pit.

"You alright?" I asked with a chuckle, eyeing how he rubbed his bare stomach.

What I wouldn't give—

I yanked my attention off him and placed another log onto the fire so we could have s'mores later. Maybe. Depended on how quickly our metabolisms made room for further indulgence.

"Why does food always taste better when it's cooked over an open fire?" he asked, and I poked at the hot coals a bit, waiting for the log to light.

"No clue but glad as fuck it does." Heaving a heavy exhale, I finally sat beside him, leaning back on my hands, gaze taking in what we could see of the sunset still streaking the sky.

Silence settled between us, a tension I recognized slowly slithering into my body. Did he feel it? The unrest inside me from my unrequited want for him? Was he even aware of how hot he was lying on the ground, arms up and hands beneath his head acting as a pillow, making his biceps pop? I eyed tanned muscle in my periphery, my desire to lick and taste his sweat on my tongue stronger than anything I'd ever experienced before. The sexy V leading into his shorts. Rippling abs. Prominent pecs with small, tight nipples.

I forced my gaze to stare out over the lake, remembering the pontoon full of people I'd seen creep by the cove's entrance today. Three women in skimpy bikinis had snagged my focus the first time they'd cruised past, but none of them had instilled that same draw inside me as that of my best friend a foot away from me.

I'd only ever had Shelly, and I wondered over Jamie's sex life. Not that it was any of my business, but curiosity had my brain buzzing.

"You must have had a different woman every night," I said, hating how the idea of that caused jealousy to twist around my stomach and squeeze.

"Nope. Not a one."

I whipped head toward Jamie to find him peering up at me, his gaze wary. "What? Why not?"

He studied me with an intensity that caused my dick to perk up.

Clearing my throat, I shifted my ass on the ground, hoping to ease the ache spreading through my groin.

"I'm demisexual," Jamie finally said, his voice low. "Never felt a connection strong enough with someone to make a move."

"Shit. You're a...virgin?" I cast a side eye, not ready to face him.

"Didn't say that."

Oh....oh fuck.

"You're into guys too?" I whispered, unable to keep from giving him my full focus.

Jamie swallowed hard before turning his face toward the sky so I no longer had access to his eyes. "Yeah."

I stared, beyond baffled, mind fucking *blown*.

"That gonna be a problem?" he asked, taking on a defensive tone when I didn't respond right away thanks to my unhinged jaw.

"I'm pan!" I blurted, my insides jittery as fuck. "I mean, I've only ever slept with Shelly, but...yeah. I'm pretty much attracted to it all. Beauty to me knows no bounds or gender, so if you're into guys, no problem here."

We both sat quiet, our breaths somewhat stuttering in and out into the tense stillness zapping between us. I had no fucking clue what to say. Couldn't ask why he'd never told me because I'd never shared my truth either.

Part of me wanted to question his sex life further, but that shit wasn't any of my business, and I didn't need to be thinking about Jamie having sex with another guy.

Eventually, I grew weary of leaning on my arms and lay down beside Jamie, watching pinpricks of light begin to break through the darkness overhead.

"Remember when we used to try counting the stars?" I asked, figuring it would be best to change the subject before shit got weirder than it already was.

Jamie chuckled. "Yep."

"The depths of the unknown, all that unfathomable distance beyond this lump of rock floating in space, is humbling," I murmured. "Kinda makes me feel inconsequential at times, you know?"

Jamie shifted, turning onto his side to face me.

My body rolled without thought, mirroring his position, and my heart rate jacked up to twice the norm.

I could still easily make out the dark blue of his eyes and the thick lashes Shelly had always envied. We'd never been this close intentionally outside bro-hugs, not with this kind of tension, the urgent need to close the gap between our bodies.

"Did you—"

"Have you ever—"

We both spoke at the same time and stalled out, our light laughs shaky with obvious nerves.

"Go ahead." I urged Jamie to continue, my pulse thrumming, butterflies attacking my stomach. Did we approach dangerous territory in sharing more personal shit than we'd done before? We both identified as queer, something else we had in common, but this yearning to explore beyond friendship thrilled yet scared the fuck outta me. I'd wanted him for so long and was nothing but softened clay in his hands.

I would have difficulty *not* being shaped however he desired.

Internally, I shook my head at myself, needing to stay on the safe side of friendship where infidelity wouldn't make me feel even shittier than I already did.

"If Shelly hadn't been in the picture back then..." Jamie's voice trailed off, and I waited to see what he meant to ask me.

"What?" I prompted him to continue, my tone nothing but a mere whisper, desperate for him to fill the thick air hovering over us like a heavy blanket.

He exhaled deeply, his gaze penetrating. "Do you think that maybe things could have been different between us?" he whispered.

Oh, Jesus. Fuck.

I swallowed hard, clenching my eyes shut. Why, of all

the times he could have spoken up about his wonderings, did it have to be when I was already married—and to one of our friends? Honoring my wife meant lying about my feelings for Jamie, but I couldn't do that to the man who I would have given anything to go back and choose instead of her.

I steadied myself before speaking raw truth that couldn't be taken back or erased from his mind. But I couldn't bear to meet his gaze. My eyelids stayed glued shut. "I only asked her out because I assumed you were straight. Didn't dare to dream I could have you."

Jamie cursed beneath his breath.

"It's always been you for me, Chaz," he whispered, his voice breaking and shattering my heart. "You're the only one I've ever wanted."

"Jamie," I choked out his name, curling in on myself enough my knees brushed against him.

He pushed hair off my forehead, and I bit back the whine rising up from deep inside my chest. "Want to kiss you so fucking bad right now."

"I..." I shook my head against stating the same, trying like fuck to focus on what was right. "That wouldn't be fair to Shelly." I grasped at the memory of my wife in my mind, the war inside me one that no man should ever have to face. Devastation didn't begin to describe the havoc wrecking my head and heart.

"Yeah." Jamie sighed heavily and rolled away, putting space between us that was cold and goddamned wrong.

For the best.

Why didn't that feel right either?

Chapter 7

Jamie

Neither of us slept worth a shit.

We didn't talk after toeing the line of friendship versus fucking. Not one goddamn word passed our lips the rest of the night. Chaz shut down, but I could sense his pain radiating outward like searing rays from the summer sun, burning my skin. Warning me to take cover. Protect myself.

Couldn't fucking do it. My insides bled, but I couldn't push for more truth between us when he struggled enough. What sort of friend would I be if I couldn't allow him space emotionally and mentally to get his shit figured out?

If Shelly wasn't in the picture, the night would have ended with one or both of us balls deep in each other. A flip fuck of the century. Years' worth of pent up lust and longing coming together in an explosive eruption of love. And cum. Fuck, a *shit* ton of cum if my throbbing nuts were any indication of how much I would fill his ass up.

My yearning intensified, and tense silence settled over the tent. The hours slipped past before exhaustion from playing out in the sun all day took me under.

I woke to find Chaz gone from his sleeping bag, a text

waiting on my cell letting me know he'd gone out to fish in the canoe before sun up. The second text required another read.

Chaz: **Regardless of everything I told you, I made a vow and need to honor it. Please tell me you understand.**

Unfortunately, I did.

Like me, Chaz was a fighter and didn't quit unless he had no choice.

And I wasn't a selfish asshole who was ruled by his dick. I just wanted the man happy. Hopefully, he would manage to find that again with Shelly, even though that meant he would never be mine in the way I found out he and I had both secretly desired for all these years.

Blowing out a miserable exhale, I stared at the top of the tent I had to myself.

Yesterday, I'd woken up to Chaz sprawled over me, heavy breaths suggesting he still slept. His cock had been hard and brushing against my thigh. In that moment, I had been a selfish prick, playing dead asleep and simply soaking in the warmth and scent of him since he wasn't aware what he'd done. Morning wood was very real, and I'd told myself he'd simply rolled toward his bed partner like he probably did in his bed every night. Unconsciously, he'd hugged my body, thinking I was Shelly.

I should have slipped away before he'd woken up embarrassed, but I hadn't been able to do the right thing and put distance between us. Soaking in his unintended affection had filled me clear to bursting with a rightness I'd never experienced before. Hadn't wanted that moment to end, so I hadn't done jack shit but pretended I slept too and was his pillow for a good ten minutes of heaven.

The second Chaz had woken, he'd gone still, tensed up

and not breathing for a few seconds before his inhales suddenly came quicker. Could have been from fear of how I might react to what he'd done while passed out, but he'd hesitated just long enough from moving away that hope thrummed through me, and I *swore* he'd intentionally ground his dick against my thigh.

For the space of a few rapid heartbeats, I'd imagined him snaking a hand down my torso beneath my shorts. I fantasized about starting out the day by devouring his mouth while we jerked each other off.

Would have been fucking perfection.

But he'd rolled and almost tripped in his haste to leave the tent.

I'd stayed put until my hard-on relented, but I'd crowded against him while he cooked our breakfast to see how he would react.

Even though his entire body had shivered from my touch, he'd been cold and standoffish, settling my mind on the fact his morning wood didn't have anything to do with who he'd clung to in his sleep. He most definitely had not sought out friction when pressing his hard cock against me.

Still, I'd felt the need to speak up, share the truth of my sexuality in case he'd realized I was awake and thought I might be all weird about what he'd done. Sure, it was a shitty conversation to explore, making Chaz possibly question his marriage, but so much had been taken away from me. I was desperate for some *good* in my life, something that would ease the ache in my chest.

Had I ruined the friendship we'd only begun to explore again?

The smart thing would be to pack my bags and head back to Boston, find work that wasn't anywhere near or included the man I couldn't have. Landing a job wouldn't be too difficult. Making connections was a possibility thanks to the couple of friends I had down there, but finding love again was off the table. No one would compare to Chaz. Didn't want anyone but him.

That idea of leaving him behind made my stomach roil, but I also wasn't about to walk out on those high school players I'd signed a contract to coach either. My assistant coach had a full-time job and was unable to take the lead, so I was stuck for the season with no chance of moving until at least late November.

With no answers other than to put one foot in front of the other in taking care of the responsibilities I'd accepted, I forced my ass out of the tent. Determination to keep my hands to myself and honor Chaz's vow to Shelly lay heavily on my mind.

Chaz sat on the canoe at the end of the cove, facing away from me, shoulders rounded as he slumped over his fishing rod. Did he feel like shit even though nothing had happened between us? Was he bummed as fuck about the choices we'd made that had led us to the path we currently walked?

I got the coffeepot going, dead set on getting back the carefree sense from the day before where nothing mattered and no responsibilities dragged us down. If I hadn't already fucked up too bad. We had a handful of hours before we had to pack and head into town. Well, Chaz needed to. He had work in the morning while I had nowhere to go until later in the week.

I heated up some sausage in a pan over the electric stovetop with plans to stir up some pancake mix as Chaz paddled toward shore. Maybe a hot breakfast would entice him to stay a little while longer.

Once he stood on land and pulled the canoe out of the water, I piled a plate high with food and set it on the table.

"Come eat," I ordered, keeping my tone light as though nothing too much or deep had taken place last night.

"Thanks," he said, tucking himself into the picnic table and allowing me to breathe a little easier.

"Any bites?" I asked, sitting across from him.

"No." He shoved pancakes into his mouth and wouldn't look at me.

I guessed we were leaving our conversation alone, but I was fine with that as long as we could move forward. "Hey, you still put those model cars together?"

A huff of laughter jolted Chaz on his bench. "God, no."

"Why not?" I asked, smiling at the upturn of his lips and the quick glance he'd gifted me.

"I don't even have time to shit, shower, and shave in peace let alone spare a second for useless hobbies," he said, shaking his head.

My heart ached even more for him, but I was determined to remain upbeat. "You know what they say about all work and no play..."

Chaz lifted an eyebrow in question while stuffing a whole sausage into his mouth.

Shit.

I tore my focus off the grease lining his lower lip as he chewed and swallowed.

"Something about having bills to pay? They're content at the end of the day?" he asked, joking. "We slay? Gotta jump into the fray? Might make us gay?"

My gaze jerked back to his at that last one.

"Shit. Was just tossing rhymes out. Didn't mean anything by it. And like I said last night, I'm pan—gay is good in my book."

I rubbed a hand over my scruffy face. "No worries."

"I was, uh, thinking I need to get back to town earlier than planned."

My chest caved in, but I wasn't surprised considering his mood. "Oh yeah?"

"Mmm." Chaz drank the last of the coffee I'd given him, and he stood, taking his plate with him. "Got a voicemail last night from a client. Car broke down, and I have to fit them in ASAP."

Unlike me, Chaz knew how to lie and didn't mind doing it.

But I would give him a pass, same as I always had. "Okay. Do you have to pack up now?" I asked.

"Yeah. I've got a shit ton of work backed up and would like to get a few hours in before Shelly comes home tonight."

Disappointment hit hard, leaving an ache radiating through my entire body.

"I'll clean up the breakfast stuff if you want to pack up the tent," I suggested, fighting to keep my true feelings from my voice.

He nodded and turned away.

It was a quiet hour between us before he dropped me off at home with a quick, "See ya later."

I didn't even get a chance to respond before he drove off, my camping gear at my feet.

Chapter 8

Chaz

I lied about that client but had more than enough responsibilities at the shop to warrant the early return. Having taken most of Friday and all of Saturday off, I'd gotten behind. Could barely afford the loan and utilities on both properties never mind pay someone else's salary. Yeah, hiring a helper probably meant we could finish up more jobs in a month, but I'd never been good with numbers. Didn't have the brains to figure out a budget that would keep us afloat long enough to get ahead.

So I continued plugging along.

Working my ass to the bone.

Hearing shit when I got home late at night.

Out of guilt over almost crossing a line that would break my vows, I asked my wife to go on a date the following weekend. She'd blinked, taking a few seconds to process my words before hesitantly agreeing. I insisted on going to Dig-In where she used to wait tables—because they didn't serve alcohol.

Tense silence settled between us as we sat at the table glancing over menus we'd both long-since memorized.

I went with my usual burger with Swiss and mushrooms, and she ordered the Cobb salad with extra ranch on the side.

"Miss this place?" I asked, hoping that topic of conversation wouldn't lead to a fight.

She shrugged, glancing around the retro diner that looked like it'd been zapped straight from the fifties to now. At least Old Man Ron had replaced the red vinyl bench seats like his daughter Addy had pushed for. Back in high school whenever we'd worn shorts, our bare legs had gotten scratched by the rips and fraying duct tape her dad had attempted to fix the seats with.

"I needed a change from the same old, same old."

I nodded, having heard the reason for her applying for a new job at the bakery/cafe downtown. Scone Haven had less on their menu and tables, but Shelly for some reason had thought the tips would be the same.

She hadn't listened to my input—what did I know of numbers anyway—and had made the switch because she'd been bored. Now, the struggle to pay bills had gotten worse.

"Those cranberry-orange scones you brought home yesterday were one of the best Kel has come up with," I said, trying again to engage my wife.

Kelly Powell was an out-of-towner who'd bought the bakery a few years earlier and had turned it into a better-than-Dunks stop for every single person in a twenty-something radius of Pippen Creek.

Shelly nodded her agreement and sipped her water, still looking around the diner rather than giving me her attention.

Uneasy silence snuck in, leaving me shifting on the bench.

Why did shit have to be so weird between us? What

had happened to that close friendship we'd once shared? The ability to bullshit and laugh about anything and everything?

I played with the straw in my Coke, swirling the ice around my cup while we sat, both of us quiet and obviously uncomfortable with each other's company.

That whole "growing apart" thing people used to justify divorce hadn't ever made sense to me. I got it now though. Too bad splitting up wouldn't work for us. We were both financially stuck with no other options on the table.

Addy approached with our meals, and I sat back as she placed my burger and fries in front of me. "Enjoy. Let me know if you need something else."

I nodded, eyeing my food while reaching for the ketchup.

"She didn't even say hi to me," Shelly muttered while drizzling her salad with dressing.

Rather than reminding her she'd left without giving a two-week's notice and probably burned the bridge between her and Old Man Ron's family, I bit into my burger.

"Could she be any more of a bitch?"

I glanced around, hoping no one heard my wife. "Shell, lower your voice," I muttered once I swallowed.

"Don't tell me what to do."

A muscle ticked in my cheek, and I focused on my dinner, regretting having pushed to eat out with her. Stomach continuing to knot, I had to force myself to finish my food.

The door opened behind me for the fifth or sixth time since we'd sat down.

"Hey, Jamie! Chief Sutton!" Shelly called all happy-like, and my breath kicked from my lungs like I'd been punched in the sternum.

Fuck. I do not need this right now.

Wiping my lips with a napkin, I straightened and turned to find both men readying to sit in the booth behind us where Addy had led them.

"Chaz," Sutton greeted with a nod. "Shelly."

"Chief." I glanced at Jamie. "How's it going?"

I could read the hesitation and wariness in Jamie's glance before he gave Shelly his attention. "It's going. Looking good, Shelly," he said, his smile forced.

"Just got my hair done," Shelly said.

I could imagine her flouncing the red curls over her shoulders but couldn't be bothered to face my wife. Jamie held me rapt with his backwards cap, the energy of his presence and the red-checkered shirt stretched over his pecs and muscular shoulders rousing my dick to life.

Fucking hell, this man.

Turning back around, I focused on my plate, annoyed I'd forgotten it sat emptied. I glanced at Shelly's oversized bowl to find she'd wiped out her salad. "You about ready to go?" I asked quietly, needing to get the hell out of there.

"You two care to join us?" Shelly asked rather than answering me.

No—please God, say no.

"Thanks, but we wouldn't want to intrude," Chief said, and I exhaled a lungful of pent-up anxiety.

"Oh, no biggie!" Shelly insisted, all sunshine and smiles. "I didn't feel like cooking, so we just dropped in real quick for a bite to eat. It's no hot date or anything."

Yeah, okay.

She stabbed me in what was left of my heart with that lie. I'd practically had to beg for her to agree when she bitched daily about us never getting out of the house together anymore.

"Maybe some other time," Jamie said, and Shelly ran with it, making plans he wouldn't say no to even if he'd wanted to.

In two weeks, he'd be coming over for dinner. She would create a delicious dish—he could bring the wine.

A few minutes later, I exited Dig-In behind my wife, hands shoved into my pockets because I couldn't stand the thought of touching her lower back or threading my fingers through hers in sight of Jamie. Not that she'd want me to do that anyway. She'd shied away the last couple of times I'd attempted some sort of affection...back in June, maybe?

But she could hang on me to put on a show whenever she talked me into going to Frenchie's and drank until she couldn't walk straight.

I dragged ass to my truck and hopped in. She shut her door loudly behind her, huffed, and crossed her arms.

"The fuck is wrong with you?" she asked, her tone bitchy as usual. "You practically cringed when I invited them to sit with us."

"Not in the mood to socialize," I said as an excuse.

"Yeah, you made that pretty clear by completely ignoring me over dinner."

"You weren't exactly chatty yourself, Shell." My clipped words revealed annoyance that would, without a doubt, start a fight.

Sure enough, Shelly ranted throughout our short three minute drive. We both slammed truck doors before stomping into the house. She went for the liquor cabinet. I headed to the guest room/office across the hall from ours.

"Straight to work!" she hollered, sarcasm heavy in her voice.

"I have bills to pay!" I yelled back, lying my ass off since I'd taken care of the house shit last week. Others statements piled up at the shop, but she didn't need to know the truth of my hiding away in the office. She could guess though. If I wasn't escaping to the shower, this room, with its small desk shoved in the corner with my computer and papers, became my hideaway whenever she went on a rampage.

The only problem?

There was no lock on the door.

Sure enough, Shelly came barging in a half hour of grumbling later, already well on her way to drunk.

I was selfish.

Didn't care I'd let her down and made her unhappy.

Wasn't bothered by the fact we hadn't gotten it on since April.

But I didn't bother reminding her she hadn't initiated sex or affection in that time either. Didn't mention my own depression and disappointment over our marriage and lack of closeness. Just kept my mouth shut in the hopes she'd run her mouth tired and leave me the fuck alone.

Took almost another hour before she passed out on our bed, her snores filling the entire single-story house that no longer felt like a home.

I grabbed a beer, stepped outside onto the stoop, and breathed fresh air into my lungs before drinking the cold brew almost in one go. I swigged the rest, emptying the bottle before descending the three cement stairs and heading into the backyard.

We had a small fire pit out we hadn't lounged beside since...who the fuck knew when. Rather than sit in one of the creaky, old Adirondack chairs set snuggly together, I plopped onto the grass, sprawling on my back.

Stars twinkled down at me, but they brought no joy.

Only memories of past camping trips and a more recent one that made my throat ache and eyes sting.

Chapter 9

Jamie

Chaz hadn't lied about the shop keeping him busy.

Two weeks passed before I saw him again and that was because Shelly had invited me for dinner when Dad and I had run into them at the diner.

Seeing them in their favorite booth they'd always sat in while dating back in high school had filled me with jealousy and a whole lot of ugly thoughts. Should have been me in Shelly's seat. Chaz would at least have been smiling at the person across from him. I would have played footsies. Slid my foot up to his groin and made him flush. Put the spark of life in his eyes that had been lacking every time I'd seen since coming home.

I was a fucking shitty friend wishing I could take his wife's place but couldn't help it.

If Dad noted my annoyance with circumstances and my mood shift from relaxed to uptight, he hadn't mentioned it. We'd discussed my lessening depression over my lost chances with the NFL and the upcoming Bobcat season while enjoying our appetizer of hot wings and blue cheese sauce. We also devoured the burgers Old Man Ron was famous for.

One topic I hadn't touched on was my best friend, his wife, how miserable they both seemed, and how I struggled to keep my focus on my life rather than theirs. During the days since we'd gone camping, Chaz hadn't reached out, and neither had I. I'd have sworn I'd definitely broken something by sharing about my sexuality. But, I'd never had a best friend as an adult who had more important responsibilities than hanging out with me.

I'd settled in my mind that I would fight through the end of the football season then decide on my next course of action since I still wandered aimlessly around in my head over what I ought to do with myself.

Shit really depended on Chaz and our ability to either get past our mutual want and put it behind us or fuck around and end up ruining his marriage and further soiling himself in his father's eyes. No way in fuck would he do such a thing. He would cling to his marriage with all his might simply to prove a goddamned point.

Couldn't blame the man though. He'd been through hell and back with his father.

Even though I didn't want to, I showed up at his and Shelly's house on Friday night with strawberry wine just for shits and giggles. My insides were a jittery mess, and wariness kept me a little closed off as was my norm.

Shelly welcomed me with open arms, her breath smelling of whiskey, voice shrill and on this side of annoying.

Chaz met my eyes for a brief second before turning away. No fucking way something hadn't gotten fucked up between us. I didn't know how to make shit better, and I forced myself to do the whole small talk/catching up thing with his wife while Chaz looked on in silence. Exhaustion still clung to him, and he appeared paler than expected considering we'd both tanned while fishing and swimming in the lake.

We hadn't even gotten to the table before Shelly had wiped out the wine I'd brought along. Like me, Chaz kept glancing at her with concern then insisted on helping get the food on the table since she was stumbling rather than walking from one end of the kitchen to the other.

Over dinner, Shelly hounded me for information like I'd expected that first night in Frenchie's, wanting to hear the gossip and about whatever trouble I'd gotten into. Like Chaz, she asked about women, and I grinned, reminding her that gentlemen didn't kiss and tell—same as I'd said back in high school when I'd taken a cheerleader out for ice cream because I feared people might start questioning my preferences if I didn't date.

"Come *on*, Jamie!" Shelly whined, her words slurred. While eating, she'd started on a bottle of white that she claimed paired well with the chicken piccata she'd made for us.

"Seriously, Shell," I argued, grinning again when all I wanted to do was assure Chaz, who'd rolled his eyes, that we were cool. Everything was fine. His wife wasn't annoying the fuck out of me.

She totally was.

My teeth ground behind my smile, and had it been anyone other than Chaz across from me, I'd have hightailed it the fuck outta there. Shelly had given me a snapshot of the woman she'd become that night at the welcome home party, and her behavior solidified she wasn't on the best path.

"How's work going at Scone Haven?" I asked about the

new job she'd started according to Chaz, hoping like hell to turn the focus off me and the total lack of women warming my bed.

While I no longer had to be wary about being gay going public, I wasn't in the mood to discuss men with Shelly either—or Chaz. Especially since that conversation would lead my mind to Zack and Elite and what it had felt like to have a semi-taste in the form of a fantasy of my best friend.

"Ugh." Shelly rolled her eyes before emptying half of her glass. "Kel's a great boss—don't get me wrong—but the pay kinda sucks. It's more of a bakery than sit-down cafe, and people don't tip like at Dig-In."

"Why'd you quit the diner? You've been there since what? Our junior year in high school?"

She shrugged. "Bored. Needed a change."

"Do you plan on waiting on customers for the rest of your life?"

"I had *planned* on being a stay-at-home mom," she stated rather snippily before sipping her wine and side-eyeing Chaz.

The desire to rip Shelly a new one had me fisting my hands beneath the table. "Ever think about going back to school?" I tossed out, feeling the need to keep the conversation off the lack of children running around their house, her obvious disappointment with her husband, and how much I was starting to hate her.

A snort ripped from her, ending in laughter. "I'm not any more college material than Chaz is. Hell, if it weren't for you, he wouldn't have even graduated high school."

While she spoke the truth, I hated how Chaz curled in on himself in my periphery at her harsh, unnecessary reminder.

My blood fucking boiled, and I saw red. "Your husband

knows cars inside and out. Could probably build one from the ground up," I stated probably too sternly, my fake-as-fuck smile fighting to stay in place. "I've never met someone who works as hard as he does and strives to succeed."

"Look in the mirror," Shelly said, completely disregarding the positives I'd pointed out about her husband.

"Yeah, and one misstep ended my dreams," I shot right back while she took another large gulp of wine. Why the fuck did I still grieve what I'd lost? How come I couldn't just fucking move on already?

She swallowed, casting another side eye at her husband. "But at least you can make time for your family and friends now."

Not exactly an upside to having your career ended, but I didn't get a chance to reply.

Shelly huffed a sarcastic laugh if ever I'd heard one. "Maybe you could help Chaz learn how to do *that* too."

"Jesus, Shell," Chaz muttered, tossing his napkin onto the table, which made me snap my jaw shut instead of chewing her out.

"What?" She turned to him, eyes widened as though surprised he was upset by her passive-aggressive bullshit. "You never have a spare minute for anyone or anything but that shop. Actually." Shelly turned her head my way, her eyes taking a while to focus on my face. I didn't bother hiding my disgust in her behavior. "You took off for a weekend with Chaz when I've been begging for us to get away for God knows how long." She almost lost her seat while looking back at Chaz. "And tonight you had *no* problem getting home for dinner when you're usually late."

"You haven't shown interest in going on a date for months," Chaz argued, his voice low, "and when I finally did ask if you wanted to go to Dig-In, you griped and bitched the whole time like you'd rather be anywhere other than with me!"

My gaze pinged between the two of them, my stomach in knots, my body heated with barely restrained anger.

"Well, you never ask about *my* life and how *I'm* doing. Everything is always work, work, work!" Shelly shot back, spittle flying from her lips.

"Because I've got bills hanging over my head," he stated through gritted teeth, his body practically vibrating.

Shelly rolled her eyes, and I wanted to throat punch the bitch. "Sure, Chaz. Sure."

"You have no fucking clue—" Chaz slammed his lips shut and stood, stacking our empty plates with more force than necessary. "Why don't you take the rest of your wine and make yourself comfy on the couch. I'll do the dishes."

She snorted, wavering as she stood. Wine splashed over the glass's edge as she attempted to top it off, but neither of us reached to help. "If you think just because you're cleaning up that you're getting any tonight, you've got another thing coming."

"*Think*," Chaz muttered under his breath as she stumbled toward the living room. "Another *think* coming," he repeated with heat in his voice. "As if I'd want sex anyway."

Still steaming inside, I grabbed the two serving bowls and followed behind Chaz, my feet itching to get me the hell out of there.

"Sorry about that," he said, setting the dirty plates in the sink more gently than I'd expected.

"Don't worry about it," I muttered, unable to bury the discomfort from my voice.

His shoulders slumped, and there was no way in hell I would leave him to clean up alone while obvious depression hung over his head like a rain cloud.

We worked together in silence, him washing and me drying, our shoulders and hands occasionally brushing against each other's, which eventually returned a sense of calm over the kitchen. Also got my dick a little too interested, but I didn't let my mind wander over fantasies I didn't dare hope would come true.

Once we finished, loud snores echoed throughout the downstairs.

"Damn." I chuckled, hanging up the towel I'd used to dry on the oven's handle. "I don't remember her snoring like that when we'd gone camping."

"It's new. All the hard shit she's been drinking." Chaz grasped the edge of the sink and dropped his head, heaving a huge exhale.

I stepped in close, needing to comfort him in some way. Probably not the smartest choice, but fuck it. Chaz's suffering hurt like fuck. "Come here."

He turned and stepped fully into my arms, burying his face in my neck, hands clinging to the back of my shirt like I was the only lifeline he had to keep his head above water.

Warmth settled low in my groin where he pressed tight against me, but I ignored the arousal swimming through my blood from the heat of his hard body against mine. I closed my eyes and held him close, giving what I could while selfishly soaking in the little bit of him I was allowed to have as his friend.

"Sorry you had to see and hear that shit," he whispered another apology, his breath hot on my skin.

I shivered, goose bumps rising along my arms, my dick thickening. "Don't worry about it. Every couple fights."

"Not my parents," he muttered.

Because his mother was a subservient, timid woman.

"You should have heard my dad and Darla go at it before she left."

"That's all we seem to do anymore."

Being the asshole I was, my mind once more went straight to the thought that Shelly ought to take off just like my mom did. Leave Chaz behind, brokenhearted so I could be the one to hold his hand and make him happy again. Especially now that I knew he wanted me.

The idea of that future sent blood to my groin. There was no hiding from Chaz what hugging him did to me, and I refused to be sorry for desiring him.

Chaz was the one to pull away but only enough to meet my gaze. Our lower halves still pressed together, and fuck me straight to hell, pain wasn't the only thing I clearly read in his eyes.

I swallowed, refusing to move even as his dick swelled against mine.

His gaze flitted down to my lips, and time slid to a stop. We hovered between fantasy and reality. Right, as I would see it, and wrong, as he definitely would after we crossed that line.

"Still want to kiss me?" he whispered.

"What about Shelly?" I hated having to remind him of the possible fallout when he already had enough shit on his plate, but honesty was what a good friend should go with.

He exhaled loudly, lips pressed tight as he studied my face.

I tried not to hold my breath in anticipation, hoping he would make the move so I wouldn't have to be doubly burdened by guilt over starting what we both clearly yearned for.

"It's not fair to her," he repeated what he'd said when

we'd been camping. "But I can't help this desire inside me. I'm so fucking lonely. Need this. Need y*ou*."

I ignored the sawing of logs from his wife and focused on the length of him that felt as desperate as mine. "Same. Always have and always will."

He sucked in his lower lip, nibbling, so I cradled his face in my hands and tugged the flesh free from his teeth with my thumb. His panted breaths warmed my mouth as he stared into my eyes.

"Jamie..."

"Yeah, Chaz. Whatever the fuck you want—it's yours. If having one taste of you makes me a bad man, then I'll gladly burn in hell."

He moved to close the distance between us, and I met him there with hungry yet gentle swipes of my lips. Fireworks exploded in my head like they'd never done before, even those few times I'd asked Zack for kisses. My pulse raced and skin came alive, every cell inside my body vibrating with need to love on my best friend. Erase all of his problems even if for a short while. Euphoric and on the verge of combustion, I ate at his mouth, desperate to dive deeper and somehow steal a part of his soul I could keep with me forever.

Flicking tongues and quiet moans flooded my senses, causing pre-cum to dampen the inside of my jeans. I couldn't get close enough. Lusted to drink him down, fucking fill him up, entwine our bodies so tightly together they couldn't be separated ever again.

Chaz whimpered, his fingertips digging into my lower back, and I didn't question the truth he wanted me too. Felt the same emotions coursing through his chest as I did.

I tangled one hand in his hair, the other to his nape before sliding my tongue into his mouth.

I didn't give a shit his breath hinted at lemon and capers. I'd never enjoyed a flavor sweeter than his underlying natural taste. Craving more, I deepened the kiss, groaning when he thrust against me.

His grasp shifted to my ass, and I rolled with his lead, working a hand between us to grab his dick.

"Fuck, I want you," I moaned into his mouth, licking in deep so he couldn't respond or attempt to deny me.

Chaz ground against me. He trembled from head to toe, his tongue fucking with ravenous strokes along mine as I squeezed and massaged his length.

My balls drew up, and I pressed my lips against his forehead panting for oxygen. "Gonna nut in my jeans."

"Jamie—*Jesus*." He bucked against me, and I captured his lips again, silencing his moans as he came. Wet heat seeped through his jeans against my palm, and I squeezed, wishing I had milked him properly, skin on skin.

"Fuck yeah." I shuddered as the first shot of spunk burst from my slit. "Shit, Chaz. Coming so hard for you—" I shoved my tongue into his mouth, groaning my release, grinding over his hip and thigh, wishing we were both naked, my cum smearing all the fuck over his skin.

Wanted it *inside* him. Down his throat so a part of me would always be in him.

We both shuddered, breathless and clinging to each other as we settled from the high of our shared release.

That line separating friendship from a whole hell of a lot more?

We'd wiped it clear from the sand between us.

And while I *should* give two shits about the woman passed out and snoring in the next room, I couldn't. She didn't deserve Chaz, and selfishly, I wished she was gone from the face of the earth so we would be free to love each other without hinderance.

Chapter 10

Chaz

Eyes clenched shut, a sticky mess in my boxers, I couldn't stop the guilt hitting me like a damned tsunami as the exhilaration of release faded.

Shelly had embarrassed the fuck out of me and made me feel like a piece of shit.

And Jamie had been there ready and waiting to take the sting of her words away with the comfort of his arms.

Once there?

Temptation had overridden my better sense, and I'd caved to my desire for Jamie, thinking that finally tasting his mouth would reveal it'd only been the forbidden aspect of having my straight best friend that had drawn me to him. I should have realized that was bullshit. After learning he was into guys, I'd been twice as desperate for his touch.

There would be no simple quenching of my thirst for Jamie.

I'd made a shitty error in judgment, giving into my lust like this. But regret? Never that. Having his mouth on me and finding release together had been the single best moment of my life. I couldn't imagine how much better it could have been without clothing separating us.

"What are we doing, Jamie?" I rasped, my heart hurting even worse now than before I knew what his tongue stroking along mine felt like.

Jamie clung to me as tightly as I did him, as though reluctant to let go. "What we should have been doing since middle school."

My pulse still thrummed, and I swallowed hard, pressing my face into his neck again. The scent of soap and the underlying musk of my best friend filled my nose. He'd skipped out on that new cologne he'd worn at the welcome home party, so he smelled exactly as I'd remembered, same as when we'd gone camping.

This—this right here is perfection. A dream come true.

Shelly snored especially loud before making smacking noises with her lips like she always did when she'd had too much to drink and crashed for the night. My wife. The woman who deserved my loyalty, and I'd failed her yet again.

Could I be any more selfish?

My eyes stung. "This isn't right."

"Please don't say this was a mistake," Jamie begged quietly, snaking his hand from between us to clutch me closer.

"It definitely wasn't smart," I tried again, still unable to pull away from him.

"I know," he whispered.

"My vows—"

"Goddamnit, Chaz." Jamie stepped back abruptly, my entire front chilling. A shiver rippled through me as I met his gaze. "That woman does *not* love you," he hissed, pointing toward where Shelly snored with every inhale.

"It's obvious as fuck you're both miserable. I won't ask why you're still with her because I know you refuse to fail in your Dad's eyes. Is she seriously not aware of all that bullshit? Hmm? You never shared that part of you with the woman who agreed to wear your ring?"

"No," I answered honestly what we'd already talked about beneath the stars while camping. "I've only ever wanted to protect her. Shelter her from my trauma since she had enough of her own."

"She's your partner!" Jamie whisper-hollered. "Made a vow to have your back, to stand beside you, same as you did with her. She's supposed to be your oak in the storms of life when you falter!"

Only one person had ever been that for me, and it sure as fuck wasn't my wife.

My throat tightened, and I blinked a few times to keep tears from welling in my eyes. Difficult didn't begin to describe the situation I'd put myself in by playing with fire. But Jamie was right. I refused to fail even worse than I already had in this stolen moment with him. This shit ended here. Now. "I think you should go."

"Chaz."

I shook my head, taking a step backward rather than throwing myself at him like I longed to do. "Please."

"Fuck." Jamie lifted his hand to rub over his face but hesitated, inhaling deeply over his palm—and groaning.

Heat rushed through me as I became aware of the wet mess inside my jeans and how he'd cupped me through my orgasm. He flicked out his tongue, running it along his fingers as though searching for a hint of my cum.

My mouth dried as I watched him, dick once more swelling. "For the love of God, Jamie, please," I rasped, on the verge of begging him to drop to his knees and get a proper taste of me.

He lifted heated blue eyes to mine. "I'll be waiting, Chaz. Always."

I worked my throat as he spun on his heel and showed himself out the kitchen door rather than the front before shutting it quietly behind him.

Knees weakening, I slid to the floor and leaned against the cabinet, my face in my hands. The stickiness inside my boxers was uncomfortable as hell, but I couldn't be bothered with seeking comfort of any sort. Felt like I didn't deserve it, that I ought to sit in the mess I'd made of myself—literally and figuratively.

Even if I had the balls to tell my parents that Shelly and I wanted a divorce, we couldn't afford to separate. We'd sold her mom's house to pay for her room at the nursing home, and the bit of savings we'd scrounged together back before marriage had been the down payment on our small ranch house outside Pippen Creek's southern end.

Lawyers would have to be involved because no way would Shelly allow me to escape with little more than the clothes on my back. We both had vehicles in our own names. Her old Camry piece of shit and my truck had seen better days a decade ago, and we'd been milking them for all they were worth. She would demand the house and everything in it, even though she couldn't afford to pay the bills that came along with the responsibilities of living on her own.

I wouldn't be able to buy again or even afford rent after she wiped me out. I could always stay at the shop because I sure as fuck wouldn't move in with my parents. A cot in the office would work as a place to sleep, but the lack of shower and full kitchen would make for a miserable existence.

Will I have to buy her out of the business?

The thought made the blood drain from my face and heart race to the point I swore it would tear from my chest.

Her name wasn't on the loan or listed in my filed paperwork, but the equitable distribution law would be in her favor. I might have to sell the business I'd bled for, but even then, I would probably only get what I still owed my father for the loan.

If that, because the fucker hadn't budged from the ridiculously high percentage rate he'd wanted in return for lending me the cash.

"Shit." I tipped my head back and slowly exhaled until my lungs emptied.

I *was* thoroughly fucked, and not in the way I dreamed of with Jamie.

"Wish I could sleep here and never wake up," I whispered to myself, on the verge of tears over the bleakness of my existence.

Shame for wishing for death rose up to choke me, and always the fighter, I forced myself to my feet and dragged my ass into the living room.

Shelly sprawled on the couch with her head at an awkward angle, her glass on the floor, wine sloshed across the small rug. At least it was white and couldn't stain.

Annoyance and disdain caused my mouth to curl into a grimace at the sight of her drunkenness. An asshole partner would have left her to sleep through the night and wake with a crick in her neck.

But I *wouldn't* quit, even though every part of me except for my pride pushed for me to move on and at least attempt to be happy while living broke on the streets. I would be Pippen Creek's first homeless citizen.

Lips in a thin line, I cleaned up that mess and maneuvered her dead weight into my arms to carry her back to the bedroom. She continued to snore in my ear, and I carefully laid her on her side of the bed. She rolled, smooshing her face into the pillow, but didn't wake.

Hands on hips, I watched her sleep.

Everything about my life hadn't panned out as I had once hoped for. Hell, I couldn't even find something positive in my reality.

Except for Jamie, the one I'd denied. He'd left me like I'd told him to, and I hated that even more.

My throat tightened again, and I turned from my wife, guilt like slimy tentacles slithering through my veins and making me feel like a piece of shit covered in flies. I needed a rainstorm to wash away the stench of failure.

I showered, scrubbing the evidence of my infidelity down the drain, refusing to think on how a single make-out session could change a man's existence.

But I couldn't.

Bed made, I had no choice but to sleep in it. There would be no easy way out, no miracle that ended in a happily ever after. As teens, we all used to joke about marriage being a ball and chain.

How fucking true *that* had ended up being.

Regardless of our actions being wrong, Jamie's kiss had felt like the key to freedom from those shackles. The memory would always remain, something to remember in my darkest days.

Chapter 11

Jamie

Football tryouts arrived and were over before I had a chance to breathe and work through what had gone down with Chaz, which hadn't been me, unfortunately. What I wouldn't have done for another chance to make him come but this time on my knees with his cock shoved down my throat.

Dreamed about it.

Jerked off to the memory of his tongue in my mouth.

Moaned his name while shooting stripes of sticky white over my abs on a daily basis.

But he kept his distance, and I honored his request, attempting to bury my focus in the job I'd agreed to take on. Unfortunately, I was so damned distraught over the Chaz situation that I didn't enjoy being on the gridiron again like I'd hoped for.

While a few of the boys who'd tried out for the team had decent enough talent, not one screamed superstar or even promised to lead us to a winning season. A girl named Gabby had shown up, determination in her eyes when she told me she was on the soccer team and was one hell of a kicker.

She hadn't lied. None of the guys on the field could keep a kickoff in bounds or came close to splitting the uprights from even twenty yards away.

Gabby making the team was the easiest decision, and I'd noticed the annoyed glances she got from a few of the other boys who'd been on the varsity the year before. That, I wouldn't allow.

The first official morning of practice, nerves a little on edge, I stood in front of our pitiful team, Coach Dave by my side.

Heat already rose off the grass beneath our feet, but I ignored it in favor of looking over each and every kid dressed in their red-and-white practice uniforms that had seen better days.

My voice shook as I began the speech I'd written and rewritten a million times, determined to let them know I expected inclusion and acceptance and that nothing else would be tolerated.

"I don't care where you're from, what pronouns you use, or what color your skin is," I stated loudly enough even those in the back would hear. "We are a team, and we will act as a single unit both on and off the field, in school and out. That means having each other's backs—*all* the time. If I catch wind of any bullying among you or even quiet, under-handed bullshit toward one another, you'll be benched. Period. I don't give a shit if you're a starter or if we're playing our biggest rival that night. Understood?"

Heads nodded, and more than a couple of, "Yes, Coach!" responses raised into the air.

"I expect everyone to give one hundred and ten percent. If the person beside you falls, you help them to their feet.

Someone's head hangs, you offer encouraging words to hype them up. We're going to work hard, sweat, and bleed together, but I promise you'll be better human beings by the end of this season."

A few hollered their agreement.

"Now get your asses in gear and give me a lap!"

The kids took off, falling into line, some sprinting because of first day excitement. True colors would show soon enough.

Coach Dave clasped my shoulder. "Great speech, Coach."

"Thanks. Was scared shitless, to be honest," I said with a chuckle, my voice still shaky.

"I appreciate the inclusion part. Gabby is my niece, and I was afraid the boys would make shit hard for her, you know?"

Dave hadn't told me details about any of the kids prior to tryouts. He'd wanted me to have fresh eyes on those returning as well as those recently graduated eighth grade, hoping things would be fair for everyone. Not that we'd turned anyone away. We needed as many kids on the side-lines as possible since a few varsity players would be on the field for both offense and defense.

"I'm happy to have her," I said, grabbing my clipboard from off the bench and striding onto the field, ready to get this show on the road. Excitement trickled in as I watched them round the final corner and sprint toward us in the middle of the field. Reminded me of all those hot, sweaty days I'd done the same, visions of grandeur keeping me focused on the goal line. A small shot of adrenaline raced through me, and I actually grinned. "Let's get these kids stretched out then see what they're made of."

Turned out, those kids were tough stock and I was

proud as fuck. Only two puked, surprising for how hard we pushed them in the August humidity, but we had everyone stay hydrated and they got breaks throughout the morning's session. We took time off for the kids to head home, eat, and rest then were back at it for a few hours after the heat had faded.

Day one had been a success as far as I was concerned. Not a single kid dropped out, and they left more wound up than I'd expected after probably having sat on their asses all summer long. While I'd been active and lifting weights, I groaned while stepping beneath the shower that night. Only a few years older than the seniors, and my body ached.

A week later into preseason practice, and I was dead on my feet. While I wasn't nearly as physical as the kids on the field, I still stumbled into the house every night, beat and fucking starved, my knee sore as hell.

Friday, Dad snickered as I collapsed at the table where he'd saved me a plate.

Chicken parm.

"Fuck yeah," I muttered, diving in without even washing my hands.

"How'd it go today?" Dad sat across from me, his after-dinner beer in hand.

With how busy we'd both been, I'd only seen him in passing, not really having time to catch up.

"Better than I expected," I replied as soon as I finished a mouthful of crunchy coating, tender meat, and gooey cheese. "Gonna have to ice my knee again though. Kinda overdid it today."

"You gotta take care of yourself, kid," Dad said, getting back up and heading for the freezer.

"I'll grab an ice pack after I eat," I said, but he didn't listen, filling a bag with ice cubes and wrapping it in a towel.

"Thanks," I mumbled when he handed it to me. Cold pack in place, I returned to the food, my insides sighing over the savory taste I barely gave myself time to enjoy before swallowing it down and forking up another bite.

Dad could cook like a damned master chef.

"If you ever get tired of trying to keep the citizens of Pippen Creek in line, you ought to open a restaurant."

He laughed and reclaimed his seat. "You think I work too much now. I'd be married to a job like that, a fuck-ton hours a day, seven days a week."

Sounded about right. Old Man Ron's truck sat alongside Dig-In Tuesday through Sunday from breakfast until dinner and had from as far back as I could remember. He and his daughter Addy shut down on Mondays along with Thanksgiving and Christmas, but that was it. Didn't seem like enough for either of them to have a life outside the diner.

"How are you feeling about the move now that the season has started? Any better than a couple of weeks ago?" Dad asked, and I considered his question while chewing, the tang of his homemade sauce making love to my taste buds.

He hadn't pried much since I'd moved home, allowing me space and quiet to work through the shit in my head. Last we'd talked had been at the diner that night Chaz and Shelly were finishing up with their date.

"Some ups but mostly downs."

"I'd hoped starting with the team would give you a bigger boost."

I shrugged, eyeing my plate. "I'm just busy right now. A little overwhelmed. Feeling a little worthless outside coaching if I'm being honest."

"Maybe you need some new hobbies. Go on another

ride along with me since it's been a while. Hang with Chaz this weekend. Grab some beers, kick back, and relax."

A grimace etched on my face. "Yeah...not sure spending time with Chaz is a good idea."

"Something happen?"

Shit. I rubbed a hand over my face and glanced across the table to find Dad's brow deeply furrowed. "You could say that," I muttered and shoved another bite into my mouth.

"Want to talk about it?"

"Not really, but going to therapy for months taught me spilling shit is better than bottling it up."

Dad lounged back in his chair. "I'm all ears, and you know I won't judge."

And that was exactly why I trusted him with my truth. Or most of it, rather. I told Dad about the camping trip, what Chaz and I had discussed that night. Also went into the whole dinner thing with my best friend and his wife and how we ended up kissing in the kitchen while she'd slept. The ejaculating in our pants I kept to myself. Skirting the truth of how we'd ended the scene wasn't lying.

"You love him."

Jerking my focus off my food I'd been staring at while sharing what bothered me, I met Dad's kind gaze. Zero trace of disappointment shone in his eyes over me making out with a married man. A small smile curved his lips, a reminder of the constant gentleness and his unconditional acceptance of me throughout childhood. I'd definitely been lucky to have him. Still was. He more than made up for my lack of a decent mother, always having my back.

"What makes you say that?" I asked, curious about how I'd given myself away.

"Please." He leaned forward, chuckling, elbows on

table. "You've been in love with that boy since middle school. Anyone with half a brain would have seen it had they paid close enough attention."

The one person I wished caught onto my feelings back then had missed it, causing us both to end up unhappy with the path we'd taken. But I couldn't blame Chaz. I'd been more focused on my dreams than my relationship status. I'd put football before him.

Mistake of a lifetime.

My face must have revealed my misery because Dad reached over and grasped my forearm. "Just keep swimming."

I snorted, rolling my eyes over Dad quoting my favorite childhood movie.

"Seriously, Jamie. You've got this."

"That's *my* saying," I reminded him.

"And I believe in you. Love him from a distance if that's all you can have. Be his friend, and available whether it's a shoulder to lean on or an ear to listen. Just keep your dick in your pants."

Heat flushed my face. "Dad!"

He sat back and shrugged. "You wouldn't want to be in Shelly's shoes, would you?"

I snorted at the thought of sharing a bed with Chaz every night. "Fuck yeah, I would," I answered honestly.

"I mean being the one cheated on."

Leave it to Dad to speak the harsh truth.

Weeks passed without running into Chaz. I knew the man was under the gun, and whenever I drove past his shop, I craned my neck to catch sight of him. Whether the sun was out and the garage doors stood open or darkness blanketed town and interior lights shone at nine at night, he slaved away to make ends meet and prove his worth to his dad and himself.

I saw Shelly every time I stopped by Scone Haven for a coffee. They made the best in town, and I didn't have any other option unless I headed south a few miles to hit the closest Dunks. Supporting local businesses had been ingrained in my head since childhood, and that wouldn't change, no matter how much my stomach turned whenever Shelly smiled at me, her eyes lighting up.

Guess she *had* slept through her husband's and my make-out session. Chaz had obviously kept his mouth shut about our actions as well or she wouldn't have acted so damned nice while waiting on me.

When I exited the coffee shop, the guilt over being the reason he had cheated on her ate at my insides even if she didn't deserve his love. Just as terrible, I couldn't help but continue wishing she was out of the picture for good.

Talk about a shit friend. Could I be any more awful of a human?

But even though we'd been the three musketeers, according to the rest of the townsfolk who'd known us back in the day, she and I hadn't ever been close. Shelly had been the tagalong younger sibling type who had followed us everywhere. Both Chaz and I had been like big brothers, even though we were all in the same grade. I wished I could pinpoint what had been the catalyst that had sent her and Chaz into a relationship, but looking back, I couldn't recall jack shit.

But as the days passed, little things began to give me a hint of joy and a better sense of purpose.

Thanks from my players for making first string when

they hadn't expected to. Knuckle bumps from Coach Dave and appreciation in his eyes over how I ran the program. Seeing Gabby excel and the guys on the team acting more like brothers to her than rivals. A few other parents offering their time to help in whatever way they could—and showing up with sliced oranges or Gatorade after practice to prove they could be counted on.

Josh, our backup quarterback and a junior, attached himself to my hip and soaked up every word I said as though thirsty as fuck to learn from my experiences in the NFL. Like Chaz, he didn't get along with his father, but unlike my best friend, Josh was out and proud, sometimes wearing mascara and lip gloss beneath his helmet.

I envied his confidence.

"God, I love that boy."

I eyed Josh in my periphery on the sidelines, his focus on first string practicing a new play, helmet in his hands. He'd spoken quietly as though to himself, and I wasn't sure if I ought to say something or keep my mouth shut.

Josh glanced over at me, and I gave him my attention, since Coach Dave was striding toward the defensive players, hollering about the missed tackle that allowed our running back to break for the end zone.

The kid's eyes stated he wanted me to interact, that he needed this discussion.

"Can I ask who?" I lowered my voice so the others on the sidelines wouldn't pick up on the conversation just in case it was a secret.

"Kyle," Josh whispered back, a soft smile curving his lips, his face lighting up at his admission.

The first string quarterback, the one he always spatted with. His best friend.

My chest tightened, and I had to swallow before replying. "Does he know how you feel?" The question choked me, causing me to clear my throat.

"Nah. He's straight." Josh sighed and turned his focus to the field again, the longing in his eyes obvious now that I was aware of who his heart wanted.

If only I'd been brave as a teen, if only I'd opened my mouth and sought out advice at his age. I refused to encourage Josh to keep quiet, and I sure as fuck would assure him that I had his back no matter his decision.

"You ought to tell him."

He whipped his head toward me. "And risk losing the only friend I have?"

"Better to have tried than to live with 'what-ifs' ringing in your mind every day." Gravel coated my tone, and I swallowed hard.

Josh studied me in silence, his gaze too damn wise for a seventeen-year-old. "Sounds like you're talking from experience, Coach."

Eyes stinging, I nodded, indirectly coming out for the first time to someone other than my father. "I chased my NFL dreams instead of a happily ever after with the guy I loved, and now it's too late. He's married, and you damn well better believe I regret that decision."

"Shit, man, that sucks." Empathy filled his steady gaze.

"It really does." I clasped his shoulder. "Most kids these days have to learn the hard way, but trust me when I say someday watching your best friend vow his love to another until death parts them will be the most painful experience of your life."

"Worse than a career-ending knee injury?"

Fucking hell, that reminder hurt but not as harshly as the constant knife in my chest stabbing at my heart.

"Yeah, kid," I rasped. "Lots worse."

"Second string, let's go!" Coach Dave hollered, and Josh took off without another word.

I watched him high-five Kyle as they passed each other, and a sense of peace settled over my melancholic heart.

If my return to Pippen Creek led to those boys finding happiness together, then all the shit I faced living in the same town with Chaz might be a little worth it.

Chapter 12

Chaz

Shelly had gone south to Berlin for the previous three weekends, but I couldn't have cared less. Her friend Tara was going through some shit, and I was appreciative of her stealing my wife away as often as she did. Offered me space to draw a proper breath and a reason to go home for dinner rather than hanging around the shop so I wouldn't have to listen to her nag and bitch until she passed out drunk.

Ever since I'd tasted Jamie's mouth, I'd been ten times as miserable than before his return. The mistake of giving into temptation pressed on my head and heart like the weight of a F-350, crushing my spine and causing every inch of me to ache.

I needed every break I could catch and didn't mind Shelly disappearing as often as she did. Made for one hell of a quiet, peaceful house, that was for damned sure.

She stayed in town tonight though because it was Pippen Creek's first home game for the high school football team. While I had zero interest in hanging with her like we'd done every year since on this night as far back as I

107

could remember, I wasn't about to miss out on Jamie coaching on the gridiron where we'd played together.

Even if we hadn't spoken for a few weeks, I would show my support from the stands along with the rest of the town.

I finished up an alignment job, and rather than lingering to clean or doing paperwork so I wouldn't get home until after dark, I stepped out into the early evening's cooling air and filled my lungs with something other than the scent of grease and oil.

A car sped past, most likely on the way to the season opener, "Go Bobcats" in bold, red letters on the back window brought a smile to my lips. When Jamie and I had played on the team, the cheerleaders had done the same. The tradition continued, as would Frenchie's being packed to the brim after the game while the players and their friends partied hard over at the pond beside a bonfire.

Chief Sutton and his officers on duty would be busy until the early morning hours, no doubt.

I climbed into my truck far earlier than usual. I couldn't remember when Shelly and I had last sat down to dinner, and it wasn't going to happen tonight because I'd made sure I would have time to get ready and nothing else.

Shelly watched TV and was dressed to go when I walked in the door. "We need to leave in a half hour so we get good seats on the fifty yard line," she said, her level of bitch voice lesser than I'd expected after I'd waited until the last second before heading home.

"I'll be ready."

I showered quickly, and we were out the door fifteen minutes later, giving her jack to complain about. I even wore a newer T-shirt, same as I had while on that date all those weeks ago because I wasn't in the mood for her nagging. The silence in the car, while better than bitching, was still depressing as fuck. At least she didn't stink of whiskey. I wished that I felt free to hold her hand atop my thigh like we'd done on this night every year since I'd gotten my license.

But I didn't, same as on our last date.

And she couldn't be bothered to initiate affection either.

We didn't have a far drive, and the atmosphere when we parked and walked through the busy gravel lot toward the school's old stadium kicked in a little adrenaline, enough to lighten my steps.

I told myself I was looking forward to the game, the enjoyment of tradition, and the hype about to hit us from the younger spectators with their face paint and signs, the cheerleaders egging them on. Music already poured from crackling speakers, coating the arriving crowd with excitement.

A grin crept onto my face, and I gave in to the thrilling swell seeming to wash over the town.

It was going to be a good night.

And my thought had nothing to do with the fact that I would see Jamie for the first time since the "incident". I'd kept my head down whenever driving in or out of town, ignoring any red vehicle in my periphery in case it was his SUV. I'd figured out of sight, out of mind. Hadn't exactly worked. Hadn't helped my state of shame or my lust-filled mind toward the man either.

But not seeking him out intentionally made me feel like I did good. Hadn't failed outwardly since that night, at least. In my mind was a whole other story, one filled with fantasies and what-ifs I focused on while jerking off in the shower or bathroom at the shop. Happened almost daily now that my libido had woken with a vengeance.

Turned out, there was nothing wrong with my dick.

109

Just my marriage.

I ignored the field while following Shelly through the gates after paying, traipsing along behind her, hands shoved in my pockets, enjoying the scent of hot dogs and popcorn from the snack shack we passed. A line at least ten deep already crowded the small building, little kids running around and roughhousing.

It seemed the whole town had thought like Shelly and had shown up early which was the norm on opening night: Grab the best seats on the hometown bleachers that didn't even span the entire length of the field.

Our feet clomped on metal treads as we climbed the stairs, and we shuffled past a few people already settled in toward a narrow opening between families.

Shelly greeted the person on her left while plunking her ass down, and I had to excuse the woman on my other side while sitting on the cold seat. Everyone scooted, making room for us, and I exhaled fully before shifting my focus to the field.

Neither team had come out yet.

I breathed easy even though we'd gotten there before for their big entrance at the field's end.

The cheerleaders had created a banner full of color and exclamation points for the team to barrel through once they'd been announced over the ancient sound system continuing to pump out music.

Shelly sat engaged in conversation with the woman beside her, face animated as though everything was rainbows and unicorns, faking like she always did, but I couldn't be bothered to do the same.

I ignored her false front, focusing inward on the tremors in my stomach and the dampness on my palms.

Was Jamie freaking the fuck out right now?

Part of me wanted to go find him, tell him he was going to kick ass, give him a good luck hug. Linger for a long time, drink in his scent, and taste his mouth—

No.

Clearing my throat, I turned toward the woman on my right.

Kathy "Babs" O'Neill was Chief Sutton's secretary and dispatch down at our small police station. She'd been playing that role for as far back as I could remember. A kind, older woman who had a spine of steel, she didn't take any nonsense from townsfolk or the officers, and treated everyone like family.

"Think Jamie's about to shit his pants?" Her question made me laugh.

"I was wondering the same thing. I would be in his shoes."

Babs glanced over at Shelly before dismissing her as thoroughly as I had. "He's a good man, just like his dad."

"One of the best," I admitted quietly.

She patted my knee. "You're lucky to have him as a friend, Chaz. I hope you're aware of that."

I swallowed hard. "I am, ma'am. Yes."

"Don't ma'am me," she fake grumbled. "Makes me feel like an old woman."

"You're far from old."

"In spirit, maybe," she argued.

The music cut off, a high-pitched squeal over the speakers—also tradition—sounded the time had come, and heart racing, I turned my focus toward the banner and cheerleaders waving their pompoms.

A loud yet muffled voice got the crowd amped up, welcoming everyone to Pippen Creek Stadium. The opposing team came running onto the field with the announcement they would attempt to beat the Pippen Creek Bobcats.

We were small but mighty.

At least, that was the reasoning for the mascot in the seventies. Unfortunately, the name didn't mean shit when it came to football. We hadn't had a winning season in any sport since the early eighties, back when our parents had been kids.

This year's captain, Kyle Danowski, barreled through the banner, fists pumping in the air, and a river of red and white flowed onto the field behind him. "In The Air Tonight," by Phil Collins, attempted to drown out the roaring crowd through the tinny speakers.

The coaches followed, jogging rather than sprinting like their players.

Jamie kept his attention set forward, face filled with grim determination. A man on a mission, he didn't fuck around but gathered the team on the sidelines directly in front of us, his focus solely on the jittery kids surrounding him.

Whatever he told them got lost in the crowd's continued ruckus and the music.

After a short time of stretching out, the team took to the field, the coin toss having us kick off.

I tried to watch the game and get caught up in our defense killing the opposing team and offense actually pulling off a few first downs. More often than not, my gaze glued to Jamie on the sidelines, causing me to miss out on the action. The man looked good. Edible. Down-right sexy as fuck. His wind-blown hair, wide shoulders covered by a Bobcat's sweatshirt, khakis form-fitting enough his ass made my dick twitch. The memory of having that body pressed fully along mine while we rutted against each other sent searing heat over my skin to the point I sweated.

Shelly ignored me, screaming her head off at every play, good or bad. She didn't understand the game even though she'd been a cheerleader when Jamie and I used to strive for wins on the same field. She'd been the cutest one in those short skirts, pompoms waving, fiery hair tamed and slicked back in a high ponytail.

The perfect cheerleader for the team's quarterback. High school sweethearts, the couple crowned homecoming queen and king our senior year. Everything Shelly had hoped for.

An ache settled in my chest as I realized nothing about the woman sitting beside me affected me in the same way Jamie did. Never had.

Still, those had been the good old days when even though we'd said life was so tough, unbearable at times, shit had been easy compared to adulting. When the only strife was learning how to accept my best friend was straight and wouldn't ever be mine. I'd thought it had been difficult settling for Shelly since I couldn't have him.

Oh, how shit had changed.

Teeth gritted, I forced myself to stay put when I wanted to escape, but I couldn't feign even a hint of excitement as those around me. My heart broke over and over whenever I glanced at Jamie. The what-ifs, all the regrets, piled up to bring back that F-350-inducing pain in my bones.

The game lasted what felt like ten hours, and the Bobcats bombed in the second half, walking away with a terrible loss. Thirty-one to three.

Gabby, Coach Dave's niece, had gotten us on the scoreboard late in the second quarter, splitting the uprights like a pro. The crowd had gone wild, jumping up and stomping on the metal bleachers. I'd managed to stand and clap, my gaze glued to Jamie's smiling face as he congratulated Gabby as she ran off the field. He'd held her helmet in his hands, face close as he said whatever a coach did when edifying their kids.

I'd never known such jealousy, a yearning to trade place if only for a few seconds with a teenage girl who had Jamie's undivided attention.

He'd patted her shoulder, and she turned toward the players around her, quite a few headbutting helmets with her.

The team didn't exit the field nearly as high on adrenaline as they'd taken to it before the game, but at least they held their heads up as though having adopted their coach's fighting spirit.

"Frenchie's?" Shelly asked as we slowly made our way out of the stadium with the rest of the disappointed yet still buzzing crowd.

I shrugged, not really in the mood for socializing, but Jamie would be there, the same as Coach Bernard always had, I didn't doubt.

"Yeah, sure."

A half hour later, I slouched on my barstool, wishing I'd insisted Shelly drop me off at home first. She'd downed a couple of shots, enough to loosen her tongue and to hang on me like she did when drunk and in public.

Yep. All was fine here, folks. We're still happy as raccoons in dumpsters covered in shit and stinking to high heaven.

Jamie arrived, causing quite the stir regardless of the town being bummed we'd lost. My pulse sped up at having him in the same room as me. The crowd surged over him, offering condolences and causing his smile to stitch into place without a hint of happiness behind it. Had he felt pressured to show up? Chosen to do as Coach Bernard had always done when he probably would have rather headed home to nurse his mental wounds? I didn't doubt he blamed himself for the loss, even though from what I'd noticed, he didn't have the best players on the field.

Eventually, he worked his way through Frenchie's crowd until our gazes caught.

Shelly grabbed him up with a hard squeeze, rocking back and forth while laughing loudly. She, at least, offered congratulations over how well he'd coached, rather than bemoaning the scoreboard.

Jamie's smile appeared a little more genuine, his eyes soft when they returned to me.

I held out my hand, needing contact desperately, and at the sparks shooting up my arm over the clasp of his palm to mine, I choked on a groan. "You did well out there, Coach," I rasped, needing to speak loud to be heard over the people chatting around us.

"Thanks, Chaz." His gaze flitted down to my mouth but jerked back up and away as though he was afraid of where his thoughts had strayed.

My lips tingled, and I pressed them together as he released my hand, wiping his palms down his thighs.

Shelly, wavering on her feet and with a second or third bottle of beer in hand, watched us, her gaze flitting between the two of us. "It's really nice having you home, Jamie." She slurred her words as usual. "Chaz needs a good friend to get him out of the shop more. Are you busy next weekend?"

"Game a week from tonight, same as every Friday, but that's about it," Jamie replied, glancing at me.

"You ought to drag his ass out the pond for a guys' weekend again. Maybe *that'll* make him smile."

Jesus Christ.

Annoyance roused inside me. "You're not my mom and don't need to be setting up play dates for me, Shell." If the woman only knew how badly I was trying to remain faithful to her, she wouldn't be trying to throw Jamie and I together, never mind into a situation where we shared a too-small tent. After having made out with him to the point of busting a nut in my boxers, I feared another camping trip would land me beneath him, his dick buried so damned far up my ass I wouldn't be able to breathe.

Desperate desire swept through me, and I closed my eyes, fighting off the blood rushing to my groin.

Goddamnit, this whole situation is fucked.

Regardless of my guilt, I wouldn't say no if he initiated. My want outweighed my morals when it came to Jamie Forester.

Chapter 13

Jamie

"I'd be up for another weekend at the pond." I agreed with Shelly's suggestion, hoping Chaz caught onto my intentional sexual innuendo.

His quick, intense stare promised he had, but he didn't turn me down immediately like I expected.

Shelly attempted to elbow him and missed in her drunken state, almost stumbling past him. I grabbed her arm to hold her steady.

"Go have fun, Chaz," she slurred, "because I'm spending next Wednesday through Sunday with Tara. Her fiancé is being a douche, and she wants to head to Boston for a few days."

"My schedule is packed, including Saturday, and I can't close the shop." Chaz's excuse caused Shelly to roll her eyes. "And Sunday, I'm going to my parents for Dad's birthday."

"When were you going to tell me about *those* plans?" Shelly asked with a little heat in her tone, and he shrugged as though indifferent.

I lay my hand on Shelly's lower back, thinking a show of affection might help keep the peace between them.

She shied away and swigged her beer, feigning interest in the crowd around us.

"Mom called while I was at work the other day, and I forgot to mention it," Chaz offered.

"Not like I'm gonna be here anyway. Frenchie!" Shelly called, waving her hand before lifting her empty bottle.

Frenchie nodded, and I turned to face Jamie, needing him to know I was available if he ever changed his mind about us. "Maybe some other weekend?"

"Yeah, maybe," he said, going for a noncommittal shrug, but he couldn't hide the heat in his eyes when he looked at me, the yearning he tried to squash but couldn't.

Selfishness rose up inside me, and I held his stare, hoping he would see how desperate I was to strip him down and flip fuck until we passed out cum-covered, every cell in our bodies sated for the first time in I expected both of our lives. Sure, he and Shelly used to be all over each other back in high school, but no fucking way could she give him what I could. The emotional connection of unconditional love and acceptance. Surely those two things when wrapped up in the physical made coming together all the better.

I lusted to find out.

Fucking drooled for it.

Shelly started chatting with the woman beside her, leaving us free to continue our stare down that promised fulfillment in every way I'd fantasized about.

Pain and weariness filled his hazel eyes and etched his brow, even though desire radiated from deeper inside him. He'd completely lost the tan from our camping trip, his skin pale yet unblemished. His full lips pressed together briefly, and I swayed toward him like he'd activated a magnetic field around his body, pulling me in one torturous inch at a time. Satisfaction awaited at the end—I fucking knew it. Could taste it—

He angled away from me, and I grasped his arm. Breath held, he studied me as I gently brushed my thumb over the sensitive skin inside his elbow.

"Y-You okay?" I asked, voice lower since I stood close to him.

He started to nod but stopped and shook his head, his focus on my mouth.

Exhaustion from denying us or pretending everything was fine in his life? Perhaps both?

I flicked my tongue over my lower lip intentionally, and his breath caught, pupils dilating exactly as I'd expected.

Fucking hell, this man.

"The last place you want to be on Sunday is with your parents," I said, pulling him in a little closer so I could speak almost directly into his ear, using the ruckus around us as a reason for being all up in his space. A deep inhale filled my lungs with his scent and stiffened my dick. "Skip out, Chaz. Spend the day with me. We can simply act like best friends or do whatever the fuck you want."

I stepped away enough to see his face, and at the blatant lust in his gaze, I dropped my hands and shoved them into my pockets to stop myself from grabbing him.

Chaz swallowed hard, and with every second he agonized over his decision, my pulse pounded.

Tonight's game had been a bigger disappointment than I'd expected, but this tension? Made up for every second. I'd had no visions of winning considering we'd faced the best team in our league, but I'd hoped to get more than three points on the board. The kids hadn't seemed as upset as I was. But then again, they played for love of the sport, most not driven to come out on top.

That thought put me back in the present and the fantasy of me cradled by Chaz's thighs while I fucked into him with slow, steady thrusts, our gazes locked, a cocoon of love wrapped around us.

The perfect fucking moment in time I wanted more than anything.

Win on the gridiron with the Bobcats included. If that made me a lousy coach, so be it. I couldn't help what my heart longed for.

"Sunday?" I pushed when he didn't respond.

At his slow nod, I expelled a heavy breath. "Your place or mine?" he asked, his tone resigned but filled with his usual persistent determination I'd always admired.

The promise of crossing another line hovered between us as real as the scent of booze and sweat in the air. Honoring vows didn't mean jack shit when it came to the same desire we shared for each other.

"Dad's off on Sunday and will be home, so yours?"

Chaz nodded again, swallowing hard and tempting me to lick up his throat.

"I'll see you then," I said, obvious intent coating my words of my plan to *see* every goddamn inch of him stripped down.

His head jerked in yet another nod, his pupils swelled and traps up tight near his ears beneath his T-shirt. "You can come whenever you want." The rasp in his suggestive tone stroked over my balls and taint, causing my asshole to clench with yearning to be filled.

Good thing I'd worn briefs beneath my khakis or I'd have been in trouble. My entire body vibrated with the need to kiss his mouth and claim him for the world to see, but now wasn't the time or the place.

I winked and turned away, counting the days until I would have Chaz in every way.

Nine, so just over a week.

Dexter walked into Frenchie's, but Dad didn't follow on his heels like usual.

I ambled over to my dad's best friend, and he flashed his grin, pulling me in for a quick bro-hug.

"Heard your kids played their hearts out tonight," he said, stepping back.

"Yeah. I'm bummed they didn't get the win. Maybe next time."

"Maybe," he agreed, but like everyone else, I was sure he didn't hold onto hope. "Buy you a beer?"

"Not sticking around, but thanks."

Dex nodded and glanced around the bar as though scoping out the possibilities for a hookup. Guess that was why he hadn't dragged Dad along for a night on the town. We sure didn't have much to choose from though. He'd have been better off using an app, which included men from down in Berlin.

Dex's gaze caught on someone, and his mouth twisted like he'd bitten into a lemon.

"You okay?" I asked with a chuckle, trying to figure out what'd set his grimace in place.

"Yeah—new guy just hired." Dex shook his hand, disgust clear on his face. "He's a punk. Gets on my last goddamned nerve."

Surprised raised my brows. "Seriously? You like everyone."

He huffed a sarcastic laugh and turned back toward me.

"Almost everyone. Christian Cole can go pound sand for all I care."

I had no clue who the fuck he was talking about, but Dex strode toward the bar a few seconds later and bumped not so subtly into a dirty blond on the stool beside him before ignoring the fuck out of the guy. Sexual tension filled the space between them. It was as obvious as Iris's blue hair where she stood behind the counter filling a pint glass for Dad's best friend.

Whoever that Christian guy was, he did more than get on Dex's last nerve, that was for damned sure.

"Going home already?" One of Dad's officers snagged me by the front door—Davidson. The single playboy the local ladies swooned over.

"Yeah, I'm done with the noise."

He chuckled. "I hear that. Been a long as fuck day. Looking forward to my bed." I doubted he slept in it by himself all that often considering the talk on the town.

"Trouble at work?" I asked.

Dad hadn't mentioned anything, but I'd only seen him at home for a few minutes before heading out the door for the high school.

"Nothing out of the ordinary," Davidson said, running long fingers through his thick, wavy hair. "Just the usual bullshit of a small town."

Which meant petty stuff. Calls about bears in trash cans. Skunks walking down the road in broad daylight. The occasional domestic issue between screaming partners. Our town drunk slumped over on the park bench and needing a place to sleep off the alcohol since he couldn't remember where home was. I'd pretty much seen everything imaginable while doing ride alongs with Dad. Nothing serious but exhausting all the same.

"Take it easy, Officer Davidson," I told him, clasping his shoulder.

"Plan on it."

Like Dad's co-worker, I too looked forward to my bed. But mostly because the sooner I slept, the sooner the next day arrived. Then the next and the next, until Sunday dawned, and like Chaz had said, I could come whenever I wanted.

Can't fucking wait.

Chapter 14

Chaz

Who was I kidding?

I'd known shit would end up this way even though it shouldn't.

Next Sunday night, I would give Jamie full access to my body. I would willingly and without hesitation surrender all of myself to him and do whatever he wanted. He would be my first outside marriage, the one I'd been madly in love with for half of my life.

Intentionally cheating on my wife would make me a piece of shit husband.

Guilt would rot my guts.

Shame would eat at my soul.

Did I give a shit about those three facts?

Clear into the following week, no, I did not. The chips would fall where they would whether it was a one-time hookup between me and my best friend or a continuous affair that went on for years. I couldn't bring myself to say no. I'd longed for closeness and emotional intimacy for too long. Had been starved for true connection with the only person I'd ever truly wanted it with, and desperation became the deciding factor.

We could both keep secrets when needed.

I stared at myself in the shop's smudged mirror while washing my hands after jerking off for the second time Wednesday morning. Feverish, bright eyes peered back at me, judgmental as fuck, but I couldn't be bothered now that I'd finally made up my mind and Shelly was gone until next week.

Nineties grunge rock muffled through the closed bathroom door. Eddie Vedder accompanied the thoughts that had rattled around in my brain since Friday night at Frenchie's when Jamie had propositioned me.

I'd understood and had willingly agreed. Flirted right back and made my intentions known.

Premeditated infidelity. Never would have guessed I'd gladly indulge in that particular sin, but I was done sacrificing my happiness for everyone else's. Not like we would get caught. Shelly would be hours away down in Boston. No one would think anything funny was going on for my best friend to stop by during the middle of the day. Locks were on doors and blinds hung over windows for a reason.

Privacy.

And we would have hours of it to finally ignore everything but indulging in what we both wanted.

Needed.

"You're a piece of shit," I muttered since that's what I should say, unable to look at myself any longer. I grabbed some paper towels and dried my hands before shoving out the bathroom door and into my office.

Papers and file folders littered my desk along with some outstanding invoices and other bills that had been piling up over the previous two weeks. I needed to pull out the checkbook and get shit taken care of, but my brain was a mess, and I was in a pickle.

What else was new?

Paying Dad for the loan needed to come first before the electric and combined internet and phone bill at the shop. Yeah, I had a landline. Had the same number from the previous owner so I wouldn't lose out on returning clients. I should have sat down to address my financial responsibilities on Monday, but I'd required hard labor to keep my body busy and exhausted so I didn't call Jamie and beg to move up our date because I was desperate for his dick.

Sitting with a pen in hand while trying to make sense of numbers hadn't ever come easy. I'd tried Monday morning for about an hour before rolling up the shop's two bay doors but couldn't pay attention to what needed to get done first. Couldn't even bring the paper in front of me into focus. As I'd often done in high school, I'd tossed my pen and strode away since there was no Jamie on hand to encourage me to keep plugging along. No kind words of wisdom, showing me different ways of getting shit to stick in my memory, speaking to my brain as though he knew exactly where mine went every time I tried to learn something new.

He'd been a lifesaver—

"Charles Henderson!"

Fuck.

My eyelids slammed shut at my father's voice calling over the music playing in the shop. The door to my office was open, so I wouldn't be able to get him gone without exchanging words. Rather than slipping into the bathroom again and hiding like I'd have done at home when I was a kid, I made my feet take me forward.

Time to face the fire I should have realized would flare up in my inability to write out a check on Monday. At least he waited two days rather than the usual one to bitch about me being late.

Dad stood, hands on hips, peering at the car I had up on the lift awaiting its new catalytic converter. He'd come from work, his gray combover perfect as always, suit coat unwrinkled even though he'd been in his office all day. His perfectly knotted tie wasn't quite tight enough in my opinion. Lips in a thin line, he oozed his usual disappointment over the vocation I'd chosen even though it fit me better than accounting ever would. Distaste intensified in his dark eyes when they landed on my smudged overalls.

I nodded a greeting, when I'd rather have told him to get the fuck out, and headed toward the second bay's car waiting for new headlights. Grabbing what I needed from the workbench, I settled in to finish the smaller job while my father spewed the usual shit.

"Your loan payment is late."

Of course he had to show up rather than texting me a reminder.

"This is the fifth time this year, Charles." His tone bled frustration, same as always.

"Haven't gotten to administrative or money stuff yet this week," I mumbled, wondering why the fuck he was so obsessed with my shortcomings. "Been busy."

"I recently learned that's what Shelly has been complaining about to your mother for the previous couple of months." Disappointment coated his words and leaked into my ears like an oil slick, black and not easily scrubbed away.

Fucking hell, that woman...Shelly had no clue the hornet's nest she messed with by oversharing with Mom. Riling up my mom meant pissing off Dad. He might be a grade-A asshole when it came to his only child, but he adored his wife and worshiped the ground she walked on. It was too bad Mom hadn't recognized the power she had over him and set him straight whenever he'd bullied me as a kid. She'd been raised to act like a fifties housewife who didn't talk back or complain, the perfect helpmate for my father.

Made me want to fucking puke and definitely had caused a root of bitterness inside me toward the woman who should have put me first.

"I'm working my ass off, Dad, trying to pay the bills as quickly as I can," I finally replied through gritted teeth.

"One would think the loan would take precedence over a tab at Frenchie's."

My eyelids slammed shut. So he *had* heard about the alcohol consumption lately. But had he paid attention to the gossip of who sat at the bar slamming back shots with friends? "I'm not the one with the booze problem, Dad."

"Is that so, son? I've heard you're often there right alongside your wife, drinking down that vile horse piss."

Only twice since July had I done that, but who was counting? Hell, I hadn't gotten anywhere near drunk either night, but that didn't mean jack shit to Dad. He only ever saw the negative, and his mind was unable to focus on anything that might resemble me getting something right for a change.

I tossed aside my tools and strode back toward the office, intent on doing what I should have done Monday to avoid this type of confrontation.

"You need to keep your wife in line before she further soils the Henderson name." His stern statement came as no surprise, but at least I managed to withhold from snorting or spouting off curses that would only make him shake his head with even more disappointment.

My hand shook as I scribbled out a check out to Clifford

Henderson, unloving father and unforgiving-as-fuck loan holder. Heat lay on my cheeks when I handed it over, gaze somehow steady on him.

He'd followed me to my office but had stopped in the doorway, glancing around my unkempt space, his nose wrinkled, while accepting my two days' late payment. "I would suggest hiring someone to help around this pigsty, but you obviously can't afford another laborer when you can barely make ends meet."

I gritted my teeth. How much had Shelly told Mom?

"Your mother said you're coming for dinner on Sunday?"

An electrical current rushed through me as the real plans I had for that day whipped through my mind, keeping me from getting pissed about his observations of my office.

"Nope, won't be able to," I corrected without feeling bad in the slightest. "I've got money to bring in so next month isn't the sixth time you have to go out of your way to even speak to me."

"Charles." He pressed his lips tight, and thank fucking hell the office phone rang.

"Gotta get that—you can see yourself out." I turned my back on Dad and settled into my squeaky chair, reaching for the phone.

Dad left without another word, disappearing out the door.

I answered the phone, my pulse still thrumming, heart in my throat. "Henderson Auto."

"Chaz? It's Sutton."

A grin split my face, and I released a huge exhale in attempts to calm my nerves. "Hey, Chief. What's going on?"

"Are you at the shop?"

Dad had disappeared through the bay's open door, thank fuck, but the worry in Sutton's tone flatlined my lips.

"Yeah. Everything okay?" I asked, my voice still shaky from Dad's little visit.

"Shelly's been in a car accident. You need to get down to the hospital in Berlin as quickly as you can."

I blinked, dust motes slowly falling in the patch of fading sunlight filtering through the shop's dirty windows.

No way I'd heard him right. Shelly was with Tara. Heading to Boston for the weekend.

My ears rang, causing his voice to muffle as he continued.

"Wh-what?" My mouth sputtered an attempt to ask for clarity.

"Shelly... Accident... Berlin hospital."

Those four words broke through, assuring I hadn't misheard. My chest went tight, and I struggled to breathe. "You're not k-kidding? I mean, you're sure it's Shelly?"

"Yeah, Chaz," Sutton assured me, his tone full of empathy. "She's in critical condition and en route to the hospital."

Fucking hell.

I stared unseeing across my office, my mind starting to race, my body cold.

"Want me to come pick you up in the cruiser?"

"N-No." Fuck. Talk about a dropped wrench in my life I did *not* need. We had no health insurance for hospital bills —I would lose the goddamned shop.

How bad are her injuries?

I finally wondered what I should have the second Chief broke the news, and humiliation kicked me in the guts for that not being the first question out of my mouth.

"She gonna be okay?" I finally asked.

"I don't know, Chaz, but it's not looking good. You need

to get down there, but drive safely. You have any trouble, pull over and call me."

I forced air into my restricted lungs, trying to get a handle on myself. "Yeah—yeah, I will."

"Want me to get in touch with Jamie? Let him know what happened?"

Jamie.

Sunday.

"Please," I whispered, my throat tightening at the sudden overwhelming need for him rushing through me.

"Drive careful, Chaz. Call me if you need assistance." Sensitivity bled through Sutton's voice, making my eyes sting with tears. Or maybe it was my desperation for his son's arms causing the emotion.

"Will do," I croaked out before hanging up and staring at the black, antique phone.

Thoughts rushed through my brain, but I focused on the most important. Why hadn't worry over my wife been my first reaction? Any loving partner would have been torn up inside and desperate for answers about their well-being. Humiliation worse than any I'd experienced before slammed into me, causing me to curl in on myself. My office chair squeaked in protest beneath me as I rocked forward, elbows on knees and head in my shaking hands.

What the fuck kind of husband was I?

An unfaithful, piece of shit one.

I moaned, running my fingers through my hair and tugging harshly. "Jesus fucking *Christ!*" I swallowed hard against the rasp in my voice and hopped up from my chair, needing to move—be proactive—anything other than do nothing like I suddenly felt guilty of since spring.

It took around two minutes for me to shut the shop down and hop in my truck, my legs weak and hands trembling along with my chin. I struggled to set my cell in its holder, but when I finally managed to do so, the screen came to life as my thumb brushed over it.

Shelly had texted an hour earlier.

Breath once more stuttering out, I picked my cell back up and clicked on the message icon.

Her typed words made my stomach turn, and I scrambled back out of the truck to heave up my dinner all over the paved lot.

Chapter 15

Jamie

Four days until I got my hands on Chaz—fucking finally.

I stood in the shower, my body amped on adrenaline even though I'd about killed myself alongside the kids on the practice field after school. My dick stood at attention, but I ignored my hard-on, determined to save it for Sunday. Edging always paid off though, so I lingered, enjoying soaping up my junk.

Felt so fucking good. His mouth or hole would be a hell of a lot better though, and I had plans to choke him with one load then fill his ass with another. I would gladly return the favor too.

Groaning, I tipped my head toward the ceiling and stroked until my balls tightened.

My cell rang, making it easier to release my hold on my dick and finish rinsing, telling myself yet again that withholding for now would be worth it. If he took a turn bottoming for me, I planned to watch my seed leak out of his hole before using my tongue to lick him clean.

But if he only wanted to top?

I wouldn't complain. I would love on Chaz however I could have him.

My insides lit with butterflies over the countless possibilities and ways we could get each other off while wrapping a towel around my waist.

Jesus, I couldn't fucking *wait*.

I picked up my cell off the bathroom counter while checking myself out in the fogged mirror and using my fingers to brush my wet hair from my forehead.

Dad had called, then texted, telling me to get back to him as soon as possible.

My brow furrowed. Pulse kicking up a notch, I tapped on his number.

He answered on the first ring.

"What's up?" I demanded, hating how my guts twisted.

"Shelly was in a bad car accident, and Chaz is headed to the hospital."

I blinked. "Huh?"

"Shelly was in a car accident—"

"Oh shit," I cut Dad off, hurrying out of the bathroom for my bedroom. "She okay? What happened?" I yanked open a drawer, grabbing jeans and a T-shirt as Dad filled me in on what little he knew. Every word caused the blood to drain from my face and my chest to tighten.

She'd been T-boned by some dude who'd run a red light. He'd hit the driver's side, and she'd been rushed to the hospital in critical condition.

My heart pounded as I struggled to get the clothes on over my damp skin. "You let Chaz drive to Berlin on his own?" I snipped my words, unable to regulate my emotions over the sudden news that chilled my spine.

"He refused the cruiser."

"I'm gonna head down there."

"Figured you would. Be safe, and let me know what's going on when you get there."

"Will do." I hung up, tossed my cell onto my bed and quickly shoved my feet into some sneakers.

"Jesus, fuck!"

I couldn't begin to imagine what Chaz was feeling. The worry. Anxiety. Fucking gut-wrenching stress that brought about an instantaneous headache. I experienced all three, and she wasn't even someone I considered a friend anymore.

I ordered Siri to get in touch with Chaz while rushing out the door, keys in my trembling hand.

The call went straight to voicemail.

"Shit—Chaz. Dad just told me about Shelly. I'm on my way—be there as soon as I can." I bit my tongue when the words *I love you* almost slipped free, hitting end instead and tossing my cell onto the passenger seat.

Both hands gripping the wheel, I raced through town, ignoring the speed limit signs. Route 16 opened up ahead of me, and I roared southward on the highway, lips pressed tight, my eyes stinging yet dry as fuck at the same time.

Bile burned the back of my throat as I considered the secret wish I'd had floating around in my head ever since I'd come home.

That Shelly would be gone. Dead.

My head moved in a slow back and forth shake of denial.

She—not like this. Please.

I choked on a sob, tears suddenly rolling down my face. It'd been years since I even considered believing in a god, but I started whispering prayers to every single one I knew the name of, begging for Chaz's wife to be okay.

"No way this is happening," I cried out, smashing my elbow into the driver side window and only hurting myself.

No whisper of assurance from any god soothed my anger. The turmoil continued to roil in my chest, making breathing difficult.

I swiped at the wetness on my cheeks, telling myself over and over, "I've got this." All three of us would get through whatever awaited, and I would change my thoughts toward Shelly. Be a better friend. Be there for them *both* and offer support in whatever capacity I could.

I had my emotions somewhat under control when I rushed into the nearly empty ER and saw Chaz sitting in the small waiting room, elbows on knees, gaze on the floor. His shoulders slumped, defeat written in his posture.

My heart seized up, skipping a beat.

Oh fucking hell.

Swallowing hard and tears once more threatening, I hurried toward him, the stench of chemicals burning my nose. "Chaz!"

He lifted red-rimmed eyes but didn't stand or burst into sobs. Chaz simply watched me approach, his face void of emotion while I swallowed convulsively to remain stoic.

Was he in shock?

I'd expected him to be an absolute mess like I was inside.

I knelt in front of him, grabbing hold of his hands and searching for a hint of what he was thinking, where his mind was—how his wife fared.

"Shelly?" I whispered, my throat closing off.

"In surgery," he muttered, his tone just as unmoved as his face. "Massive internal injuries. Doesn't look good." He pressed his lips tight and glanced toward the doorway, eyes still dry as a bone.

"Fuck. Jesus, Chaz." I threw my arms around him and squeezed, but he stayed passive in my arms, a limp fish who'd been out of water for too long. There was no point in lingering. Chaz was past accepting comfort of any sort. Releasing him, I slid onto the chair beside my best friend, grasping his hand in mine, refusing to break contact if only for my own sanity.

He squeezed—proof of life—but didn't speak. Thankfully, he didn't pull away.

"I'm here, Chaz," I rasped. "Whatever you need, okay?"

"Thanks, brother."

We sat in silence, my mind stewing and continuing with those goddamn prayers on repeat as the minutes ticked past. More than anything, I wanted to wrap my pinkie around his but didn't feel the freedom to do so. Wasn't sure he'd allow it anyway.

The occasional sound of the automatic doors swishing open around the corner to admit people into the hospital reached us. At least we had the small waiting room to ourselves and didn't have to attempt conversation with strangers.

A code broke the stillness from the overhead speakers, taking me back to the hospital in Texas. A blown knee wasn't *shit* compared to this kind of trauma.

That purpose I'd been searching for hit me like a goddamned Mac truck. I'd been too blinded by my woe-is-me attitude to see the truth.

My sole reason for breathing was to stand by my loved ones. Help them on the journey they'd chosen for themselves even if it didn't include me being by their side. A job just afforded me the ability to exist on earth. It didn't matter what occupation I ended up with or even where.

I would support and edify those I cared about no matter the situation. Whether they returned my love or not.

My ass grew numb, as a sense of peace settled into my heart. The newfound revelation didn't rid my mind of worry though. If anything truly happened to Shelly, I would never forgive myself. Couldn't even begin to imagine—

A guy in scrubs appeared in the room's entryway. Same as my best friend, the doc showed zero emotion.

Chaz at least straightened, seeming to ready himself for the worst. He dropped my hand and clasped his knees, knuckles turning white as he stared unblinking at the man.

"Mr. Henderson?" the doctor asked.

"Yeah," Chaz rasped.

"I'm sorry, but your wife passed while on the operating table."

Static hit my ears, and I only caught bits and pieces of his explanation.

Internal injuries beyond repair.

Crushed spine.

Wouldn't have lived a full life even if she'd survived.

Chaz didn't twitch or blink, unlike me who couldn't sit still due to the clenching of my guts. I cringed forward as though stabbed in the stomach.

"Her pregnancy wasn't far enough along to tell the sex of the baby, either," the doctor continued. "You have my deepest condolences, Mr. Henderson."

Pregnancy...

Chaz continued to stare as though frozen.

Oh fucking Christ—Jesus!

My chest caved inward, wetness rushing to coat my eyes at the horrid news dropped in Chaz's lap. After all this time, years of trying...his determination to fulfill Shelly's dreams...

Chaz returned his gaze to the floor while my mind continued to stall out on partial thoughts.

The doctor left us once more in silence, and I bit my tongue to keep from losing my shit.

This wasn't possible.

Couldn't be.

I—fuck!

My body shuddered, my heart thumping heavily in my chest. My palms sweated, and the dinner I'd wolfed down threatened to make an appearance.

Was this God's way of punishing me for my selfishness?

Needing...I wasn't sure what, I reached for Chaz's shoulder and clasped on tight in a show of support even though I seemed more desperate for it than he did. Warmth radiated from beneath his mechanic coveralls, and I closed my eyes, wishing our souls could connect so I could understand what he was going through. How he felt. The thoughts in his head.

How could I be there for him if he didn't speak?

Unsure of how to comfort him, I simply stayed put, fighting off emotions while he sat unmoved and somber. Restlessness attacked my legs during the long moments of shameful reflection and not knowing what to do. My agitation grew with every quiet tick of the clock, the hopelessness causing me to open my mouth.

"Chaz?"

"I-I need a minute."

"Want me to contact your parents? Tell the nursing home staff in case Shelly's mom is having a lucid day?" I had to move, keep me from spiraling further into the shame rotting my soul.

He huffed what sounded like a snort. "Dementia never sounded so good." Chaz heaved a heavy exhale and nodded. "Yeah—I would appreciate that," he whispered. "Thanks."

I squeezed his shoulder and stood, anxious for space while wanting to stick close. "Be back in a few."

I breathed deeply, trying to get myself under control. Maybe I would call Dad and have him reach out to Chaz's parents so I could sit in privacy for a few minutes and lose my shit without anyone seeing.

The automatic doors opened as I approached, a guy a decade or so older than me running past, sobbing out of control.

That was what I had expected from Chaz, even though he and Shelly had been on shaky ground. Hell, any sort of emotion would have been nice, giving me some sort of hint into how Chaz was handling the situation so I could figure out how to help him.

He fared better than me, that was for damned sure.

I exited the building and turned left, breathing in the cool evening air, closing my eyes against the parking lot lights and the flashing ones of an ambulance. "Siri, call Dad," I croaked into my cell.

"Jamie?"

"She's gone, Dad," I gasped out the words, my heart breaking along with the floodgate holding back tears. "C-Can you tell the Hendersons?"

"Jesus—I'm so sorry. How's Chaz holding up?"

Like a goddamned oak while I crumpled beneath the crippling weight of guilt.

"Still in shock, I think," I managed to answer in between sobs.

"Don't worry about making calls—I'll get in touch with his parents and the nursing home. You just go hug that boy of yours tight. He'll need you now more than ever."

I nodded even though Dad couldn't see me. If he knew that I was responsible for her death—

No.

I wasn't so stupid to believe I'd been behind the wheel of the car who'd smashed into her, but goddamnit, how many times had I wished her gone?

Hanging up, I slumped to the cement sidewalk, leaning against a wall, head in my hands. In my current state, I wouldn't be any help to Chaz. I ran my hands through my hair, biting my tongue until I tasted blood.

Chaz would hate my guts if he ever learned I'd wanted his wife out of the picture so I could have him all to myself. He could never know the truth. It would wreck us for sure.

How the hell did we move on from this?

Could we?

Chapter 16

Chaz

Emotionally dead, I replayed the surgeon's words over and over in my head, wishing I could at least bring myself to anger since grief refused to hit like it ought to. My sense of shame intensified over my inability to cry or rage over the loss of my wife.

And...a baby?

After thirty some months of trying, she finally conceived?

How the hell was that even possible? We hadn't—

A man sprinted into the ER, rushing past the waiting room's entrance. "T-Tara!" the man sobbed. He choked on his own spit, sputtering in his distress as he stumbled forward.

"One minute, honey," the reception said. "I'll go get her."

The man paced past where I sat, frantically yanking at his too-long, dark hair, mewling whines of anguish slipping past his lips. "Please, God...*please*." He turned leaking eyes to the ceiling but didn't stop walking or even bother wiping the wetness off his face.

Why did empathy fill me for the pain he suffered while I couldn't shed a shingle tear for myself? Disbelief or denial seemed like the reasonable answer, but I knew she was gone. Believed what I'd been told. Maybe I was in shock. Unlike when I'd first gotten the news, I didn't have difficulty breathing, and my heart beat steadily without pain. The fuck was wrong with me? What kind of spouse was I?

Widow.

Even that word whispering through my brain didn't rouse the type of emotion pouring from the frantic man nearby.

The doors leading back to the triage area clanked opened, and the man spun around. "Oh, God."

A blonde woman in pink scrubs met him halfway across the distance between them, and they fell into each other's arms in view of where I sat. Their shared sobs echoed in my ears, and I cringed, wishing I could disappear and give them privacy.

"T-Tell me she's okay. Please," the man begged, clinging to the back of her shirt.

"I'm so sorry," his friend whispered.

He wailed, slumping to the floor, lost in his grief as I ought to have been. The nurse went with him, wrapping him in her arms.

My throat ached for the man and the loved one he'd lost—

Fuck.

Tara.

Shelly's best friend was a nurse and lived in Berlin.

I stared at the two hanging on each other in shared grief, my brain stuttering briefly.

Need to get out of here.

Can't—breathe.

143

Standing, I walked past them on stiff legs, ignoring the two on the floor, my focus on getting outside where I could fill my lungs with fresh air.

Shelly had been traveling to Berlin a hell of a lot since midsummer. Visiting her best friend, my ass.

That man sobbing his heart out had been in love with my wife.

And she'd been pregnant.

Ice chilled my bones, keeping me blessedly numb.

The automatic doors swished open, and a quick glance revealed Jamie a ways down the sidewalk to my left, sitting on the cold ground, head in his hands. I longed to go to him but needed to be alone in silence for a while, to find a place to allow myself to fucking *feel* something other than nothing.

My work boots scuffed on the cement walkway as I headed right. Once around the corner of the building, I stared up at the night sky, cloud cover blocking out stars that would have brought me a sense of peace or at least a good memory to possibly take away the horror of my life my emotions hadn't yet caught up with.

My cell burned a hole in my pocket.

Closing my eyes for the span of a single heavy heart-beat, I pulled it free.

Shelly's message from earlier in the day shone back at my eyes, bright in the darkness.

Shell: **I found out this morning that there are men who can keep their promises. Tomorrow, I'm meeting with an attorney to file for divorce. Please do something right for a change and don't make this difficult for me.**

I re-read her first sentence twice. Her meaning hadn't

computed when I'd been anxious to get to the hospital, but I understood now.

That man on the hospital floor had given her everything I hadn't.

If I'd done more, listened to her griping, and changed my behavior, neither of us would be where we currently were.

Me standing alone outside a hospital, her body growing cold on a metal gurney.

Why didn't sorrow send me to my knees?

Was there something more I could have done to keep our marriage from falling apart? Had my actions or lack of them been the reason she'd sought out another lover? I hadn't hated my wife, so why wasn't I a crying mess?

Sighing when a good husband would have been half-mad with grief, I dropped my head. I put my cell where I wouldn't be tempted to reread her text over and over since I didn't need additional agony when my thoughts were a swarm of angry bees.

"Chaz?"

Leave it to Jamie to find me when I needed him most.

But I didn't deserved his comfort or his faithfulness considering the lines I'd crossed with him. Yeah, Shelly had cheated too, but that didn't make what me and my best friend had done behind her back right.

We'd chosen an unethical path, and even though my act of infidelity hadn't caused Shelly's death, I couldn't help but feel somehow responsible. I'd vowed to love and honor. Cherish. Care for her in sickness and in health—emotionally as well as physically.

I'd failed in keeping every single promise I'd made on our wedding day.

My throat swelled as Jamie drew nearer, and I swallowed down tears of self-pity as he tugged on my arm with a soft touch.

"Come here."

I went willingly, allowing myself this one thing, a single hug wrapped in strong, warm arms. He smelled like soap and natural underlying musk.

Home.

But I refused to buckle to want, to show how desperate I was to lean on him, soak in his strength, and lose myself to an onslaught of emotions that hovered beyond reach.

Jamie cradled me against his hard chest, his exhales hot on my neck.

I shivered, eyes clenching shut at the raw need far beyond lust clawing through my insides.

While now free to pursue the man I loved, I deserved to wallow in my loneliness for how badly I'd failed my wife. I'd done nothing to stop the train wreck we'd headed toward, and she in turn sought out the happiness that I hadn't supplied.

Who could blame her?

If I'd been as miserable as she'd been, I'd have done the same.

I *did* do the same.

Fucking hell, my head hurt, and I wanted nothing more than to curl up in a ball and feel sorry for myself. *And* her. She'd lost even more than I had.

Shit had to get done, and I needed to pull up my boot straps and see to my responsibilities.

"You got in touch with my parents?" I asked with a deadened tone rather than revealing evidence of my emotional downward spiral.

"I called my dad, had him reach out to them," Jamie said, his voice low and steady, reassuring as always.

I exhaled loudly as though emptying my thoughts of everything but necessities, nodded, and stepped out of his arms. Gaze on the ground, I shoved my hands into my pockets to keep from clinging to him. I could stand on my own two feet and *would*. "Thanks for being here for me, Jamie."

"Of course—always."

Fuck, that word. I used to love hearing it on his lips.

Now it brought just as much pain as the other one I hated—failure.

I swallowed hard, determined to remain steady and in control. "Why don't you head north," I suggested when I wanted to slump back against his chest and fade away into oblivion. "I can imagine I've got a long night ahead of me—papers to sign, calls to make, that sort of shit."

"Chaz."

I forced my focus upward.

Pain and empathy filled his dark blue eyes, and I clenched my jaw to keep my overwhelming yearning for him contained inside my body. "What can I do to help?"

"Go home," I croaked out. "Give me space to make sense of this mess. Figure out the next couple of days and the laundry list of responsibilities ahead of me. I've got to go see Shelly's mom. Bury my wife. Not get so backed up on work that I lose the shop."

Fuck.

How was I going to pay all the bills—and the ones racked up thanks to today's accident?

I was so screwed.

"Let me—"

I shook my head while straightening my spine. "No. I...I need to do this on my own."

147

"You don't have to prove jack shit to your father right now, Chaz," Jamie snipped.

"This isn't about him."

"The fuck it's not!" His eyes blazed, and while I appreciated him having my back, I had to prove to *myself* that I could take care of shit like a real man, that I didn't need *anyone's* acceptance of myself but my own.

A shitty time to recognize the truth of how badly I lacked self-confidence, but I wouldn't quit until I found what I'd been missing.

"Please, Jamie," I begged, wishing I could make him understand all the shit sloshing around in my head.

Jamie pressed his lips tight, thankfully not arguing further. "Okay." He finally relented even though his eyes stated he hated doing so. "I'll go, but I'm available if you need me, no matter when."

I nodded that I'd heard, not as an acceptance of his offer he'd clearly meant with all his heart.

He leaned in, and I allowed one last hug, his lips branding my forehead.

Fucking hell.

I gritted my teeth, refusing to pull away from his tenderness that would have me caving to weakness. Healing wasn't going to be found by Jamie's mouth or his dick. I needed to walk this journey on my own.

He left me there as I'd asked for, and cold seeped into my bones until I felt brittle—fragile—like a simple fall to the ground would shatter me into pieces.

Hours passed in a blur of doing shit exactly as I'd expected to have to do.

When I got home, I could barely see straight. Rather than slamming back a couple of shots of whiskey to fuck with my eyesight even more, I crawled into bed and passed the fuck out. Who expected emotional exhaustion to be worse than stress? I slept, but nightmares haunted my mind, not allowing the kind of rest I desperately needed.

The doorbell rang in the back of my consciousness, but I ignored it and whoever wanted to poke into my life and bother me right now. Didn't matter they meant well—I wanted them fucking gone and leaving me the hell alone.

A long, hot shower rid my body of the filth from work on Wednesday. Shelly would have bitched if she'd been around to see me climb between the sheets un-showered after a long day in the shop.

Why didn't my eyes fill with tears at the thought?

Silence hung heavy over the house we'd shared, but I couldn't be bothered to hate the absence of another living soul inside the walls. Talk about making me feel even shittier.

I brewed coffee.

Nibbled on toast.

Ignored my ringing cell.

The quiet should have had me huddled over in despair or at the very least teary-eyed. Instead, I sat on the couch, staring at the TV's dark screen, my eyes dry as a fucking bone.

Shelly had an affair, and while I hadn't fucked Jamie, I was no less guilty of the same. We had both broken our vows to each other, so why didn't that truth ease my conscience?

It was the pregnancy that bothered me the most, even more than my wife's death. Did the guy even know she was —*had been*—married? Had he just not cared and was so desperate to love her, fulfill her desires, that he would fall into bed with her and give her all the happiness I hadn't been able to?

"Fuck." I rubbed a hand over my face and lifted my coffee mug for a sip.

It was empty.

Grumbling, I stood and shuffled into the kitchen, realizing as I did, that I'd never bumped the heat back up last night when I'd gotten home. I'd put it down the morning before since Shelly was leaving and I didn't need the house to be as warm as she preferred.

Used to.

How long before my brain caught up with past tense in reference to my wife?

I was a widower.

Hard stop.

No one other than Jamie knew anything different about the state of my heart, and Shelly's lover and Tara didn't live in Pippen Creek. Nor were our lives intertwined now that my wife was gone, so the truth of the entire affair would fade into oblivion.

Hopefully, someday, my shame would do the same and allow me at least a slight bit of peace on this earth.

The doorbell rang, and I cursed. Who the fuck would bother me this morning?

I peeked out the window.

Mom. Holding a casserole.

Not in the mood but also not having a choice, I unlocked the door and motioned her inside. At least she'd come alone.

"Charles." She set her dish on the side table alongside my keys before throwing her arms around me.

I kicked the door shut and returned her hug, able to at

least take some comfort from one of my parents. Mom smelled like roses, same as always, her short stature only bringing the top of her head to beneath my chin.

"How are you?"

I shrugged while stepping back. Mom clung to my arm, her hazel eyes wet with tears. She'd never been the nurturing sort, so her empathy surprised me.

Maybe I didn't know my mom all that well after all.

"Hanging in there. Coffee?"

"I'm good, but thank you for the offer." She retrieved her casserole and followed me into the kitchen, her ballet flats whispering over the floor compared to my heavy foot-falls. "It's tuna noodle," she said, setting the dish on the cold stovetop. "Your favorite."

Yeah—from when I'd been in grade school. Now? I couldn't stand the shit. Even worse, she'd started adding peas a few years back, which made me want to vomit. But I would never admit the truth and hurt her feelings.

"Thanks, Mom." I retrieved another full mug of coffee and leaned against the counter as Mom settled at the table.

"Your father had to work today, but he wanted me to extend the offer to see to Shelly's wake and funeral since money is tight for you."

I took a few sips while digesting that bomb, hating that I never had enough funds for normal responsibilities never mind the hospital bills that would start showing any day. I doubted Dad offered out of the kindness of his heart though. There was no such thing inside that man. He probably figured I wouldn't do the memory of his daughter-in-law justice. That I would just have her cremated without any ceremony or offer her friends the chance to pay their last respects as a good, upstanding citizen of Pippen Creek ought to.

Getting shit over with as quickly as possible was exactly what I *would* have done so her death wouldn't drag on and intensify my shame over not being able to grieve.

"He can do whatever he needs to," I finally agreed.

Mom smiled, her tears gone as I guzzled down more coffee. "The community has already come together. Babs started a meals-on-wheels type thing online. Sign-ups filled within an hour, so at least I won't have to worry about keeping you fed. Scone Haven has begun a fundraiser for burial expenses, since she'd told her boss Kel that you didn't have life insurance on each other."

I wouldn't pass up free meals or the gift of having not to worry over money for something else I hadn't considered. Both acts of kindness gave me more free hours at the shop without additional stress.

Speaking of...

"I appreciate it." I set my empty cup aside, wanting to be alone even though my mom meant well. "Sorry to cut the visit short, but I have to get to the work."

Mom blinked, her spine straightening. "What? No! Charles, you need to grieve!"

"I'll do that in my own way when I can," I explained. "I've got bills to pay, and the clock is ticking."

She pressed her lips into a thin line. "Charles Clifford Henderson."

I hadn't heard my full name fall off her lips since child-hood, but I didn't cringe as I would have as a kid.

"Even in death you can't make time for your wife?"

Talk about a low blow. What a way to make me feel even shittier—bring up Shelly's bitching behind my back.

A muscle ticked in my cheek as I fought to keep from scowling or even worse, cursing both her and my mom out.

"She's gone, Mom." I barely refrained from hissing the

sad, fucking truth. "Shelly is dead. It no longer matters where I spend the bulk of my days since she's not around to complain about it."

Mom gasped, her eyes wide.

I rubbed a hand over my face, scrubbing at the scruff on my jawline. Perhaps I'd gone a little too far. Mom hadn't ever been so brutally honest with me. She'd lost her only daughter-in-law and was probably hurting more than I was.

"I know it sounds harsh, but let me figure out how to move forward now that she's gone, okay? Please give me space—and tell everyone calling and knocking on my front door that while condolences are appreciated, I need to be alone."

It took her a few seconds, but she nodded and stood. "I'll see myself out."

I didn't address her slightly petulant attitude or voice while she did just that. With how I'd spoken to her, I deserved it.

The door shut behind her, leaving me exactly how I wanted to be.

On my own.

I picked up the casserole and emptied the contents directly into the trash, my mind already going to the car on the lift I hadn't been able to finish the day before.

Chapter 17

Jamie

I texted Chaz a few times a day even though he never responded. While I couldn't begin to imagine what he was going through, I hated that he shut himself off from everyone who cared for him.

Kel over at Scone Haven had raised more than enough money to help with the burial. Dad's secretary, Babs, had set up meals for Chaz, making food one less thing he had to think about or plan for the coming days.

A local cleaning service had offered their services free of charge for the next couple of months too. Knowing Chaz, he'd decline that offer since he didn't like nosy people all up in his space.

Apple Acres Farm along with The Market had donated groceries and fresh produce, probably more food than he could eat in a year. The Outdoor Shop had mailed a gift card in the hopes of giving him something to indulge in once he was ready to move on.

And me?

I got in contact with the hospital and made sure that all bills were sent to me. Chaz didn't have health insurance, and I had more than enough in the bank and investments to cover the costs of her ER visit, tests, surgery, the morgue stay—everything.

Reducing Chaz's financial difficulties was penance for sinning against his wife but also the only way I found to help him. Honoring his request for space hurt like hell.

The bay doors at the shop no longer stood open during regular business hours, the colder September air requiring a heated interior to work comfortably. But that meant I never caught sight of Chaz while intentionally driving by to check on him from afar.

Friday night, we had an away game and got crushed forty-something to zilch. Regardless of the shutout and losing season, we plugged onward, the kids and Coach Dave able to keep more upbeat than I managed.

My mood dragged over having to be apart from Chaz when he suffered.

Saturday morning's outlook didn't pan out any better, dark skies bringing in depressing rain storms that matched my spirits as I sat at the kitchen table drinking coffee and attempting to eat cheesy scrambled eggs because I needed nourishment. Thoughts of Chaz made engaging in normal, necessary activities difficult.

He had finally succeeded in giving Shelly what she'd always wanted, and both his wife and child had been ripped away from him.

Thinking about their intimacy made it even harder to eat or sleep, so I attempted to keep my focus on his heart rather than mine.

Chaz's loss not only left him without a deserved sense of accomplishment but what had to be gut-wrenching devastation too. I couldn't imagine his emotional state, and every time I tried, I broke down into tears. Then guilt rose to choke the air from my lungs, and I found myself begging those gods again for their forgiveness.

The wake was set for Tuesday night. Babs informed me when I dropped off Dad's lunch he'd forgotten. He was out on a call, so I hung out for a little while, having nothing better to do, listening as Babs filled me in on the town's gossip.

The Hendersons had taken care of the funeral plans and had intended to pay for it as well until Kel had stepped in with his fundraiser. Scone Haven was in need of a new waitress with Shelly gone, and Babs joked that I would look good in an apron.

Smiling, she leaned onto her desk, chin propped in her hand, eyes twinkling with mischief over the receptionist's counter between us. "Imagine the tips a boy like you would get from all us older ladies around town."

I chuckled. Babs's flirting was the only thing that had made me smile in days.

"There's lots of cougars around here, but I can imagine you'd prefer a woman closer to your own age," she continued.

Hardly, but I wasn't in the mood to out myself at the moment since she was definitely fishing. If I told Babs my sexual preference, me being gay would be the talk of the town from now until Christmas if not longer. A few pride flags waved in front of businesses and attached to houses, and no one seemed to care a lesbian couple owned and ran Frenchie's, so I wasn't concerned what people would think.

It was simply a private issue that wasn't anyone's business but my own.

While I hadn't heard anyone discuss Dad's bisexuality, I wasn't sure if he'd ever shared his truth with anyone but me. His best friend Dexter and Kell were also openly gay and had dated for a short time, or so I'd heard. Who knew with gossip in a small town like ours.

"I'm considering a job down in Berlin," I offered Babs news to talk about. "Once the football season is over, I'll need something more permanent with insurance, a 401k—all the good stuff."

"You were smart to finish your degree in engineering before skipping off to the NFL. Your daddy is proud of you."

I nodded, glad for myself I'd chosen that route. Otherwise, I'd really be up shit creek without a paddle because my contract money wouldn't last forever. "Heard from Coach Bernard?"

Her smile widened. "He called just yesterday, high on living his retirement dream."

I could imagine. Who wouldn't want to travel across country and relax after being stuck in one place his whole life? "Think he'll ever come back?"

"He better!" Babs straightened, a glint in her narrowed eyes. "Or I'll have his hide."

"Why's that?" I asked with a smile at her spunk.

"He promised me a ring on Christmas and the rest of his days until death parts us!" She whisper-hollered even though the station was close to empty except for Officers Davidson and Jones on the building's other side.

I blinked. "Why, Kathy Babs O'Neill. Since when have you and Coach been an item, and how is this not the gossip of the century?" I asked, my voice low too.

She glanced around, checking that the others in the office were busy at their desks before shifting forward, beckoning me closer with a crook of her finger.

I leaned onto the counter with crossed arms, having entirely too much fun when I should have been wallowing in the shit of my current circumstances. Babs was a breath of fresh air.

"I know how good you are at keeping your own secrets, so you won't spill mine."

A punch of adrenaline hit me, straightening my spine. "What are you talking about?" I asked, my smile dissolving.

"Oh, please. You think you did a good job hiding who has owned your heart since you were young boys?"

I blinked.

Jesus fucking Christ.

The town gossip had seen and actually kept her mouth shut just like Dad.

"Spill your secrets, Babs. You have my word I won't say shit to anyone." That was the only admission to her assumption she would ever get from me.

"Coach and I were an item long before he married his wife."

"Are you shitting me?" I asked, failing to keep my voice down.

"Shh!" She glanced around the building again. "It's a terrible secret, but yes. He pissed me off way back when, I dumped him, and he snagged hold of Rose Gibbons, got her pregnant, and had to marry her so her daddy wouldn't take a shotgun to his balls."

Well, goddamn.

"I won't lie and say that he and I didn't flirt on occasion during the years they were married. I'm no saint, and neither is he," she continued, "but we didn't fall into bed together until after she passed in March."

I stared. Babs had always been known for her wildness, in her late sixties and single her whole life, but Jesus. "You mean you loved him and waited for him to be free again?"

"Bet your last dime, I did," she whispered. "And I won't

admit to being sorry about rumpling his bedsheets before Rose's body was cold in its grave either."

"Babs!" I snorted a laugh, amused rather than repulsed by her frank, almost morbid admission.

She shrugged. "Life is short, Jamie, and when you love someone and are willing to set aside a few years for them, why drag out the loneliness once you finally have a chance to be happy?"

A few years. More like forty if not more for her. The fact I couldn't be patient for a couple of months but pushed Chaz to have an affair brought back that shit feeling inside me again.

"Why didn't you retire along with him and go see the southwest together?" I asked, needing to change my thought patterns.

"Pfft. I love the man, but being stuck in a tiny camper for months on end?" Grimacing, she shook her head.

"As if marriage after he returns is going to be any different!" I joked.

"I'm kidding," she said, still smiling. "I would have loved to go with him, but there's no way I could just up and leave last minute like he wanted with winter fast approaching. I also wasn't going to ask him to hold off until I trained someone even though I had every right to."

"You're a good woman, Babs."

She lifted and dropped a shoulder as though not sure she agreed.

"I'll see you Tuesday night?" I asked even though I expected the whole town would attend Shelly's wake at the only funeral home in town.

"I'll be there," she promised, her eyes filling with tenderness. "Now, go take care of that boy of yours."

Shit, she sounded like Dad.

"I can't until he's ready," I said, my chest heavy.

Babs reached over the counter and patted my arm. "It won't be nearly as long as I sat twiddling my thumbs—I can promise you that."

I sure as fuck hoped not, but for Chaz?

Yeah. I'd told him I would wait forever, and I'd meant it.

But fuck, walking into the funeral home on Tuesday night after football practice and catching sight of him in a new suit and tie, hair slicked back, hazel eyes just as empty on his pale face as the last I'd seen him at the hospital on Wednesday?

Every part of my being yearned to pull him close and hold him. Whisper that I was his whenever he was ready to move on.

But I paid my respects first to the closed casket, my throat thick as I chose to remember some of the good times Shelly and I had shared while with Chaz. She'd been an upbeat, sunshiny soul once in our teenage years, always attempting to make our best friend smile when he'd gotten down in the dumps. She'd been an unbelievable caretaker to her mother before they'd had to hospitalize her, never once complained or bitched about the dementia that had slowly made her mom forget who she was—or at least, that was what Dad had told me. Who knew what went on behind closed doors though.

The scent of roses, her favorite flower, lay thick in the air, suffocating and taking me back to her and Chaz's wedding day. White petals had decorated every surface that afternoon, their sweet scent overpowering, burning my nose and etching in my memory the moment my best friend had said *I do* to someone other than me.

I stared at Shelly's casket, humiliation rising up over my bitterness and resentment in the prior weeks, the wish to have her husband all to myself. My throat ached over my selfishness, and I offered up a prayer for her soul, begging forgiveness once more.

Blowing out an audible exhale and not feeling the slightest bit better about my shame, I finally turned my attention on the two-person receiving line.

Chaz, dressed all in black, waited for me, hands clasped in front of him, Shelly's mom in a wheelchair to his right.

"Chaz," I said, moving to stand in front of him, hand extended.

He clasped my palm, and we both leaned in for a bro-hug, the stiff material of suit coats between us uncomfortable and unwanted. I breathed him into my lungs, the underlying scent of his shop, and my eyes stung.

Swallowing hard, I stepped back, clasping his shoulder while retaining my hold on his hand. "I'm sorry for your loss." I offered the proper condolences although they seemed meaningless. "For both of them," I tacked on quietly in case he hadn't told anyone about the pregnancy.

A muscle ticked in his jaw, and he nodded. "Thanks for coming."

He'd given me nothing more than the same greeting as everyone else, and although his lack of enthusiasm over seeing and touching me stung, I reminded myself he grieved and probably didn't yet have space in his heart for more.

This time, I would be patient and not push no matter my longing to ease his suffering.

People in line behind me made me release my hold and move on when I'd rather have stood by his side offering my support.

I knelt in front of Shelly's mom, but her gray eyes were vacant. She didn't recognize me, nor did she acknowledge the condolences I spoke over losing her only child. Standing, I nodded at the nurse seated slightly behind her before making my way to the second row of chairs facing forward.

Even though I couldn't stand beside Chaz, I planned to sit there until the last person paid their respects. And if he still wasn't ready to talk, then I would continue to wait, same as Babs had for the love of her life.

Chaz was worth it. Always had been, but I'd been too blind, and now we both paid the price.

Chapter 18

Chaz

I was too aware of Jamie seated mere feet from me, and I struggled to focus on thanking people for coming as they passed by me after a moment or two by Shelly's casket.

We'd had to keep the lid closed due to her injuries, but I'd been forced to see the damage to her body in order to properly identify her at the hospital. I'd barely made it to the bathroom before puking my guts up that night, the sight of lacerations and swollen features haunting enough she visited me in my dreams, telling me to *look* at her, that I was to blame for what had happened.

My swimmers had been the problem exactly as she'd screamed about, the fallout of which had brought us to this point.

She'd made her choice to fuck another man, but she never would have been down in Berlin on Wednesday if I'd been the father of that baby in her belly. Failure number six-thousand and fifty-three or what the fuck ever, proven true by irrefutable evidence.

No one knew about the longed-for pregnancy as far as I was aware, and our corner of the world never would.

According to her text, she'd only found out that morning, and I had to wonder if she'd had a chance to tell Tara or the baby's father.

I'd been at the shop all day every day since the accident, thankful Dad had seen to the funeral arrangements so I was free to lose myself in work rather than stewing in truth and lies. Whiskey helped me with the quiet hours at home, probably more than was healthy, but I couldn't fucking deal with the constant thoughts in my head. Especially those which made me feel even *more* guilty.

Relief.

No one hounded me about being late. A shrill voice no longer ranted every day about what I did or didn't do. There was no more gaslighting. No arguments. Just quiet—what should have been peacefulness—but my brain didn't allow such a thing.

"Why am I here?" Shelly's mom asked loudly, startling me along with a lot of the people in the hushed room. "I just don't understand! I want to go home!" Her whining sounded just like Shelly, but I forced myself to think about my mother-in-law's complete lack of memory rather than get pissed off she disrupted what was supposed to be a few hours of respect for her last known relative.

It would have been for the best if she'd stayed at the nursing home, but Dad had insisted she deserved to be present for her daughter's wake. It'd been two years since she'd recognized Shelly in a moment of clarity and even longer that she remembered I was her son-in-law.

"I want to go home!" she hollered again, growing agitated in her wheelchair.

The nurse attempted to soothe her, at least getting Shelly's mom to lower her voice.

Dad approached and spoke quietly to the nurse before

glancing at me, his gaze stating his intention to remove her from the room to stop further disruption and embarrassment.

Whatever. He'd been the cause of it by insisting she be present. Her being there was begging for trouble. Might as well let him handle the situation because I had zero patience for it.

I nodded, and they wheeled her away, allowing me to breathe a little easier.

The line waiting for a moment of prayer over Shelly's casket continued out the door where the trio left, and I expected it spread down the hallway and into the parking lot beyond. I appreciated everyone showing respect for Shelly, but continued condolences wearied me.

Pippen Creek's funeral home wasn't exactly large, so when a townsperson was ready to be laid to rest, the place packed out. An hour in, and my feet were pinched by uncomfortable-as-fuck dress shoes, and the tie choked me. I was to the point of ready to complain along with Shelly's mom. But I had no excuse for the outburst wanting to erupt from beneath my skin.

Zero.

I grew tired of saying "thanks" and drumming up smiles for people I held in high esteem or truly appreciated seeing. Countless arms hugged me, perfume and cologne clinging to my nose and causing nausea to brew in my empty stomach.

I checked my watch discreetly while waiting for the next person kneeling beside Shelly's casket and making the sign of the cross over their chest. One hour to go. I would get through this then head home for a double shot of whiskey to help my exhaustion drop me into bed without further thought and hopefully nightmares.

My gaze roamed the room—skipping over Jamie—and snagged on a blonde rounding the corner.

The sight of the nurse from Berlin leached the blood from my face as I tried to pay attention to the person moving to stand in front of me and offer their sympathy. How much had Tara been involved in Shelly's life? Obviously, she'd known of Shelly's affair, her interactions with that man in the ER proof enough she'd been a trusted confidant to them both about their secret relationship.

I kept an eye on her as the line slowly moved, my focus on her rather than the people attempting to comfort me with meaningless sentiments, no matter the intent behind their words. They echoed one after the other, their compassion falling on deaf ears.

Tara stood before the casket, her lips murmuring as though offering a goodbye that shouldn't have been forced onto either of them. Her shoulders lifted as though inhaling a bracing breath, and she turned toward me.

Our gazes caught, and I waited, my stomach tight and pulse heightened.

"I'm so sorry for your loss," she murmured kindly even though she probably hated me out of loyalty to her best friend. Who the hell knew what kinds of stories she'd heard about our miserable home life.

I nodded my thanks while noting her red-rimmed eyes.

"We've never met, but I'm Tara," she said, extending her hand. "Shelly's friend from Berlin."

Accepting her greeting, I nodded but had no fucking clue what to say. Ask forgiveness for being a shitty husband to her bestie? Offer my own condolences over the loss of someone she had loved probably better than I'd been able to?

Her smile wobbled when I didn't speak, and our palms

fell away from each other's. "Here." She pulled a card from her bag and held it out to me. "If you ever wanted to meet up for coffee sometime..."

"Thanks," I managed to say, accepting the card and tucking it into my pocket.

A small smile, and she moved off.

I caught Jamie eyeing her as walked away, his brow furrowed and eyes thoughtful.

"Chaz."

I turned to the next person in line and actually smiled. "Hey, Babs."

She threw her arms around me, squeezing me tight, offering me one of the few hugs I didn't mind being forced to accept. "Not sure how I feel about all of this to be honest."

Huh. Definitely not what I'd expected her to say.

"Don't let this loss stop you from living, boy," she continued beside my ear, keeping her voice quiet. "You've got so many years ahead of you that can be filled with joy. Deal with whatever it is you need to, then move forward. The sooner the better for everyone involved."

I didn't take offense at what some might call insensitivity. That was Babs's way, how she always offered advice, her intentions coming from an accepting, loving heart.

"Thanks, Babs," I said as she released me.

She glanced over at Jamie, who watched us from where he still sat like a sentinel, hands clasped lightly on his lap. His intense focus sent a shiver over my skin, and I tore my gaze off him to meet Babs's understanding and too-knowing eyes.

"You have a good friend in that young man. Best you let him help you through these times. No need to face grief on your own, and no one will judge you for finding comfort in a man who would move heaven and hell to see you smiling again. It's been long enough as it is."

I nodded, my throat tight.

She moved off and was replaced with another person from the seemingly endless line.

Babs's words echoed long after she walked away. The town gossip was intuitive as fuck after spending thirty or so years behind the police station's receptionist desk and wasn't easily surprised.

And her advice? Golden to anyone else standing in my shoes and looking for an excuse to stride forward without a backward glance.

But too much shame had its hooks in me, keeping me from even glancing at the man she'd given me her blessing to fall into. I could feel his eyes on me though. The want between us hadn't faded in the midst of what should have been grief far beyond what anyone should ever experience.

The finality of Shelly's death had settled over me upon seeing her bruised and broken face. I'd accepted her absence from my future. And I hated myself for the relief that mingled with sadness over the passing of someone who'd once been a good friend to me.

Another half hour slid by, the warmth of the room dictating I rip off the restrictive suit coat, but I gritted my teeth and dealt with the misery of being in a place I wished to flee from.

Still, they came.

Business owners, local officials, including the chief who clasped my back when hugging me. His comfort, the fatherly affection I'd enjoyed as a kid, was the first to threaten tears to my eyes all night.

"If you need anything..." Sutton didn't have to say more, the promise of his support already assured from years acting as a stand-in father when mine couldn't be bothered to take an interest in his only son.

"Thanks, Chief," I managed to reply past the lump in my throat.

My gaze caught Jamie's as his dad moved on, the empathy and love in his eyes causing a whine to build in my chest I struggled to contain. Now was not the time for the dam to break, for me to reveal to the world who my heart beat for while my wife's no longer did.

I would stand on my own two feet through this. Retain privacy for the embarrassing feelings and thoughts in my mind. Allowing Jamie in right now, accepting his help and comfort as Babs had told me to, would only worsen my sense of humiliation, not make me more confident like I wanted to be. I couldn't begin to imagine my father's horror if he learned the truth of both affairs, or how he would react to my moving on too quickly.

One step and supportive town's member at a time.

I hastily wiped the wetness from my cheek, cleared my throat, and readied for the next in line.

It was him—the man from the ER.

My dead wife's lover and the father of her longed-for child who never had a chance to draw its first breath.

Rage should have consumed me as he paused beside Shelly's casket, hands clasped in a white-knuckled grip before him. Pale and haggard, he looked like he'd slept about as good as I did in his black suit and tie that had cost a shit ton more than what Mom had bought off the rack for me. His body twitched nonstop either from absolute exhaustion or from fear for showing up in Pippen Creek where, if anyone knew his truth, he would be crucified for betraying one of their own.

As if I hadn't done the very same thing.

Still, the absolute balls on the man made me feel...less than. I could respect the hell out of a guy who would face down an entire town to offer a final word to the woman he'd adored. He was the type who would move mountains for his lover if he'd been able to.

My attempts to please Shelly paled in comparison.

Humiliation kept me still and quiet when most husbands would have smashed their fist into flesh and bone. Besides, I refused to cause an outburst that would disrupt the crowd as thoroughly as Shelly's mom had done. Wouldn't give my father the satisfaction of seeing me fall apart like he probably expected my weak ass to do.

I allowed my wife's lover his last moments with the woman he'd wanted as desperately as I had always longed for Jamie.

If my best friend's body had been inside that casket—

Fuck.

Pain ripped through my chest, catching my breath.

Couldn't even go there or I would lose my shit worse than Shelly's lover did while saying his goodbyes with tears streaming down his face.

Swallowing conclusively, he finally turned away, his gaze downcast as he skipped out on the receiving line made up of only me. A sense of urgency overtook me—

"Excuse me," I murmured to whoever waited to offer their condolences next, my focus on the man's retreating form as I hurried after him.

He exited to the right, and ignoring the long line and curious eyes to the left, I did the same, hot on his heels. Compulsion to take a step toward healing moved my feet faster than they had all week.

"Wait!" I called out the second the funeral home's door shut out prying eyes.

A pause, and the man strode faster across the filled lot in an attempt to leave me behind.

"Please!" I cried out while running after him, not above begging for just a moment of his time. I felt I deserved that much, at least.

His hand shook as he hit a key on his fob, the lights on a Mercedes feet away from him blinking along with a beep. He grabbed the door handle but glanced over his shoulder at me.

Dark eyes filled with anguish met mine, his features and body tensed for confrontation.

I held up my hands to show I meant no harm, slowing to close the distance between us in an unaggressive walk.

He stayed put, his gaze wary, shoulders hitched near his ears.

"You're—*were*—my wife's lover," I stated quietly without a hint of anger in my voice. Easily done since her infidelity hadn't hurt.

He didn't speak, simply waited for me, probably expecting that fist another man would have used to break his nose.

I wanted closure but not for me. I wasn't the one who'd been devastated by Shelly's death in the way a normal, loving husband would have been.

"You made her happy. Gave her everything I couldn't." My rasped admission of failure didn't hurt as I peered into his wet eyes. Instead, a sense of gratitude eased through my chest at knowing Shelly had found what she'd always wanted. It wasn't fair she didn't get the chance to enjoy that life, and for that, I would always mourn.

Still, the man didn't speak.

"She was going to meet with a lawyer on Thursday to divorce me so she could be with you—the father of her unborn child. Were you aware she was pregnant?" I asked in no more than a pained whisper.

I didn't believe it to be possible, but his face turned an even whiter shade of pale, his eyes widening and flooding with tears. "Wh-What?"

My goddamned heart broke for the man as his shattered in front of me.

A hard swallow allowed me to continue. "She was a few weeks along, and it'd been months since she and I..."

The man barely drew a breath as his eyes unfocused, and tears spilled down his cheeks once more. He *hadn't* known, which meant Tara probably hadn't either.

"I'm sorry for your loss," I whispered, my tone as broken as his spirit.

He choked on a sob, and I clasped his shoulder before turning and walking away. I'd hoped speaking to him would lighten the emotions attempting to hold me back from living, but my heart lay heavier with grief.

Chapter 19

Jamie

For the next three weeks, Chaz ignored my text messages and everyone else who reached out to him. With how he shut himself off completely, the town grew concerned. A few people besides myself had attempted to interact with him outside of his shop, but he refused each and every invite to get out of the house during his down-time. Rather than starting at the beginning stages of grief, he'd jumped straight to the end with immediate acceptance before sliding backward, seemingly stuck in depression from what I'd seen and heard from Babs and Dad.

I found myself still bogged down in self-loathing for wishing Shelly was gone and anger over her death draining Chaz of life along with hers. Dad told me everyone grieved differently, that each stage passed as a person slowly came to terms with their new reality.

Wanting to push Chaz along made me feel even more like a shit friend, and the fact I couldn't do a goddamned thing to ease his suffering created more bitterness in my heart for a woman whose body now rested in a cold casket.

Powerless, I stood on the sidelines, only allowed to offer

encouragement to Chaz via text—if he even read my messages.

My football team was another matter. They heard me loud and clear. Listened and attempted to stride toward victory. We continued in our season's losing streak, but at least we'd managed to tack points onto the board in recent games thanks to Gabby and her golden foot. The lack of talent otherwise lay like a stifling blanket over my already shitty mood, even though I'd known what I was getting into when I agreed to take over Coach Bernard's job. I told myself daily "I've got this."

I'd begun to feel like I lied to myself.

Waiting for Chaz to decide he could live again wore me down. I'd never been a patient man, always proactive, and with how every part of me ached for him, those steps Chaz needed to get through in order to move on dragged like molasses in winter.

Slow. As. Fuck.

How the hell had Babs survived all those years without losing her shit?

Unlike those Hallmark movies I longed to live in, weeks didn't leap forward with scene breaks. A blink left me standing just as lonely and helpless as a second earlier when I'd wished to be transported into the future where Chaz was willing and ready to love again.

Where guilt and shame no longer shrouded every thought and action.

Needing to do *something*, I bought a bunch of gym equipment and set it up in Dad's garage, dedicating most of my free time to getting into the best shape of my life. While I had no say over Chaz's emotions nor could I steer the journey he was on, I was able to control my own forward progress. But I knew better than to push myself too hard, too fast. Modifications for some weight training I used to do while in the NFL had to be done, but at least I made gains toward losing the pesky pounds that I'd put on due to lack of motivation since my return to Pippen Creek.

I sent my usual daily text to Chaz after practice on Thursday night, but rather than begging for him to hit up Frenchie's for a beer with me, I simply informed him that was where I would be. Maybe his not having to please someone else but rather be prompted on his own to socialize might get his ass in gear. Less pressure, which had afforded Chaz to make decisions easier in the past.

Iris manned the place by herself, and rather than spilling my woes to her like needy patrons usually did, I asked questions to keep the focus off me and my misery. She leaned on the bar, eyes twinkling while she told me about her and Frenchie's "meet-cute" as she called it. The whole damsel in distress on the side of the road with a flat event. Frenchie had come riding in on a black stallion—Harley Davidson style—and changed out her tire. She had insisted on repaying the bad girl goddess with dinner, but it was realizing they shared a similar tattoo on the same body part that had her tumbling head over heels.

What that was exactly, I didn't ask because the flush on her cheeks and hint of shyness in her gaze made it clear I would be better off not hearing details.

One of the town drunks sat at the other end of the bar nursing his beer while listening in on Iris's tale, two couples sat at high tables, oblivious to anyone around them and making me envious as fuck, and a few newly-legal drinkers hung around the pool tables, shooting the shit and attempting to sink balls into pockets while buzzed.

It was the perfect night for Chaz to show up. No nosey people to get in his space and cause him discomfort. Just me being my anxious self and a smiling bartender who wasn't known to judge a single soul.

The door opened behind me, and Iris smiled. "Welcome to Frenchie's!" She called out the usual greeting over my shoulder.

Tingles of awareness crept down my spine, and I stayed put, my focus on my beer rather than drawing even more attention to the man who'd stepped inside. Relief swept through me along with a shot of adrenaline that had my heart racing. I'd made the right call in not pushing.

"This seat taken?"

I chuckled and glanced over at Chaz, my pulse thrumming regardless of his appearance.

He was too pale, dark circles beneath his eyes, but not as closed down as last time I'd seen him at the wake. The terrible, too-large suit had been replaced with his usual worn T-shirt and baggy jeans. Still damned edible as always.

"It's all yours." *As am I.* My chest fluttered as I attempted to calm my racing heart.

Chaz slid onto the barstool.

"Good to see you among the land of the living, Chaz." Iris poured three shots of Shelly's favorite whiskey, passing one to both of us and holding up the third. She didn't need to speak a word.

We slammed back the drinks in a moment of silence, the burn I wasn't used to causing my eyes to sting. At least I didn't land in a coughing fit. Then again, that would have probably put a smirk on Chaz's forlorn face.

"Now that's out of the way, what can I get for you, sweetheart?" she asked Chaz, her tone soft and empathetic while setting her glass aside.

"Just a Sam Adams OctoberFest if you have any?" Chaz said.

"Sure do."

Iris retrieved a cold bottle, popped the cap, and set it in front of him. "Give me a holler when you're ready for another." She patted his forearm on the bar before ambling off to check on the guy at the other end. She leaned onto the counter to occupy his attention and ears.

I could have kissed the woman.

"I've missed you." I decided on honesty about my feelings in the hopes he would follow my lead.

Chaz grunted and took a long pull from his beer. He immediately went for the label once finished, picking at its edge.

Spinning a quarter turn on my stool allowed me to semi-face him. His hair hung over his eyebrows and ears, and my fingers twitched with need to brush the dark, soft-looking waves back so I could get a better view of his face.

"How are you holding up?"

"Okay, I guess." His brow furrowed, and he still wouldn't give me his attention.

Maybe it would be best to steer clear of any topic focused on his recent loss. "Busy at the shop?" I asked.

"Always," he answered without hesitation and immediately cringed at the word.

"What's that look for?" I asked, unable to help myself because I hated the disgust crinkling his face.

"Nothing," he muttered as his brow smoothed over. He sucked down another third of his beer and leaned forward, elbows on the bar.

"Chaz."

"Hmm?"

"Christ, man, would you look at me? Please?"

He closed his eyes, lips in a thin line. "I'm not doing well, Jamie. Need numbness to return before I lose my goddamned mind. Didn't show up here to spill my guts or evaluate how I'm feeling or what I'm doing to cope." Chaz drank the rest of his beer and reached for the bottle of whiskey Iris had left sitting nearby as though knowing he would be wanting more.

I held my hand over my shot glass when he offered. It took three shots back-to-back and another five minutes of absolute uncomfortable-as-fuck silence before he finally gave me his eyes.

Their hazel depths swirled with a toxic brew of pain and deep sadness I ached to ease for him.

"Want to get out of here?" I asked, my voice low.

He glanced away immediately, started to shake his head.

"Not for that," I hastened to correct the way I realized his brain had gone. "I just meant...shit." Scratching at my scruffy jawline, I eyed him, simply wishing to protect him from embarrassment in the event he broke down in public. "This isn't the place to get drunk, Chaz. If you're in the mood to get wasted, then let's crash at your place. We can talk—or not. Whatever you need. And I'll make sure you don't do anything stupid and that you fall asleep in bed rather than hugging the toilet."

"Not ready to have what happened in the kitchen last time," he said, sounding broken far beyond his loss.

My entire body ached to soothe his obvious guilt over the best night of my entire existence. "I'll keep my hands to myself. Promise."

He stood and went for his wallet, but I clasped his wrist to stop him. "I've got it."

I tossed a couple of twenties onto the bar, called a "see ya later" to Iris, and followed Chaz out the door.

Stars hung low in the cold air, a million pinpricks flooding across the expanse overhead, disappearing behind the mountains to the south. My breath fogged on a deep exhale of thankfulness for Chaz taking a step in the right direction in allowing someone to be a part of his life. Thank fuck it was me.

"Hop in," I told him, motioning toward my SUV in the front parking spot.

"I'm okay to drive," he muttered.

"The fuck you are. It might only be a mile down the road to your house, but you slammed back four shots and one beer all in a matter of what? Twenty minutes? We'll get your truck tomorrow."

He climbed into my passenger seat, and we drove in silence to the southernmost end of town. My heart beat heavy the entire time simply from being with him. The close proximity was right in ways nothing else ever had been.

Chaz was it for me. Always had been, always would be.

Telling myself I could be as patient as necessary, that I would honor his boundaries, I pulled into his empty driveway, determined to keep shit on friend level rather than lust and fucking.

Chaz and Shelly had bought a small ranch-style home, and when we walked through the side door into the kitchen, rather than smelling like lemon and chicken when I'd been invited for dinner, staleness met my nose.

The house felt...vacant. Completely abandoned of life.

Like a tomb.

A fine layer of dust covered the curio cabinet on the right, dishes piled in the sink to the left, and a few articles of clothing draped over the chairs half-pushed in around the table. I didn't bother mentioning the mess Chaz hadn't cleaned up. Doing so would make me sound like his nagging wife, and he didn't need another reason to drink more than I already expected him to in the coming hours.

We kicked off our shoes, and he grabbed a bottle of whiskey and two tumblers from a cabinet, nodding toward the living room.

I sat on one corner of the couch and nursed my drink while he swallowed down a couple more shots, the quiet oppressive like a too-heavy barbell across my shoulders.

Chaz slouched on the other end, body wilted and head downturned. He focused on the empty glass clutched in both of his hands.

"I don't want to be here anymore, Jamie," Chaz whispered, his voice ragged and slurred from all the alcohol he'd drunk. "I'm not strong enough to do this."

Chapter 20

Chaz

J amie didn't react to my admission, and I reached for the whiskey to pour myself another shot, lost in my misery and the wish to escape it.

He tipped his glass back with intention and held it out for a refill.

I couldn't be bothered with another dose of guilt over him drinking with me when I knew he preferred water to alcohol.

"I was so focused on succeeding and proving my Dad wrong that I ignored Shelly when she needed me most."

Failed in knocking her up too, but I wouldn't ever admit that humiliation to another soul.

I eyed the amber liquid in my tumbler, the whiskey loosening my tongue. I'd had zero intention of even talking about my dead wife, but here we were, and I was well on my way toward drunk off my ass.

"Hard work equals success was my motto," I continued to spill my guts, "but I forgot to pay attention to the most important thing that mattered—my marriage."

"Her death wasn't your fault," Jamie murmured. "And

the grief might be making you feel like you have to escape permanently, but I want you here. Can't live without my best friend, Chaz. Lots of people would be devastated if anything happened to you."

I slammed back the shot and poured another, ignoring his words. "I was stupid to think it would ever work." Jamie didn't know I spoke of marrying Shelly when I'd desired but couldn't have him, but I'd come to realize with every passing hour as my sorrow grew that I didn't deserve the happiness I'd always hoped for.

Those days, like my wife, were long gone.

Even if my childhood dreams came true, I would eventually let him down like I did with everybody else. I couldn't stomach that heartache becoming reality.

"I ignored the red flags. Worked harder to prove my worth rather than paying attention to what Shelly needed from me. Hell." I huffed an unamused snort. "If that isn't the definition of failure, I don't know what is."

"You *aren't* a failure," Jamie argued, but I was beyond hearing thoughts other than my own toxic ones loaded with self-hatred.

"You'll never convince me otherwise, so don't bother," I muttered and drank another shot.

We sat quiet for a few minutes while I wallowed in the shit of my existence. The worthlessness of being here. Everything I had managed to fuck up.

"When I tore my ACL, I thought my life was over," Jamie said, reminding me of the other shitty thing I had in my brain—secret thankfulness for that injury that had brought him home to me.

Jamie could share his pain if he wanted, but no amount of whiskey would make me uncover my feelings over his early return. He'd hate me if he knew I hadn't been all that upset by the news his career had ended.

"It took months of therapy to get my head set straight. Coming back here made me face parts of my past I'd feared. Regretted." Jamie released a heavy exhale. "I'm slowly learning we can go on after our hopes get completely crushed."

Did he think that was what Shelly's death had done to me?

It had never been my dream to raise a brood of children with her, but I would never admit to that either. It'd simply been what had been expected of supposed high school sweethearts from a small town. I'd chosen second best and had gone along for the ride rather than speaking up about what I yearned for or where I saw my life in fifty years.

Sacrificing my love in believing it would never be returned had been my ruination.

I swigged straight from the bottle, my eyelids closing.

"Have you considered talking to someone, Chaz?"

I shook my head. Hadn't he heard me when I said I didn't want to? Guilt upon guilt caused my body to feel heavy, but there was no escaping its weight, and no therapist could ease or erase that shit.

Leaning back, I rested my head against the couch, whiskey bottle in hand between us. Thoughts sloshed around, attempting to wade through the mud in my mind, but the blessed alcohol made them just as intoxicated as I was.

My friend numbness had returned, thank fuck.

"What's the smile for?" Jamie asked, his voice fuzzy in my ears.

"I'm drunk," I slurred, not having realized my lips had tipped upward.

183

"You'd better be for how much you drank." He pried the bottle from my fingers, but I couldn't be bothered to care.

I'd gotten where I'd hoped to be, which was well on my way to oblivion, where self-critical and negative reflections couldn't reach me.

"Remember the first time we tasted whiskey?" he asked.

I did—but didn't want to reminisce over memories that would do nothing but send me spiraling even deeper into the depression I'd been battling.

"I almost admitted my feelings for you that night," Jamie said, seemingly determined to discuss us.

Fuck.

My stomach turned over with sudden violence, and I rolled off the couch, intent on crawling back the hallway to the bathroom.

"Shit—Chaz. Hold on." Jamie grabbed my arms and eased me upright on noodle legs.

"Gonna puke," I mumbled, hating that he had to hold me when I needed distance.

We stumbled forward, and I lurched toward the bathroom, wishing I could purge myself of emotion as I did the contents of my stomach all over the toilet, wall, and floor.

Minutes or maybe an hour of hacking later, my cheek rested on the toilet seat as I lamented the alcohol gone from my system that meant thoughts and emotions would return sooner than I wanted. But not yet. My vision still swam, the spins keeping me company.

"You ready for me to tuck you in now?" Jamie asked from behind me somewhere.

"She was going to divorce me," I said without intending to, but Jamie would never know why. I couldn't stand the idea of him realizing exactly how badly I'd failed her.

"That's why she went to Berlin. Meeting with a lawyer then celebrating her future freedom with Tara in Boston."

Or maybe she'd planned to be with her lover the whole time. That was probably who she'd been with whenever she'd spent the night in Berlin anyway.

I couldn't rouse two fucks to give about that though.

Whatever his name, he'd made her happy, and I was still thankful she'd finally experienced the joy of seeing a positive pregnancy test after dozens of heart-wrenching disappointments. But now she would never hold that child. Kiss its chubby cheeks. Shower it with love like she'd always dreamed of doing.

Tears ran down my cheeks. I'd wanted that for the woman who used to be a good friend. We both could have moved on with that existence without turmoil. Divorced, her remarried and living the dream she'd always wanted. Me and the love of my life eventually becoming more than best friends. Everyone getting their happily ever after.

The grief over what could have been fucking sucked. Even intoxicated, I couldn't escape my emotions.

Jamie sat behind me, his hand heavy on my shoulder, assuming I cried over the loss of my wife, but there was a shit ton more to my tears than her death.

I took comfort in my friend's proximity, the warmth of his hand through my shirt a sturdy pressure, assurance of not being alone even though I could have sworn that was what I wanted before I'd started to drink hours earlier.

The ache in my chest intensified. Why couldn't I just hide for the rest of my life where no one had to witness my weakness?

"Need to piss and go to bed." I sniffled, attempting to stand up on wobbly legs so I could escape him.

Jamie clasped my arm and helped me to my feet. "Okay?" he asked when I swayed, wrestling with my zipper.

"Huh?" I asked, still drunk off my ass even though there was jack shit left in my stomach. "Fucking jeans—buttons broke," I slurred, my eyelids fluttering shut. I stumbled sideways, felt myself falling, and he grabbed hold of me again to keep me upright.

Passing out would be great right about now.

"Jesus, Chaz. Lean on me."

Unable to do anything else, I did as told.

Jamie made short work of my button and zipper. "You got this?"

I snorted, having no fucking clue what he'd even asked about.

Jamie fished my flaccid dick out, and I emptied my bladder when he told me to.

"You're the best," I mumbled when I realized I lay on my bed, my shoes tugged off by his large, capable hands.

Jamie didn't respond but continued to strip me down to my boxers. "I'll leave some water and Tylenol on the bed stand."

I hummed my appreciation, my eyes refusing to stay open.

"I'll be on the couch if you need me."

"Don't go," I mumbled as drunken darkness tugged hard on my body and mind.

"I don't plan on it."

"*Stay*." I tried again to tell him what I wanted.

"I said I would, Chaz," Jamie muttered. "Just close your eyes and sleep."

"Want you. Here." I managed to pat the mattress next to me before sweet unconsciousness slid over me like a warm blanket on a cold night.

Chapter 21

Jamie

I stared at the ceiling into the early morning hours.

Being stone-cold sober and lying in bed beside my best friend who seemed incapable of returning my love anytime in the near future was absolute torture. Somehow, I'd managed a few moments of rest but woke before dawn, restless, grumpy, and horny as fuck.

The pillow I clutched to my face smelled like Chaz. Heat from his body mere inches away radiated like the sun's rays attempting to singe my skin. Taking off my shirt had probably been a mistake, but I was burning the fuck up from the inside out, the heat centered in my groin.

I could be a total perv and jerk off while lying beside his passed-out ass, goddamn luscious thing that it was.

I'd left the bathroom light on in case he needed to hug the toilet again during the night, so lifting a single eyelid allowed me to check out his peach-like globes. He'd inadvertently gifted me the view when kicking at the blankets and shifting onto his stomach a few minutes earlier.

Black cotton hugged the swells perfectly, tempting as fuck. I could imagine what it would feel like sliding my lubed dick up through his crack, rubbing over his virgin hole. Teasing him. Poking and prodding but denying us both penetration. While I would love to fill up his ass with cum, the thought of seeing my spunk shot over his ass cheeks and back hit me harder for some reason. Marking him as mine would be more satisfying than unloading inside his body where it couldn't be seen.

Jesus.

I swallowed hard and rolled, staring at the ceiling again, determined to keep my hands to myself because it was what he'd asked for, and there wasn't anything I wasn't willing to do for Chaz.

Drape a cold wet towel over his neck while he puked his guts up. Wipe his face off once he finished. Clean the splatters of vomit off his toilet and floor. Hold his dick while he emptied his bladder. Wear fucking jeans to bed because I always went commando and couldn't very well sleep on his and Shelly's bed *naked.*

I'd finally gotten my hands on Chaz's cock, and he'd been too goddamned drunk to realize it. At least I hadn't been turned on by the experience, which I'd kept as clinical as possible. Didn't mean I wouldn't mind helping him out again like that in the future. A lot. Every fucking day if he would allow me to. While I wasn't into water sports, if I was ever lucky enough to shower with him, I wouldn't care if he took a leak over my feet. Wouldn't be any different than smearing my cum over his skin like I'd been focused on a second earlier, right?

That thought of my spunk on his back shot lust through my dick again, and I groaned, moving onto my stomach for needed pressure since I wasn't about to put my hand on my throbbing length while less than a foot from my best friend.

I shoved my arms beneath the pillow and filled my lungs with his scent.

My entire groin ached, balls tight, stuffed into uncomfortable-as-fuck denim.

Chaz grumbled nonsense as though I'd disturbed his sleep, and he rolled into me, arm flopping over my back, leg slotting between mine. Even through my jeans, I could feel the heat of him and the full length of his morning wood pressed against my thigh.

Eyes clenching shut, I swallowed a moan as he snuggled in closer, bare chest against my side, face in my armpit.

Jesus fucking Christ, this man would be the death of me.

Did I do the right thing and slip from beneath him, escape to the bathroom, and jerk off without him knowing?

Hell no.

Same as when we'd gone camping, I stayed put and gladly allowed Chaz to use me like a body pillow while he slept.

This ought to be us every morning, I mused, daydreams flooding my mind, making me even needier for the man. Warmth radiated between us, and I couldn't help but soak in his nearness, how he clung to me as though desperate for comfort—

Fuck.

His unconscious move to snuggle had nothing to do with me.

He thought I was Shelly.

Pain spread through my chest, settling in the back of my throat, and I did what I should have the second Chaz had reached for me.

I slid from his grasp, and my feet hit the cold floor as I sat on the edge of the bed, elbows on knees, head in my hands. My dick throbbed, angry and insistent. Might as well take care of that shit before Chaz woke up. Coffee and breakfast would be a good idea too since he probably had a full day's worth of work waiting for him at the shop.

My release into my hand turned out disappointing and unsatisfying. There was no marking of skin other than my own, and I washed the spunk from my fingers and palm, watching it disappear down the bathroom sink. It would have looked better all over Chaz's fine ass.

Still restless as hell inside and sporting a chub that refused to relent, I made my way into the kitchen and set to doing what little I could for Chaz.

Coffee being the first task.

The scent of fresh brew flooded the room as I next searched through the sparsely filled fridge for breakfast stuff. He had a couple of eggs but not enough for scrambled —and no cheese. A box of half-full pancake mix sat in the tiny pantry, so I set about mixing enough batter so we both could have a decent-sized stack. A partial box of frozen sausages allowed for two a piece, and they sizzled in a small pan on the stove. Real maple syrup and OJ would have to suffice as the rest of our meal.

I heard Chaz long before he made an appearance, and he must have left the bathroom door open because his morning routine sounded throughout the house as though he couldn't give two fucks he had company. The scent of sausage and coffee had to have traveled back the hallway, letting him know I hadn't yet left.

The toilet flushed after his long-as-fuck piss, then the sink ran as he washed up and brushed his teeth while I dished up our food and set the plates on the table.

I heard him head my way and filled a coffee mug,

thrilled that I could *finally* help him out. Even with some-thing as little as this.

He stumbled into view a second later, obviously hungover, eyes bloodshot and scratching his junk through his boxer briefs. Fucker hadn't put on another stitch of clothing. He seriously tried to off my ass.

"Thanks for sticking around," he said without meeting my eyes, accepting the cup of coffee I held out to him.

"Thanks for letting me be here for you."

"Sorry if I said or did anything weird last night." He sipped, a low hum of approval rumbling his chest and causing my dick to twitch.

"There's nothing you could say that would ever make me think you're anything less than perfect," I assured him or hoped to at least.

He made a disbelieving noise and sipped again, and I wondered if he realized he'd been plastered to my side like the morning we'd gone camping.

"Sit," I ordered, needing to move the fuck on from memories that would give me another boner.

Chaz collapsed into the chair I pulled out for him, and he eyed breakfast. "Looks good."

"Eat. You'll feel better."

We chowed down until the plates were scraped clean, and I got up to refill our coffee, my dick finally deflated.

"Got a full schedule at the shop today?" I asked while sitting across from him again, planning on light and comfortable conversation.

"Yeah."

"Plans tonight?"

A grimace thinned his lips. "I agreed to dinner with my parents. Put my mom off long enough."

"Want some company so the bullshit remains at a minimum? You know I don't mind running interference."

"Thanks for the offer, but I've owed them this visit for a while now. Especially since Dad took care of all the wake and funeral details. It was partially fear over having to be with him that had led to me wanting to get smashed last night." A hint of humiliation coated Chaz's admission.

"You've got this."

Chaz snorted. "I'm a stubborn bastard, but I'm not a fighter like you, Jamie."

I wanted to argue but didn't.

He glanced up at me long enough I caught the wariness in his hazel eyes, but he quickly looked back down at the scarred wooden table, retreating into himself again.

"How are you feeling?" I asked, my tone careful. I had no wish to pry, but I was here and had the opportunity to check in without him being able to ignore me.

"Fine."

I curled my fist to keep from reaching for his hand because that single-worded answer was a lie if ever I'd heard one. "Call me after the visit with your parents if you need to. Anytime, day or night."

"Will do."

Taking the hint he wasn't in the mood to talk, I got up to clear the table. "Why don't you go shower for work," I suggested. "I'll clean up our breakfast stuff and get out of your hair."

Chaz opened his mouth but closed it again before nodding. I guessed that meant he didn't want me to stay.

Regardless of the sting of rejection, I watched that ripe peach encased in black cotton flex with every footstep he took away from me.

Eyes lifting to the ceiling, I begged whatever god might

be listening for the patience and understanding I'd been lacking lately. Babs had lasted forty-some years without losing her shit. I would find a way to do the same even if it meant carpal tunnel and a raw dick.

Lube—I needed to refill my jerk-off stash at home so that last possibility didn't happen.

I added a stop by The Market to my small mental list for the day that included only one other thing. Worrying over Chaz's visit to his childhood home and hoping it didn't intensify his feelings of wishing to be gone from existence.

That loss would wreck me more than a torn ACL ever could.

Chapter 22

Chaz

I'd lain in heaven, suspended in time while wrapped around Jamie's hard body. Wishes to freeze that moment forever had whispered through my mind as I had become fully conscious. Hungover like never before and playing the sleeping idiot with morning wood had been easy.

Jamie had been tense, but it'd been at least five minutes before he finally pulled from my clingy limbs. I'd let him go, still feigning sleep, the scent of his musk thick in my nose from where I'd buried my face in his armpit. A body part I hadn't known could cause arousal *and* comfort.

Might be a new favorite place to linger if I could ever allow myself to seek out happiness.

The second he'd left the bedroom, reality crept into my throbbing brain, bits and pieces of the night before playing out in my head.

He'd taken care of me as no one had ever done, the same as I used to for Shelly when she went overboard with the booze.

I'd loved her in some ways but not the kind that could

ever last a lifetime where happiness tended to shroud the bad. Perhaps a part of me did grieve her passing. I'd considered my heart while Jamie banged around in the kitchen, searching out emotion beyond pity for the woman I'd failed.

Beneath feeling shitty about myself, I was sad her life had ended at such a young age. We'd had some good memories that had been overshadowed by the rough patches of the past year. She deserved for me to focus on those rather than the negative as I tended to do thanks to childhood trauma. Overall, she hadn't truly been a bad person. Just not right for me. We would have been better off staying friends, never crossing the line into a relationship that had been bound to fail from day one.

Because of me.

My head was a fucked-up place to lose myself in. Maybe I really did need help, some direction to get past this. If such a thing was even possible.

Jamie had cooked us breakfast, and even though my stomach wasn't exactly happy with me, I would need sustenance for the long day and evening ahead.

Maybe a few shots of whiskey for courage after work too before heading to my parents.

Hadn't been able to look at Jamie fully while sitting across the table from him. I couldn't bear for him to see the true extent of my depression. I hadn't lied the night before about not wanting to be here anymore. A magic wand to erase every single one of my failures would have come in handy, but I could be satisfied with at least being numb again.

Tears slid down my cheeks while I showered, longing to lean on Jamie in every way I could, making me feel like I wasn't strong enough to stand on my own two feet like I'd been determined to do. He'd been my oak as a kid, and going through this shit without him was damned near impossible. It'd been difficult to stop myself from arguing when he'd said he would get out of my hair.

It would have been easy to accept his offer to run interference with my parents. Having the comfort of him nearby would have made dinner with them bearable, but I wanted him too much. Couldn't be this weak around him, especially not in front of my dad who would easily sniff out my true feelings. No doubt, he'd give me shit for disrespecting my recently deceased wife and warn me not to spoil our name by moving on too quickly. He wasn't a homophobe, as far as I was aware, but seeing as how he couldn't be pleased, he'd find a negative to point out.

Babs had told me to lean on my friend in my time of need, but look where that had almost landed me. Clinging to him like an octopus in my bed would have eventually led to sated balls if he hadn't pulled away.

But I wasn't ready emotionally, no matter how badly I wanted him.

Not yet.

Work passed too quickly, but I couldn't complain over the lot full of vehicles that kept me busy. Since I would be seeing Dad that night, I wrote out my loan check—three days early. Handing it over would keep him from having to stop by the shop next week after he left the office. Who knew...maybe being on top of shit would get him to say something kind to me for a change.

While I would have preferred having a couple of shots before heading to my parents, Dad had a bloodhound nose and would know if I'd been drinking, so I abstained.

Showing up sober had my guts in knots, but at least I had a check that might help things remain pleasant enough I could eat, thank them for their help with

Shelly's wake, then take off immediately afterward without issue.

Mom met me at the door promptly at six as I'd been instructed to arrive, kid gloves in place while offering a gentle hug. She avoided questioning my current level of grief.

I was so sick of the goddamn carefulness everyone took around me, like they thought I was some fine china or such shit. Sure, parts of me felt broken inside, but I wasn't about to let the world see how poorly I handled my emotions when not numb. If only I excelled at fake smiles like my father.

Yet something else I couldn't seem to get right.

"Dinner will be ready shortly," Mom said as I followed her back the tiled entryway toward the pristine kitchen.

"Charles." Dad greeted me from where he carved the chicken Mom had roasted for our dinner. He wore an apron over his starched shirt, his actions with the fork and knife precise like a chef's.

The only thing *he'd* ever failed at?

Being a good father to his son. It didn't get much worse than that, and I had to remind myself whenever those goddamned comparison thoughts crept through my mind.

"Got this month's payment," I told him, setting the check on the island, shoulders back, feeling a hint of pride in myself for the first time since closing on my house.

Dad nodded and continued on with his task as though unimpressed I'd put pen to paper before its due date.

I should have known better to expect anything other than indifference over my finally meeting an expectation, but his dismissiveness still stung.

Fuck him and his high horse.

I turned away from him, done for the night and ready to

leave. "What can I do to help, Mom?" I asked even though I could see the dining room through the archway. She'd already set the table, had ice water poured and everything.

"If you wouldn't mind carrying in the potatoes." She handed me a white serving bowl, steam rising off the fluff of white and glob of butter at its center.

It'd been days since that meals on wheels thing had ended. I hadn't had a warm, home-cooked meal since, but I'd only agreed to dinner because it was long overdue.

We sat at the dining room table built for eight, Mom and I bracketing Dad at the head like we used to do every night when I'd been a kid.

Dad said grace while I grimaced over the bowl Mom had set down beside my plate.

Fucking peas.

After his deep and reverent, "Amen," Dad nodded as though giving us permission to begin.

I managed to keep the disgust off my face this time even though I hated their old traditional values of the man ruling the roost.

Made me want to vomit.

"How are you doing, Charles?" Mom finally asked what I'd expected the second I had walked into the house.

At least one of my parents showed concern of my well-being, but having zero wish to repeat the last conversation she and I had in my kitchen, I decided to keep it short like I did with everyone else who asked.

"Fine." I scooped mashed potatoes onto my plate even though my stomach wasn't feeling up to food no matter how good it looked or delicious it smelled.

Her disappointment in my answer lay heavy in the air. Imagining her pursed lips was disheartening enough, so I didn't bother glancing across the table.

"We heard you were at the bar last night."

I closed my eyelids briefly, fighting off the need to shake my head. Of course they would catch rumor of the grieving husband finally showing his face outside the auto shop—and find my choice of where I decided to socialize distasteful. Dad's tone made that clear as the brilliant green balls of shit in the bowl beside me that I ignored.

"I met up with Jamie for a few drinks," I said, not feeling the slightest bit guilty.

"A few?"

I ignored Dad's inquiry. He obviously already knew I'd been slamming back shots of whiskey. Choosing dark meat, I stabbed a thigh off the platter of chicken and set it onto my plate. "Gravy, please?"

Mom handed the boat over, and I covered everything on my plate. "Have some peas," she suggested with her mom tone I didn't often ignore.

I shoved a mouthful of potatoes in my mouth instead. Creamy, buttery perfection coated my tongue, but I struggled to swallow while waiting for the disproval to rain down.

"You have a reputation to uphold, Charles."

There it was, right on target and on time.

Dad's stern voice sounded as though I were nothing more than a child, his words exactly as I'd heard from him steadily throughout my life. "Henderson is a respected name worth protecting."

"There's nothing wrong with going to Frenchie's, Dad," I said even though I knew better than to argue with anything he said. Annoyance and feeling at the end of my rope had given me the balls to stand up for myself for a change, so why curb my tongue? "Everyone else in town has

199

gone there at one point or another," I tacked on before he could speak.

"Not everyone," he snipped, and yeah, he had a point. He and Mom hadn't ever stepped foot into that place. "I would appreciate it if you considered possible consequences before making that kind of decision in the future. As a grieving widow, you don't want people believing you need alcohol to cope. A Henderson ought not to show such weakness."

"And *I* would appreciate if you would mind your own damned business," I shot back, the words spewing because fuck him and fuck being treated like a stupid kid.

Dad's hands paused in cutting into his chicken breast, and he cast a glance my way, one eyebrow raised. Red crept up his face and clear over his bald head he attempted to hide behind that ridiculous comb-over. "*Excuse* me?"

Talk about a patronizing-as-fuck tone. Shouldn't he have been a little more sensitive considering I *was* recently widowed?

It had taken having my entire existence turned upside down for me to finally find some balls, and I. Was. Done.

"No." I set down my fork and whipped my cloth napkin off my lap, tossing it onto my barely touched plate. "I don't think I will excuse your words or condescension. While I appreciate you taking care of Shelly's wake and being laid to rest, I'm twenty-four, not ten, and like you said, a widow. Pretty sure that means I'm a goddamned adult who can make his own decisions. Thanks for dinner, Mom, but I'm not hungry. I'll see myself out."

"Charles Clifford Henderson!"

I ignored Dad and stalked up the hallway, grabbed my coat off the rack in the entryway, and shrugged it on.

Mom sat silent as usual. Anything to keep the peace.

Rather than storming outside like a pissed off teen as I was sure Dad expected, I shut the door quietly at my back, leaving them both behind.

A weight shuddered off my shoulders, and I stomped down the stoop, something that felt a lot like another shot of pride simmering inside me.

For half a second, I'd been tempted to spill the truth of Shelly's affair and her pregnancy—that would have shut Dad up for sure—but I didn't want to tarnish her reputation. I also wasn't so selfish to use her sins to make me look better in eyes that would never see me as anything other than a failure.

Most likely, Dad would have pointed out she'd committed adultery because I hadn't paid her enough attention, just like Shelly had complained to Mom about.

Nope. I was done and didn't need someone reiterating what I already knew deep in my marrow.

I might not have been capable of forgiving myself and moving forward, but at least I'd taken a step in the right direction. It had felt damned good too.

Perhaps I would find even more freedom in doing what Jamie had suggested...talking to someone and hopefully rousing the will to keep persevering in whatever life that would offer me a sense of purpose. While I didn't believe I deserved happiness, I would be content, at least, with that.

Chapter 23

Jamie

Chaz never called, so I assumed dinner with his parents had passed uneventfully. I texted twice over the weekend and never heard back. I'd thought we had some sort of a breakthrough, him coming out to Frenchie's, but his silence suggested he still wanted space.

I continued to send him daily messages telling him I was thinking about him and had an ear if he ever needed someone to talk to.

With every day wondering over how he fared and hating the distance between us, I found the football practice laborious. Pretty much everything became more of a drag than enjoyment, even working out. Coach Dave managed to keep the kids upbeat while I struggled to focus. Depression crept in stronger as I struggled to hold onto that sense of purpose I thought I'd found in Pippen Creek. Why did I stay when Chaz clearly didn't want me around?

A complete week of silence on his end, and I slouched in Coach Bernard's office, still unable to call it mine even though a new whistle hung around my neck on his iconic, frayed, red cord. The kids had cleared out after practice, and I sat alone, staring at some plays Coach Dave had jotted down in scribbled, black ink.

He should have taken over as head coach, and I began to question not remaining in Boston to carve out a new life for myself far from where I'd known nothing but heartache awaited me.

Knee aching, I stretched my leg out and rubbed the tenderness from having pushed a little too hard during my leg workout earlier in the day.

A bark of laughter reached my ears, and I strained to listen, having thought for sure I'd been left alone in my misery. Sure enough, I caught a quiet murmur of voices a few seconds later.

Ready for the meatloaf and baked potatoes Dad had texted me sat waiting in the oven, I decided to head out and clear the locker room on my way.

"Come here," someone whispered.

The quiet command sounded so much like me that I had to smile, but I pulled up short when I rounded a row of lockers.

Josh grasped Kyle's neck and yanked him in, their mouths meeting eagerly.

I stood silent, unsure if I should sneak back how I'd come or—

"Shit." Kyle jerked away from Josh, the blood draining from his face as he caught sight of me. "It's n-not what it looks like!" he hastily sputtered.

"Kyle." Josh's low tone only caused his best friend to shake his head, eyes growing wild with fear.

"A m-mistake!"

Josh's shoulders wilted at his best friend's claim.

My chest caved in for the boy.

"Nothing wrong with a couple of friends kissing in my

book," I said with a shrug, hoping to put Kyle at ease. "Also nothing wrong with two boys falling in love and wanting to be together either."

"Seriously, Coach—this was a one-time thing. Not gonna happen again." Kyle grabbed his bag and took off, leaving Josh behind.

The kid slumped, gaze on the floor while reaching for his own backpack on the bench beside him.

"If you love him," I murmured, "then love him. Put him first. Sacrifice it all to be with the guy you want. You might lose friends and family, but would he be worth it?"

"Fuck, yeah he would," Josh muttered.

I clasped his shoulder, angling him toward the exit.

We stepped out into the cold night.

Kyle leaned against the brick wall, head tipped back and eyes closed. "Sorry," he whispered, tipping his face our way. A parking lot light lit him up from above, casting shadows over his anguished face. "It wasn't a mistake. Definitely not a one-off if that's still okay with you, Josh?"

A relieved sigh, and Josh dropped his bag and threw himself into Kyle's arms.

The two boys hugged, and I swallowed hard at the sight before locking up for the night.

When they finally released each other, a flush flooded Kyle's cheeks.

"So—homecoming?" Josh's tone sounded more like a nudge for an answer over something they'd discussed already.

Kyle glanced at me, and I forced a smile. He turned toward his best friend. "Yeah, Joshy—yeah. I'll go with you."

My heart soared even as my throat went tight as fuck.

"Go on and get out of here," I managed to say past the

lump in my throat. "And no more shenanigans in my locker room."

The boys clutched hands and hurried toward Kyle's Jeep, and I stood in the cold, barely aware of the nip of the wind as I watched them drive away.

More than anything, I wished I could go back in time and make a move on Chaz like Josh had obviously done with Kyle.

I had considered telling him my truth while in high school, warred over it in fact.

It'd been during the summer after our sophomore year, and with butterflies making my heart flutter, I'd gone over to his house thinking that might be the day for honesty. I'd found him and Shelly lip-locked in their backyard, the first display of PDA even though they'd been "dating" for a few months.

My chest had cracked wide open, and I'd stuffed down the emotion stinging my eyes. I'd told myself I was going to play in the NFL one day and that no team would want to draft an out and proud gay man anyway. Besides, if he was all up in Shelly's curves, he wouldn't be interested in a hard body and dick.

Unrequited desire noted and squashed. At least, I'd attempted to ignore the feelings inside me.

Fucking impossible.

Yearning for Chaz ruled me regardless of the heartache we'd both endured. I was more than ready and willing, but would his mind ever be free so he could return my love even though nothing physical now stood in our way?

With every passing day of silence on his end, I feared a bleak future without him as a lover or friend.

My face must have shown my defeat because Dad eyed me while setting my plate in front of me at the table.

"Stay the course."

I rolled my eyes at him while shoveling a too-large bite of meatloaf into my mouth.

"What?" he asked, sitting across from me with a cold beer.

Still chewing, I shook my head. "How do you do it? Read my thoughts when I don't speak a damn word?"

"You're my son. I can always tell when you're struggling with something. We've talked the losing season to death, so I'm assuming this is about Chaz?"

I nodded and spooned up a pile of sour cream onto my steaming potato. "He's completely shut down. I don't know what to do. Fucking hurts that I can't be there for him. Hurts even more than the fact he isn't interested in me."

"I doubt that last bit is true."

I shrugged. "Sure as hell seems that way," I muttered. "Makes me want to stop texting to check in with him. Ignore him for a few days. See what happens—or doesn't."

"Don't stoop to manipulation, Jamie." Rarely did I hear disapproval in Dad's voice, but that order? Loaded.

I huffed and exhale before digging into my meatloaf again. "Wouldn't really do that. Just feeling..."

"A little moody? Sulky?"

A grunt was my reply, and Dad chuckled before sipping his beer.

I eyed the man who'd always been my oak. He'd gone through some shit with my mom, and even though she wasn't in a cold grave, she'd disappeared from our lives as thoroughly as Shelly had Chaz's.

Had Dad mourned even though Darla had been a piece-of-shit wife and mother?

Not that Shelly had treated Chaz any better in my opinion. She hadn't deserved my best friend any more than my mom had Chief Sutton Forester, a highly respected man loved by almost everyone in Pippen Creek.

"How did you deal with Mom leaving? I mean, were you heartbroken? Go through those five or seven stages of grief?" I asked, watching Dad closely. I'd been fourteen, too caught up in my own bullshit to consider what he might have experienced in the wake of her abandoning us.

He glanced around the dining room with its lived-in manliness, the lack of her touch. It'd been over ten years since she'd taken off, and in that time, we'd both done a few purges to rid the house of any evidence she had ever existed.

"In some ways, I suppose I did. Her actions had completely blindsided me, but by then our marriage had been over for years."

"It's been a decade, Dad," I said, studying the furrow between his eyebrows. "Think you'll ever be ready to move on? Trust someone enough with your heart that you'd try again?"

A half-smile curved Dad's lip for the briefest of seconds before dissolving completely. "Doubt it." He took a long pull from his beer.

"Aren't you lonely?"

"Sometimes."

"Do you ever hook up? I mean, you haven't been celibate since then have you?"

Dad shifted, his face actually flushing.

"Oh shit." I chuckled. "Who is she?"

"Would you be grossed out if I said he?"

I huffed. "Come on, Dad. You know better. Wait. Dexter?"

"What?" Dad blinked, his head jerking back as though I'd slapped him.

"Dex," I repeated. "He's hot. Ever cross that line?" I

waved my fork in front of me as though drawing one in the air.

"No—*hell*, no. He's as far from my type as can be."

"And what's that?" I stabbed into another bite of meatloaf and chewed while Dad gathered his thoughts. We'd talked about sex aplenty, but I'd never pried into his personal life. But now, it felt good to be open with him about adult shit.

"Someone who needs me," Dad finally said, twisting his bottle in his hand and taking a sip. "*Wants* me as a partner. Let me care for them."

Mom had always been independent as fuck. Probably wouldn't have married Dad if she hadn't gotten pregnant her senior year of high school.

Dad had tried with a woman, so why not dick? Maybe even a younger guy in need of a daddy.

I grimaced at the thought that had come out of nowhere. "What?"

"Just thinking that a younger guy might be a good bet for you." I went with honesty as always.

Dad hesitated a second but nodded, seemingly unsurprised.

"Someone needy, but that's...yeah, no." I shook my head even though it looked like he'd given some thought to what I'd suggested already.

Dad finished off his beer and got up to retrieve another one.

I went back to my food, putting Dad's sexual future way the fuck in the back of my brain where it belonged. Better to be rid of it altogether, but shit had been spoken out loud, so yeah. Not happening. Still—where my mind had gone for Dad? Gross.

"There's a position down at city hall in Berlin that

might be of interest to you," Dad said, letting me know he was done discussing his own sex life too. "I could put in a good word if you're unsure about what to do when the season is over."

I'd talked to Dad about looking for something to keep me busy, but Pippen Creek didn't have anything to offer someone with my degree. Hell, they were only hiring waitstaff or shelf stockers over at The Market. And the apple orchard where I'd worked two summers while in high school wasn't in need of seasonal helpers since the place pretty much shut down until spring.

"It's only a half hour away," Dad said. "Easy commute."

I nodded while continuing to eat.

"Might be good to get some space."

"Sick of me already?" I joked.

"You know what I mean."

Yeah, I did. Being close to Chaz but not having any access to him was wearying. I'd been the one pursuing him, so maybe it was time for me to step back fully—and not do it out of manipulation but honoring his wishes.

Hopefully, Chaz would work through his grief and eventually reach out to me again when he was ready.

And if he wasn't?

That was something else I would have to learn to deal with alongside all the other disappointments I'd experienced in my twenty-four years.

Chapter 24

Chaz

I kept my front porch light off on Halloween. Didn't even put up any decorations in the front lawn like Shelly used to do every year trying to outdo the neighbors around us who went overboard, in my opinion.

Whiskey was my sole company, but I limited myself to two drinks that night. Dry-eyed, I sat and listened to neighborhood children's laughter outside for two hours, recalling the happier memories we'd had when trick-or-treaters came to our door.

Jamie, Shelly, and I had spent every Halloween night together from fifth through twelfth grade, flitting from porch to porch and filling pillowcases with candy. The best year had been when we'd all turned sixteen and went as the Three Stooges. We acted like morons, snort-laughing while running down Pippen Creek's roads.

I did miss Shelly in some ways. The friendship we'd had prior to our relationship becoming more had meant a lot to me. Even though she'd basically tagged along with Jamie and I wherever we'd gone, she'd been a welcomed breath of fresh air. Sunshiny and upbeat alongside my best friend.

They had been a double dose of happiness for me once upon a time.

Our tears had mingled when we'd had to put her mom in the long-term care facility. She'd clutched my hand that afternoon when we'd driven away from the only family member she had remaining. I'd been determined to knock her up after that Friday afternoon.

Heaving a sigh, I set my empty glass aside and focused on the tightness in my chest.

Grief was a fucking funny thing but far from amusing. Different reasons for it weaved throughout my brain, but I realized not all of what I experienced stemmed from being upset for her and the life she'd missed out on.

I might have fucked up, but I was starting to believe the therapist I'd been seeing for a couple of weeks when she said I wasn't at fault. I was coming to understand that it was okay to grieve for myself over the loss of my wife too. Doing so wasn't selfish like I'd thought it would be considering my infidelity I'd yet to discuss with anyone but her.

A tear slid down my cheek, and I let it drip onto my old T-shirt while slouched on the couch. There hadn't been a big breakdown or agonizing sobs over my own loss as I'd done while hugging the toilet when feeling sorry for Shelly, and that was okay too according to my therapist. People dealt with loss in different ways. I needed to allow myself to feel the emotions, let them happen, and accept them.

The guilt was just as real, understandably so considering my failing to fulfill Shelly's dreams and how I'd fucked around with Jamie behind her back, but I was learning not to let it rule my life. A slow process for sure, but I would get there eventually.

I'd been to therapy three times, and it actually felt good to unload to a complete stranger who wasn't from Pippen

Creek and didn't know me or other townsfolk. She would never judge me or tell my parents about my shit. Or about how I was desperately in love with my best friend and wasn't ready to pursue a relationship because I needed to love myself first.

My fourth online meeting was the day after Halloween, and I left the shop early again, actually anticipating talking with her.

We discussed the self-confidence I'd been building, and she recommended stretching myself a bit more. Start opening up again to friends and loved ones. Sharing my grief rather than hiding from or stifling it because I didn't want to be vulnerable with others and show that supposed weakness as Dad had called it.

The first person I thought allowing back in—as a friend for now—had his final home game on Friday night.

I showed up early and sat on the fifty-yard line.

Babs was there, same as she always was in support of our Bobcats. She smiled, hugged me, and welcomed me to the land of the living. Nothing was said after that about Shelly or questions about how I was doing. She simply chewed my ear off about the town's latest gossip, keeping my brain occupied until our team tore through the banner held by the cheerleaders.

Jamie and Coach Dave trotted behind the players, the energy not nearly what it'd been the last game I'd attended with Shelly. Still, grim determination lined both coaches' faces when they rounded the boys up on the sidelines for a quick pep talk.

I couldn't tear my eyes off Jamie.

He once more wore khakis that fit his ass snugly and made my mouth water. A thick fleece, red and sporting the school's logo, covered the bulk of his upper body, but I'd memorized every inch beneath. Lusted to touch and sample the dips and swells of his muscles. Maybe even shove my nose in his armpit again. Lick over his skin and get a proper taste of him.

It'd been weeks since I'd gotten myself off out of sheer need to empty my balls, but he'd been front and center in my fantasy while doing so.

Guilt had accompanied my spunk shooting from my dick and hadn't disappeared down the drain like my cum had.

Technically, I was free, but my head wouldn't allow my heart what it wanted. Remorse and a desire for betterment constrained me, but I wasn't sure how to let go of the self-imposed shackles that were stronger than any ball and chain I'd imagined being imprisoned by before.

The heaviness of those thoughts carried on throughout the game the more I looked at Jamie. And with every touch-down from the opposing team, Jamie's shoulders slumped further. I wished I could hug him.

A shutout ended the season, but with it being senior night, the crowd didn't disperse right away.

One-by-one, the graduating players strode across the field on the arms of their parents or loved ones, waving or fist-pumping the air as their name announced over the tinny speaker. Kyle, the starting quarterback, got the biggest round of applause, his backup, Josh, a close second and hot on his heels.

The guys lined up along the edge of the field in front of the stands, and the whole town offered thanks and the edification the kids deserved for fighting so hard. They hadn't once given up, and according to Babs, had the best season team-wise in years. They had only won one game, but their comradery soared.

Jamie stood behind his quarterbacks, a smile on his face, pride in his eyes as he watched the two boys in front of him.

Kyle and Josh turned toward each other, laughing. Josh said something in Kyle's ear—and they were suddenly kissing. Full-on lip-lock, Kyle holding the back of Josh's neck in a firm grip as though desperate to keep him in place. Not that Josh appeared to have any intentions of backing away. He clung to Kyle's jersey with both hands.

I stared, my heart pumping as their mouths moved over each other's in view of everyone.

That bit of news hadn't gone 'round the town. Even Babs gasped beside me before whistling shrilly along with dozens of other folks.

My gaze went to Jamie behind the kissing boys.

His smile had faded, and he watched with such longing in his gaze that pain knifed at my heart. He lifted his focus, eyes settling on me without surprise, as though he'd been aware of my presence the entire game.

Ears muffling, I could only hear the whoosh of blood rushing through my body as our gazes locked. Want carried on the cold air between us, intensifying the puffed white exhales from both of our lips. My body leaned forward to erase the distance, but the team suddenly crowded around their coach, hiding him from my sight and returning me to the reality of the cold biting my nose and the chilled metal beneath my backside.

I swallowed hard and turned away to find Babs peering up at me.

Her kind eyes said it all—not to wait, to take what happiness I could while I still had the chance.

While half the town headed to Frenchie's, I was too amped up, too hyped on desire and fear to be in a crowd. Temptation to text Jamie and...I didn't know what else, made my fingers itchy to pull my cell from my pocket, but I didn't.

I drove home in silence and entered the tomb-like house that no longer felt like a home.

At least I'd been taking better care of the place the previous couple of weeks, vacuuming and doing dishes rather than allowing them to pile up. I'd even scrubbed the bathrooms the day before, so the place smelled somewhat lemon-like.

I eyed the whiskey I'd left on the kitchen table. A few shots would chill me the fuck out, but I needed to learn to cope without the alcohol. Emotions were healthy, I'd been told, and I ought to let them happen. Feel them. Hell, the therapist had even suggested talking to them as though they were my children, as though nurturing them would create a better relationship between us.

Sadness over wanting what I didn't deserve was the most prominent. Yearning for connection attempted to over-rule the first, a not-so-sweet war between my head and heart.

If Jamie stood before me—

Headlights flashed on the wall, and I moved toward the front windows as a red SUV pulled into the driveway, causing the motion-detecting floodlights to flick on across the yard.

My mouth dried, pulse thrumming with unsteady beats.

We hadn't spoken in a couple of weeks. He'd finally given me the space I'd asked for, and every necessary second without him had sucked.

Eyes closing, I rested my forehead on the front door, hand gripping the handle.

Silence settled in my mind, all thoughts of being torn in two directions going quiet. Hadn't we been headed toward this moment for our entire lives? Whether proper or too soon to be ethical, this was always where we'd been meant to be.

I wasn't sure I was ready, but I couldn't say no any longer.

He knocked quietly as though knowing I waited a mere panel of wood away, heart in my throat.

Refusing to give in to the shame wanting to creep into the back of my mind, I pulled the door inward.

Dark blue eyes shadowed by the overhead light atop the stoop met mine. Emotions poured through them and off his body. Pain. Longing. Perhaps even his own sense of guilt.

"Can I—"

I grabbed the front of his fleece and hauled him inside, causing him to stumble into me.

Our mouths slammed together as our bodies collided, hard and hungry. We were desperate with aching desire, making the show those two boys had gifted the town on the sidelines look like child's play.

Somehow, the door shut behind him, leaving us alone in oppressive silence broken by heavy breathing and low moans. Jamie held my face in his warm palms, moving my head at an angle so he could plunder my mouth, own me with deep strokes of his tongue along mine.

My legs went weak, and I clutched at his thick fleece, his strength kept me upright.

How could this kind of lust be healthy? This consuming craving to connect on a spiritual level far beyond the caressing of flesh?

I had to touch him. All of him.

I shoved my hands up the back of his shirt, hot skin meeting my fingertips. Mapping the muscles along his spine and across his shoulders, I submitted to his kiss, to whatever he wished to do with me.

Jamie Forester owned me in that moment, and no amount of shame or guilt would convince me we were in the wrong.

Maybe later, but right now?

"Want your dick, Chaz." Jamie's statement lit my insides on fire.

There was no stopping us.

Chapter 25

Jamie

I'd acted on instinct, driving to Chaz's rather than Frenchie's where I would be expected to show up. Discretion and honoring my best friend's wish for space could go to hell.

Seeing Josh and Kyle kiss in front of the entire town, coming out loud and proud to tell the world who they loved, had hit me like a bullet to the chest. My heart had stalled out, and my breath ripped from my lungs.

Lifting my focus to Chaz right where I'd somehow known he'd be, I found his gaze promising me we had both secretly wanted the same back then—and now.

Intense ache didn't begin to describe the draw toward him, the need to claim him reminiscent of how my players had each other. Chaz was always meant to be mine, and even though circumstances had led to the passing of miserable years apart, we were both finally in a place where nothing physical stood between us.

And neither of us were at fault for that truth.

His hazel gaze had latched onto mine, desire flaring,

burning through my groin and causing goose bumps to break out over my entire body. There was no question he experienced the exact same need as I did. Yearning etched on his face, his parted lips waiting to be tasted. Pink cheeks begged for my hands to cradle them with the tenderness he deserved.

Desire had dictated my actions, and his face upon opening his front door had lit me up inside as quickly as his hands had yanked me over the threshold.

"Want your dick, Chaz," I whispered hotly against his mouth, getting straight to the point because we'd waited long enough.

"Jesus." He gulped and ground against my hard length, fingertips digging into my ass. "Fuck, yes."

I forced my hands off him only to yank my fleece off overhead, taking my shirt along with it. We came together again, and I tore at his worn T-shirt until it ripped down the middle, allowing me to touch his skin.

Groaning over the heat of his chest against mine, I ran my hands over his back as he did the same to me, both of us grabbing hold of each other's ass cheeks at the same time. I considered the bedroom for all of two seconds but dismissed the thought of the bed he'd shared with his wife.

Kicking off my shoes, I tried to keep our lips plastered together. Didn't want to give him space or any downtime to rethink where we were headed either.

He pushed off his jeans with shaking hands and stumbled in his haste to kick them away along with his shoes. I finished stripping first and squeezed the base of my granite-like cock, pausing to look him over fully for the first time without having to hide how the sight of him affected me.

Pale skin, blemish-free, stretched over muscle and bone.

His build was a little more slender than my own but no less sexy in my mind. A trail of dark hair started at his navel and spread downward, untrimmed and wild around the base of his dick. Pre-cum pearled at the slit and slid along his length as I stared. He was a leaker, and I needed a taste.

I snagged his balls and dropped to my knees, diving onto his dick without warning.

"Oh fuck—Jamie!" Chaz grasped at my hair and yanked me closer, his hips thrusting to stuff my mouth full. His cockhead lodged in my throat, and I swallowed, unable to groan over how perfect he felt on my tongue, the salty tang of him coating my taste buds. "My God...Jesus. Fuck—sorry." He jerked back, but I moved with him, taking him into my throat again, hungry as fuck for his dick.

A deep groan rumbled from both of us.

"G-Gonna come if you don't stop," he panted, and I slowly backed off, tongue laving over the vein running up the length of his shaft.

A quick little suckle on his slit, and I crawled around him on hands and knees toward the couch. Kneeling on the edge, arms along the back, I presented my ass. "Fuck me, Chaz. My ass is yours to do with what you want—always has been."

"I-I don't have any lube."

A rush of air left my lungs as I realized I wasn't a hundred precent sure he'd be into fucking me like this.

"I can take you without it." I spat on my hand and reached around my backside, smearing the slickness over my hole.

Chaz cursed, shuffling closer as I spat for more.

"Put your hands on me," I said, pushing two fingers into my ass as deep as I could. "Spread me open."

Warm palms clasped my cheeks, and he groaned as I arched my back to show him where I needed him, sliding my fingers in and out of my ass.

"Spit on my hole," I ordered. "Get me good and wet."

"Jesus, Jamie."

"Do it."

A glob of warm wetness hit my crack and dripped over my taint. I gathered his spit, shoving it up my hole.

The head of his cock brushed over my hand, and a whimper escaped me.

The need to be filled had never been so great or consuming. I pulled my fingers out of my ass and wrapped my hand around his stiff length.

Goddamn, my man was a leaking faucet—good news for me.

I smeared his pre-cum over his shaft, getting him slick. Wouldn't work as well as lube, but here we were, and I was done waiting. Situating his firmed tip at my hole, I bore down, pushing onto him.

He popped through my ring, and I hissed, holding still.

Hands clasped at my hips in a sudden death grip, fingertips digging into flesh. "Fucking *hell*." Chaz groaned the words and shuddered hard.

Goose bumps erupted over me as I focused on where he split open my body, the sting everything I'd hoped for and more.

"Fill me up, Chaz. Want every inch of you shoved up my ass," I said the second I was ready to take more. "Need you in me. Please," I begged, not giving two shits I revealed my desperation to finally be with him.

Another curse spilled off Chaz's lips, but he pushed forward, slow and steady, until his groin kissed my cheeks.

Still, he shoved as though desperate to go deeper, pressing my chest into the back of the couch.

Fuck. Yes.

I moaned, my ass stinging. It'd been too goddamned long since I'd been with a man, and the raw ache and discomfort of being stuffed too quickly electrified me.

Chaz, my best friend, the man I'd loved forever was finally inside me, owning me in ways no man had ever done. There would never be anyone else. Ever.

Shivers raced over my skin again. I was a live wire ready to explode, sparks igniting along my nerve endings.

"So goddamn tight." He groaned, his fingertips digging into my hips. "You're strangling the fuck out of my dick, Jamie."

"Fuck me," I begged, trying to squirm on his cock. Needed him to send me tumbling head over heels into what was going to be the best climax of my entire life. No. Fucking. Doubt.

He hissed and smacked my ass cheek with a sharp crack that sounded as good as it felt.

"Ah, fuck," I arched, my cock bucking against my abs as I squeezed my hole around his girth.

"Hold still, goddamn you." Chaz growled and gripped me firm again. "Want to enjoy this, not blow like a teenager, and you got me there already with how perfect you feel. Jesus Christ." He slowly pulled out, dragging his length from of my clenched asshole until only the tip stayed lodged inside me.

I whimpered at the loss. "Chaz..."

He thrust in, forcing a grunt from my lungs. Not nearly enough lube, but fucking hell, he fit me perfectly.

"More—give it to me. Every goddamn inch."

No more words filled the heated air around us. The

smacking of his groin against my backside, the grunts and groans of two men in the throes of passionate fucking, created the most spine-tingling music I'd ever heard.

Chaz angled his hips and leaned over my back, face in my armpit, rutting into me like a crazed animal.

"Fuck yeah—right there," I groaned as his pounding thrusts rubbed his cockhead continuously over my prostate.

He was a fucking god, and finally mine.

Love you.

The words whispered through my head, and tears welled. Slamming my eyelids shut to keep from crying, I reached for my straining dick that jerked and spat out pre-cum with every slam of Chaz's body into mine.

I could have come hands-free, but the noises Chaz made clued me in he wasn't going to last. Wanted my hole to suck the cum out of his shaft and milk him until he filled me the fuck up. Needed to be flooded with his spunk, have it soak into my flesh so he would always be a part of me.

"Give me your cum, Chaz—fucking now, goddamnit."

White light flashed behind my clenched eyes, and I hollered as spunk shot up through my length.

"Fuck!" Chaz buried deep as my hole squeezed around him. His cock bucked inside me but didn't release. "Oh fuck, fuck, fuck." He croaked and swallowed harshly, hips stuttering as I splattered his couch with thick spurts of spunk.

Groaning, I arched on instinct, wanting to be bred like a bitch in heat.

"C-Coming," he whispered. "Jamie..."

The heat of his cum painted my insides as he bucked, his cock pulsing inside my ass.

Perfect. So goddamn, utterly *perfect*.

Spent and body going limp, I sagged against the couch, my cum smearing all the fuck over everything.

Chaz wrapped his arms around me and stayed buried deep, one last shudder rippling him over my back. A few more curses spilled from him, and I found myself grinning, riding the high of a lifetime.

I squeezed my hole around his girth, wishing he could stay inside me forever.

He shuddered again, trying to bury deeper. "You killed me," he grumbled, breath hot in my pit. His tongue stroked me there, causing me to shiver.

"Mmm," I hummed my enjoyment and appreciation of a him delivering the ass-fucking I'd been desperate for, even if it hadn't been hours long like I'd have preferred. Not bad for a quickie, but next time would be ten times better. "Give me a few, and I'll return the favor."

He huffed a snort and started to pull out.

I sighed at the loss of his warmth, the fullness of having him inside me. My hole gaped, the wetness slipping from me making my dick twitch sooner than it normally would.

Tentative fingers slid over my taint and up over my stretched pucker.

"Shove it back in," I ordered, feeling too damned empty for comfort.

Chaz retreated rather than obey.

I looked over my shoulder.

He stared at the spunk on his fingers, his face void of color. "Oh, fuck. We—we didn't use a c-condom."

"I told you it was okay," I assured him, shifting to perch on my hip. "I trust you, Chaz, and I was tested after the last guy I was with. There's nothing to worry about."

He swallowed hard and shook his head. "I didn't... We shouldn't have—"

"Don't you *fucking* dare," I hissed, anger roused like a flash of lightning. I wouldn't let him go there, ruin the most memorable night of my entire life. Finally being with him, sharing intimacy far beyond fucking even if it had been a quick and harsh coming together, was a dream come true. He would *not* fuck this moment for me.

"Jamie."

"No, Chaz. Do *not* lessen this, do *not* regret this. Please!"

"The fuck did I do? My fault," he whispered at the cum on his fingertips as though lost in his head, and fucking hell, did I want to grab hold of his arms and shake the shit out of him.

"The fuck it is!" I shot back, annoyed, hurt, and beyond pissed. "Shelly didn't deserve you, Chaz. She's the one who planned to leave. She was down in Berlin that day because she wanted to be there. Her actions were not a direct result of anything than her own thoughts and decisions!"

Chaz shook his head as though he refused to believe a single word I said. If he'd heard me at all. His shoulders rounded, his face stricken with grief.

Empathy rushed through me, cooling my blood in a blink, and my throat swelled, my eyes stinging. "Chaz."

He wouldn't look at me but stood like a statue, dick flaccid and glistening, cum coating his hand and holding his gaze riveted.

"You aren't to blame," I tried again, the sudden urge to let him know he wasn't alone in his feelings of guilt rushing through me. Mine had to be ten times his. Maybe if I told him the truth, he might be willing to do the same, and we would be able to continue moving forward.

"Don't you think I feel guilty as fuck for wishing Shelly was dead?" I whispered, sharing my deepest shame. "That she would be gone from this earth so you would be finally be free to be with me? That I would be able to love you how I've always dreamed of doing?"

The blood drained further from Chaz's face, causing a sickly pallor, and he blinked, lifting his focus upward. "You...*what?*"

Humiliation flooded through me at the horrified surprise in his eyes, but I needed to be honest about the hurt I'd been hiding from him. He wasn't the only one living with guilt that ate at a man's insides. If outing my shameful secret helped him, I would gladly uncover my sins.

"Why would you want that?" Chaz asked, his voice low. Broken in a way I'd never heard. "*Why*, Jamie? She was your friend!"

Was. Had been.

But my desire for Chaz had long-since overshadowed whatever kindness I'd felt for his wife who had treated him like trash when he'd always been an unpolished diamond in my eyes. He was the one who held my loyalty, not Shelly. *Never* Shelly.

"I told you I would burn in hell if it meant having you." I reached for him, but he yanked away, putting even more distance between us as he gave a slow, disbelieving head shake.

"You—Jesus, Jamie!" Shuddering, he turned his face from me as though he couldn't stand the sight of me. "Fuck!" Chaz stormed to the other end of the living room but stopped in the hallway, wrapping his arms around himself as though trying to keep his insides from spilling out onto the floor between us.

Hazel eyes welled with tears, his face a sickly gray, leached of life.

Nausea erupted in my stomach, and tremors took over my body. "Chaz—"

"D-Don't." He held up a hand, and the hurt in his gaze constricted my lungs. "How..." He swallowed hard. "How could you betray her—*me*—like that?"

I should have kept my mouth shut and taken the truth to the grave where it wouldn't have caused any damage. Here I was, hoping to protect Chaz from more pain, and all I'd done was make shit worse.

Mistake?

You bet your fucking ass it was.

"I'm sorry," I croaked.

"Get out of my house," he stuttered, choking on the words as tears slid down his face.

"Chaz, please."

"Get. Out!"

Pain ripped through my chest as easily as my hands had his shirt what felt minutes earlier. Lightheaded and reeling, his cum dripping from my ass, I grabbed my clothes and struggled to tug them on, unable to find any words that would make this right. Every thought escaped me other than giving Chaz exactly what he had demanded of me.

I shoved my shoes on, fumbled to pick up my keys from where they'd fallen to the floor, and turned toward the front door without looking at him again. Couldn't bear to see the additional pain I'd caused, how my horrifying admission had let him down when all I'd hoped was to set him at ease.

What had I expected? For him to say, "Yeah, me too"? He'd loved Shelly enough to marry her. Of course he would be horrified to hear his best friend had wanted her gone.

The damage had been done, and now there was nothing I could do or say. I'd fucked up beyond redemption.

Chaz didn't utter a word, and I shut myself out of the

home he had shared with Shelly. My lungs ached to scream into the cold night sky. Hand fisted around my keys so hard the metal bit into my palm.

I'd always prided myself on my loyalty, and I had broken faith with him in the worst possible way.

I didn't deserve Chaz's love.

Or forgiveness.

Chapter 26

Chaz

My best friend...he'd wished my wife was dead.

What the actual *fuck*? That was not the man I'd known since childhood, not even close.

He'd wished her gone from Pippen Creek, no longer a part of my life. Well, he'd gotten what he wanted, and the woman's heart along with her unborn child's no longer beat. And the father of that baby was probably broken beyond repair.

And me? I was just downright pissed over his betrayal of both me and my wife.

Anger seared through my veins, devouring all other emotions in its path. I clung to the rage as it burned the others to ash easily blown away on a wind through my mind.

How could Jamie Forester stoop to that level of shittiness? Hell, I'd wanted my freedom more than he ever could, and I'd never once hoped something bad happened to Shelly.

I'd striven to make things better even though we'd been miserable.

Hadn't I?

Second-guessing started up in my brain, loud as fuck between my ears. I remembered the negativity and complaining she'd heaped on my head every night when I got home. Pleasing her had been an impossibility.

What more could I have done? Surely, there'd been something I'd missed, some way of easing the tension and conflict between us.

I needed to quiet the voices in my head and had demanded Jamie leave because I couldn't stand the sight of him in that moment.

What had been a beautiful moment turned into a nightmare.

Any trace of happiness I'd felt while being with Jamie had been torn away by the evidence, the goddamned reminder of my failure, on my fingertips. I'd been too far gone in my lust to think shit through, and the mistake of not using a condom could have put Jamie at risk.

I wasn't sure of the timing of Shelly's affair. Had she been fucking the guy before we stopped having sex? Was I unknowingly carrying around some nasty disease?

I should have told Jamie what she'd done the second the sight of my cum brought reality crashing back into me but couldn't bear the humiliation of another man giving her what I couldn't. I would drive into Berlin tomorrow and get tested. If everything was okay, there was no reason I had to reach out to the man who had betrayed not just her memory but me as well.

The door closed behind him with a click that sounded a lot like a final nail in a coffin. Wrong fucking simile or metaphor—or whatever—but there the fuck it was.

Whiskey called for me, a quiet whisper promising numbness from the pain ripping through me, but I'd been trying to abstain. Deal with shit like a strong human, not some weakling who didn't deserve the Henderson name.

"Arg!" I hollered and ripped at my hair, uncaring that sticky wetness still clung to my fingers. "Fuck!"

I wanted to punch something. Kick a wall in. Tear down the house around me.

Teeth bared, I growled at the empty room, my pulse speeding and muscles quivering. Fists at my sides, I looked around for something to destroy without hurting myself in the process. Had to keep my hands healthy. Work depended on it.

Nostrils flaring, I closed my eyes and sucked in oxygen, a low keening noise filling the air.

"Jesus fucking *Christ!*" I hollered. A quick stomp around allowed me to snatch my clothes up off the floor, I kicked my shoes toward the rack where Shelly had demanded I always leave them by the front door, and I stalked up the hallway.

I tossed my clothes in the hamper and yanked the shower faucet on, stepping beneath the spray before it heated up to distract me from my thirst for alcohol.

"Fuck!" I clenched my jaw against the ice-cold water pelting my skin. Having something to focus on helped me to draw breath even if it stuttered through chattering teeth.

I closed my eyes and willed myself to still, searching out that numbed peace that had settled over me when the surgeon had informed me of Shelly's death.

The water warmed, running over tense muscles that refused to relax.

Soap.

Scrub him from my flesh.

Watch the reminder of being inside his body and the connection I'd found euphoria in disappear down the drain.

A sob ripped from me unexpectedly at the finality of Jamie being gone, and I gulped to fill my lungs. Another anguished howl spilled from my lips, and I slumped onto the shower stall, head hanging as water beat on me.

I hadn't thought my sorrow would ever make itself known in such a violent way, all-consuming and agonizing, attempting to cut off my ability to breathe. I'd been stupid to think grief meant crying for what Shelly had lost and the friendship she and I had once shared. Neither compared to how Jamie had fractured my heart.

This...this is what true heartache feels like.

A few weeks' worth of therapy helped me set my head straight somewhat, allowing me to at least go through the motions beyond mere survival in my renewed misery. So did having a negative test result in my hands. We were safe. I hadn't put Jamie's health in danger, thank fuck. Didn't change my disappointment or anger at him for what he'd dared to wish though. I couldn't begin to think about forgiving him any more than I could myself.

I ignored the passing of Thanksgiving that I used to spend with Jamie before he'd left for college. Shelly and I would to go to my parents for the holiday, but I couldn't be bothered to return Mom's text asking me to join them. Considering the outcome of our last dinner as a family, I didn't expect a calm or enjoyable visit.

I'd made the choice to completely cut their toxicity out of my life, which had been easier than expected. While my mother hadn't exactly been toxic, her silence proved her inability to love me above herself. Yet another pile of shit to share with my therapist.

I spent that Thursday at the shop instead since I was bogged down with both large and smaller jobs that would keep me busy for most of the winter.

It was time to hire someone. While I couldn't figure out the numbers in my attempted budget, I had no choice. People wouldn't wait forever for their vehicles, and there weren't enough hours in the day for me to get the work done on my own. Having to believe that the faster I moved cars through the shop, the more money I would make, I put an ad in the local flyer.

Of all townsfolk to answer, Josh, Jamie's backup quarterback from the season, had come sauntering into my office the Saturday after Thanksgiving, asking me to take a chance on him. He'd spent his childhood tinkering alongside his dad on small engines—lawn mowers, motorcycles, ski mobiles, and such. He also knew how to change oil, rotate tires, and he had even done a brake job with his dad once. While he was only available after school and on Saturdays, no one else inquired about the position.

Having no other options, I hired the kid, thankful at least that I didn't have to pay him top dollar. The fact he was openly gay and that I could provide a safe place for him made the choice even easier.

Someone young and full of life brought a tiny bit of sunshine to the shop. Josh enjoyed blasting pop music, singing along with his favorite artists. While I doubted I could ever be converted into a Swiftie as he claimed to be, I could appreciate the woman's music and often found myself humming along with the catchier tunes.

Having someone involved in my tiny corner of the world felt...good. And with every passing day and hour spent spilling *all* my secrets to my therapist, the emotions churning inside me began to quiet. I could go minutes,

Lynn Burke

sometimes up to an hour without thinking about Shelly or Jamie.

"Joshy!" A voice called over the music playing on Josh's Bose speaker, and I stepped out from beneath a car up on the lift.

Kyle, Josh's boyfriend, stood inside the shop's door, face red from the biting cold outside, a grin on his face.

Josh dropped the ratchet he'd held, the clatter on the floor making me smile rather than frown over his disregard for my tools. He threw himself at Kyle, who wrapped his arms and legs around the kid, spinning him around like they hadn't seen each other in weeks, when earlier, Josh had told me they'd gone to the movies in Berlin the night before.

Their lips locked, and I looked away, an ache growing in my chest over their complete freedom to love without hindrance or issue.

It had been because of their kissing that Jamie had followed me home. It had been because of Kyle and Josh that I'd finally gotten a taste of what an intimate relationship with my old best friend could be like. Addictive in the moment, but his usual brutal honesty afterward was more hurtful than anything I'd ever experienced.

One of the highest and lowest points of my life, a dream come true and regret all wrapped up in one untidy package no person ought to have to lug around on their shoulders.

Forgiveness would be key in moving forward, according to my therapist, but not just for Jamie or even my parents. For myself. While I could finally admit without questioning that I hadn't been responsible for Shelly's choices that led to her death, I still hadn't been able to pardon myself for putting my own thoughts and needs above hers, which had led to her loneliness.

Wasn't sure I ever would.

Kyle took off a few minutes later, and Josh was all giddy, pink cheeks, and sparkling eyes as he ambled over toward me.

"Sure you don't mind him stopping by like that? I can tell him to wait for my lunch break."

I shook my head. "No. It's fine." While I attempted to smile, I failed.

"You all right, Mr. Henderson?"

"Chaz," I repeated what I'd been doing since Josh had started working for me a couple of weeks ago.

"Still—you okay?" Josh pushed.

"It's...bittersweet, I guess, seeing you with your boyfriend."

"Can I be nosy and ask why?" He leaned against the workbench, arms crossed while I eyed the exhaust I'd installed on the car overhead.

The kid was always poking into business he had no right to, but for some reason, I didn't mind him being up in my personal space. I expected it was what having a younger sibling might be like, and I didn't hate it. The kid was only six years my junior after all. I'd come to care about the boy who was an open book, sharing bits and pieces of him that took me outside of my own head.

"I was in love with my best friend once, just like you."
Still am.

"But weren't you—" He swallowed the rest of whatever question he had as though realizing he might be nosey about a sensitive topic.

"*Before* I married Shelly," I tacked on, expecting that's where he'd been headed. Satisfied with the job I'd completed, I moved from beneath the car and started to lower it.

I could feel Josh's eyes on me and gave him my focus

when the lift settled to the ground. Like me, he wore a navy-blue jumpsuit, grease-stained and filthy. His dark hair was a ruffled mess, from Kyle's hands or lack of a brush before coming in to work, I had no clue. Hadn't really checked the kid out when he'd arrived a few hours earlier.

"What's on your mind, Josh?" I grabbed a towel off the bench beside him and wiped my hands.

"You played ball in high school with Coach, didn't you?"

A million memories of uniforms, the gridiron, and ass slaps flooded my mind, but I pushed against them, refusing to linger on what would only bring more pain.

"Yeah." I tossed the rag aside.

Josh studied me, his eyes revealing he put puzzle pieces together in that crafty brain of his.

"I didn't have the balls back then that you do," I said. "Didn't want to chance heartache, so I chose the safer route."

He nodded, proving my assumption of what he'd figured out. "Coach said watching you marry someone else hurt worse than his knee injury."

That news hit me like a punch to the gut, ripping the air from my lungs. Jamie's truth tore through me, leaving a gaping hole behind.

The day his knee ligaments had torn to shreds had ended his lifelong dreams, and he'd told Josh losing me had caused him even *more* pain?

Fucking hell, why did agony stab at my heart and tighten my throat?

"It's a good thing you found the courage to tell Kyle how you felt," I said, my voice nothing but gravel and regret.

"Didn't want to live with the what-ifs." Josh shrugged. "Best decision of my life because it turned out in my favor.

Maybe it'll work for you two this time. Won't know if you don't try, Mr. Henderson." He walked off to finish the job he'd been taking care of before his boyfriend had shown up.

What-ifs.

There were a shit ton of those in my head I'd been attempting to move on from at the insistence from my therapist. Couldn't change the past, only stride forward. My goal was to live with less of those pesky questions in the future, but I wasn't sure how to go about doing that.

One foot in front of the other, I'd been telling myself lately.

I'd begun to get my own groceries again instead of having The Market deliver. I'd even swung by Pedro's Pizza to pick up dinner one night last week rather than having it dropped at the shop like I sometimes did.

Sunday morning, I woke feeling restless, my mind busy as usual but with Josh's words added to the mess. I needed a break from cars and their parts too.

Kel's face lit up when I walked through the door of Scone Haven, the scent of freshly baked deliciousness and coffee thick in the air, making my mouth water. "Good to see you, Chaz."

I dipped my head in greeting while approaching the counter.

He leaned on it, blue eyes kind without a hint of pity, his white apron a little stained from his earlier baking in the kitchen out back.

"Thanks again for the fundraiser," I said even though I'd managed a phone call not long after Shelly's death to offer the same.

"It's the least I could do." Kel's gaze flitted over my face. "How are you?"

He wasn't a nosy gossiper, so I didn't mind the question from my wife's old boss. "Keeping busy. You?"

Kel shrugged. "Might have finally found a replacement for Shelly. Younger kid, new to town who used to work as a barista in North Conway. He starts tomorrow, so we'll see. Want your usual?"

"Please. Thanks."

He poured my black coffee into the biggest cup he had and handed it over along with one of the cranberry orange scones I could easily eat a dozen of.

The door pushed inward behind me, letting in a blast of cold air.

I could sense the person behind me before Kel glanced over my shoulder and greeted Jamie by name.

My pulse kicked up, and the fight-or-flight part of my brain went haywire.

Instead of taking off—I'd gotten out of the house for a reason, goddamnit—I dropped a ten on the counter and moved to the far corner where a table sat empty. A few patrons greeted me as I passed them by, but no one asked questions or attempted to pull me into conversation, thank fuck. It was enough I'd chosen to come out and be among the living.

Unless they stopped by my shop for a job, small talk with old acquaintances was another step for a different day.

I sat with my back to the counter, closed my eyes, and sipped my coffee, enjoying the heat sliding clear down to my empty stomach. Ignoring the buzz over my skin from being in the same room as Jamie wasn't an option, but I would bear it until he left.

But of course, he approached, the hairs on my arms standing on end when he appeared in my periphery.

"This seat taken?"

Shaking my head, I gave my cup all of my attention as Jamie settled into the chair across the small table from me.

I had some shit to work through and wasn't ready to forgive, but I refused to be an asshole or cause a scene by telling him to leave me alone when the deepest parts of me didn't want him to. At least anger didn't still burn bright in my chest like it had that night. Would have been nice though not to feel that sense of loss and emptiness that had taken over me ever since Josh shared with me what Jamie had told him.

Tension was a thick blanket over us, the kind of silence that stifled and made breathing difficult.

"Chaz—"

"Don't," I mumbled, stopping him from apologizing.

His heavy exhale let me know I'd been right in assuming he'd been about to do that very thing.

"Fine. Onward it is," he muttered. He inhaled deeply and held it a second before opening his mouth again. "I'm moving to Berlin."

Jamie's statement hit me like that goddamned F-350 again, ripping the oxygen from my lungs and sending me into a spiral-like panic. Same as when my best friend had informed me he was headed to Boston College, I couldn't speak. Couldn't breathe.

I clutched at my coffee cup. This time, there was no Shelly for me to cling to in hopes of filling the void his absence would leave behind.

Chapter 27

Jamie

I'd seen Chaz's truck parked outside Scone Haven and hadn't been able to squash hope rising inside me. If he was learning to live again outside his home and shop, he might be willing to forgive me and get us back on track for where we'd always been headed.

Considering our connection and unbelievable chemistry, Chaz and I could have something beautiful. Long-lasting. We'd shared explosive passion, and I struggled to believe my honesty had ruined my chance of him returning my love.

I didn't doubt he'd blamed me for his wife's death in those days since I'd seen him last. How could he not? Putting myself in his shoes reiterated the mistake I'd made in sharing my secret with him. I would hate him too if he'd wished the woman I loved enough to marry would disappear off the face of the planet.

The weeks of silence between us had passed in a haze of hurt and remorse, and I'd clung to memories from our one night together that would eventually fade from my mind like the ache in my ass days after he'd given me what I'd begged for. Nothing had held meaning since then. Seeing my team's players around town, Josh and Kyle, holding hands and looking like they were on top of the world, hadn't offered a single spark of happiness. Neither had homecoming, where I'd heard they'd gone together and danced the night away.

That Hallmark movie moment belonged to those two boys, not me.

Working out and taking care of my body no longer lay at the front of my mind. I'd begun to slack off, the entire week after Thanksgiving a tumble down the eating-shit cliff thanks to Dad's cooking and Dexter bringing the best cranberry cheesecake I'd ever had in my mouth.

Twice since Chaz had ordered me from his house, I rode along with Dad around town in the cruiser while he attempted to cheer me up, but I couldn't be dragged from the pit I'd tumbled into.

Dad had suggested that perhaps it was time to move on, that distance and the passing of days and eventual months might allow for some healing. I'd admitted to the shitty wish I'd had and how spilling it had ruined my friendship with Chaz along with the possibility of him ever allowing me to love him in the way I yearned to do.

So when the job offer from one of Dad's contacts down in Berlin's town hall had come through via email, I'd considered taking it even though I'd filled out the application while pissed off and wanting to disappear from Pippen Creek forever. Getting my own place down there rather than commuting had sounded like a damned good idea at the time. Maybe some sort of satisfaction in working 9-5, putting that engineering degree I'd earned to use, could be found.

But I needed closure first even if it seemed that Chaz wasn't willing to give it to me one way or the other.

The silence between us grew heavier with every passing moment.

"Chaz?" I prompted him for some sort of response to my declaration.

Still, it was another full minute before he spoke, his tone barely audible. "Why?"

"Why move?"

He nodded, refusing to take his eyes off his coffee cup.

"Got a job offer from their town's building department, so why not? There's nothing keeping me here." I studied his down-turned face and how he swallowed, his Adam's apple dipping slowly. That hope that had brought me through Scone Haven's door rekindled to life inside me. "Is there any reason I *should* stay?"

"This is home—your Dad is here—those kids on the team adore you."

He didn't lie, but I dreamed of more.

"You've encouraged and changed a lot of lives," he continued. "You're loved, Jamie."

"Am I?" I pushed, wanting to hear his truth more than any of the others he'd pointed out.

"Of course you are!" he stated sharply, finally gifting me the vision of his beautiful, pain-filled hazel eyes I found myself drowning in.

My heart beat heavy in my chest, every thump for him. He owned me, body and soul. Always would.

"What about you, Chaz?" I whispered, needing verbalization of what I swore I saw in his gaze.

"What about me?"

I sat in silence, watching him until he glanced away.

Weak sunlight filtering through the bay window behind

him caressed his strong profile like my fingers itched to do. Snowflakes fell beyond, their pristine white covering the muck and dirty slush from previous storms.

Dad had told me that if I was gifted the opportunity, that I needed to share the rest of my heart with Chaz. While sitting in a public space with other townsfolk close enough to listen wasn't ideal, time ran short. Berlin's town officials expected me to start after the first of the year, and a lot of details needed taken care of between now and then if I accepted their offer.

That decision rested on the man across the table from me.

"I told Josh that if you love someone, you put them first," I said, keeping my voice low. "Sacrifice for them. That's the kind of love I desire, Chaz, and you're who I want it with. But being here in this town with distance between us... Fuck." I ran a hand over my face, my throat aching. I was no Babs. "Seeing you and not being able to have you hurts more than anything." I went on. "Goddamn knives pierce my chest over and over until I bleed out. I know I don't deserve your forgiveness, but it's what I want. What I *need*. And if you can't give me any of that, what's the point of sticking around where there's more pain than happiness with every breath I take?"

Chaz didn't respond, simply went back to studying his goddamned coffee cup.

Answer enough.

An audible exhale emptied my lungs and slouched my shoulders. My eyes stung, but I couldn't tear my focus off his thinned, pale lips I would never taste again.

Loneliness for life appeared to be my future, and there was nothing I could do to change that fact no matter what pep talk I offered myself. There was no winning in this moment, only a chance to escape the pain and attempt to survive.

"I'm the one who needs space now," I managed to whisper before sliding out of my seat.

Every step putting distance between Chaz and I was agony. A slow peeling of skin away from muscle and bone, wounding me in ways that would never fully heal.

He didn't call out to stop my leaving, and the door shut firmly behind me.

The cold outdoors slapped me in the face, its bitter chill stealing what little air I had left in me. I stood alone on the walkway, Christmas music filtering in from somewhere along Main Street, twinkling lights in the fire station's windows across from Scone Haven attempting to make the atmosphere festive.

As a kid, I would have tipped my head back and caught snowflakes on my tongue, but I couldn't be bothered to search out even one second of happiness thanks to the heaviness in my heart. I wanted to curl up in a ball and throw a massive pity party for one.

Head down, I trudged through the thickening snow toward my SUV, fighting to focus on the immediate future.

Accepting the job offer, making it through the holidays, then packing up my shit and moving out of Pippen Creek for good.

Chapter 28

Chaz

My therapist had suggested a lot of things in the weeks I'd been seeing her, and while I'd implemented a few recommendations, the one to confront my loved ones and share my feelings was a hard limit.

I cleared the house of Shelly's belongings, donating everything to Consider Consignment over on the far end of Pippen Street. I painted the entirety of my house's interior, rearranged the furniture, and even splurged on a new bed and linens since I hadn't needed to pay a weekly tab at Frenchie's.

While proud of myself for continued advancement in moving on by creating a new space that was solely my own —and a lot more comfortable—I couldn't bring myself to speak to my parents.

Or Jamie.

I wanted him more than anything, loved him regardless of his betrayal of the friend we'd shared, but I wasn't ready. Something inside me stalled out when it came to him. Perhaps I still felt I didn't deserve happiness. Or maybe that seed of bitterness deep inside me needed to be completely rooted out before I could stomach facing him again.

Sitting alone in my living room on Christmas morning, I stared at the small tree I'd bought for myself, a sense of thankfulness snaking through my chest for the first time in months. The scent of fir filled the air, a smell Shelly had hated along with the pine needles littering the floor as the tree eventually gave up the ghost no matter how much one watered it.

I'd used multi-colored lights rather than the white she'd always insisted on for our fake fir. The branches of what I called my Charlie Brown tree were sad in their scarcity but beautiful to me because it was exactly what I'd always wanted and hadn't been allowed during the years of my marriage.

While I had created a new beginning in my immediate surroundings, a weight still held me back, and I'd begun to hate it. Being around townsfolk again, seeing the world continue to revolve and how people found happiness in the small things made me yearn for the same.

I wanted to be free to live my life.

Today, I could take one step as my therapist had said that might make others easier in the future. Forward progress didn't have to be in leaps and bounds.

You've got this.

Jamie's motto whispered through my head, bring a sad smile to my lips and an ache in my heart.

My cell lay in my hand, screen dark, but the text from Mom still etched in my mind. An invite to Christmas dinner.

I toyed with my phone, going over in my head what my therapist had suggested in our last session. Telling my parents the truth about Shelly wouldn't be an attempt to tarnish her reputation. I'd clearly cared about her too much to do that intentionally. Sharing everything I'd kept from them also wouldn't be selfish because I wouldn't use her supposed sins to make me look better than Dad saw me. Nothing would ever change his mind toward his failure of a son, but I'd emptied my house of the bad memories. It was time to clean out the closet, air the dirty laundry, and own my failings.

Attempting not to overthink as I did these days, I showered, shaved, and put on some nice clothing. Armor, perhaps, but whatever. At this point, I didn't care if Dad frowned at my appearance or not. I made an attempt, and that was winning in my eyes, same as when I'd mailed out last month's payment two days early.

Mom answered the door as usual, her eyes lighting up at finding me on the front stoop with snowflakes in my hair and on my eyelashes. The nostalgic scent of ham and sweet potatoes, the traditional Christmas dinner, rolled over me.

"Charles!" She threw her arms around me before I made it over the threshold.

My throat went tight, and my eyes stung, and I returned her greeting, although with slightly less enthusiasm.

"It's so good to see you." Mom stepped back while I shrugged out of my coat, a quick swipe of her fingertip to the corner of her eye ridding her of a tear. "I wasn't sure you would come."

"Considering how I left last time, I didn't expected an invite," I explained, hanging up my coat on the rack.

Mom glanced up the hallway toward where I could hear Dad puttering around in the kitchen. "I apologize for his—"

"Don't," I cut her off, refusing to hear from her lips what

ought to be on Dad's. "Does he know you asked me to come over?"

"Yes." She lifted her chin in a show of backbone I'd never seen before. Her eyes even flashed with stubbornness I recognized in myself. "I told the man if he didn't like you showing up, he was welcome to fly to Florida to spend the day with your grandparents."

I stared. "You...*what?*"

"Needless to say, he folded immediately."

Goddamn. Mom *had* found her backbone. Dad had cut his own toxic father out of his life years earlier and refused to talk to the man.

A chuckle rumbled in my chest. "You finally realized who really rules this roost, huh?"

"I've always been aware but never felt the need to spread my wings or ruffle feathers until recently. And trust me, I've done so countless times since he and I were alone on Thanksgiving. I've failed you in too many ways to count."

"Mom."

She held up her hand. "I'm sorry, Charles, for not standing up for you or putting you first. You should have been my focus, not attempting to please a man who continues to live under the trauma caused by his own father."

Dad didn't have it easy growing up, but his past experiences weren't an excuse for how he treated his own son. I expected Mom was intelligent enough to recognize the same.

All we could do was move forward as I'd been attempting to do.

I hugged Mom again, a little bit more tenderly and

appreciative. "I forgive you." I offered what she needed to hear, and a weight slid off my chest.

One down, one to go.

Not that I would ever forget even if I managed to somehow forgive the biggest obstacle to my self-worth beneath this roof.

Dad's face didn't betray jack shit when he turned around from plating the candied sweet potatoes to find me in the kitchen. "Charles."

"Dad." I nodded in greeting, holding my face in the same stoic mask as he did.

"Dinner is ready, so please make yourself at home," Mom insisted, handing over the platter of spiral-cut ham with its clove and brown sugar glaze.

We had been eating the same meal this time of year since I could remember, and my mouth watered once we sat at the table in our usual seats. The chair on my right was empty, but only a small snaking sense of loss walked through my mind.

I would miss some parts of having Shelly around but wouldn't allow grief of any sort to dictate my life any longer.

The lack of peas, however, made me smile.

"You seem happy," Mom noted.

"No peas," I answered honestly, and Dad actually barked a laugh.

I jerked my head toward him, and he coughed, wiping his smile away as though ashamed by his outburst. "You hate them too?" I asked him.

He glanced at Mom—and nodded.

"Clifford!" Mom exclaimed, eyes wide. "Why didn't you say something sooner?"

"Because you love them, and I didn't want to hurt your

feelings," Dad said, his cheeks a shade of pink I'd never seen before.

"Well." Mom huffed and slid a slice of ham onto her plate before handing the platter to me. "Perhaps a little more *honesty* in this household might be a good idea from here on out."

Agreed, one-hundred percent.

"You've been speaking your mind for weeks on end, woman," Dad said but with softness in his tone rather than chiding. "It's been...refreshing in ways I never would have expected."

"On that note," I said, taking three slices of ham because I was hungry for a good meal, goddamnit, "I've been seeing a therapist since October, and I've learned more than I expected. Need to share a lot too." I handed the platter to Dad, whose lips returned to their usual thin line. "Getting help isn't weakness, Dad. It's being responsible and taking care of yourself when things around you are beyond your control. She's shown me how to put my...well, shit, into perspective."

Mom didn't chide my language, nor did Dad argue my statement.

We finished plating our food and began to eat while I decided how to best state the truth I'd been living since marrying Shelly.

"Would you rather wait for this discussion until after dinner?" Mom asked, but I got the sense she offered out of sensitivity toward me rather than demanding I keep the peace until we finished. She probably wanted me to fill my stomach before walking out again if that was where the conversation ended up.

Seeing as how we didn't have anything else worth discussing until this was out in the open, I shook my head.

Might as well get shit laid out on the table now so I could enjoy apple pie and coffee afterward.

Hopefully.

"Shelly was having an affair."

Dad's fork clattered to his plate, and he gave me his full attention, brow furrowed and gaze searching.

I refused to feel the blame I expected he thought to push onto me and continued before he could open his mouth. "She was pregnant with another man's child and planned to divorce me."

"Charles." Mom's voice broke.

"Our relationship was on the rocks for years. My inability to give her the family she wanted, the fights, my staying away from the house to escape—" I cut myself off, refusing to put Shelly down. "I failed her in many areas of our marriage. Definitely wasn't the best husband, that's for damn sure."

Both of my parents stared at me, Dad's face struggling to remain stoic, Mom teary-eyed and lips trembling.

"I'm not pulling shit out of my closet to make her look like the bad guy but being honest so you know how I'm feeling. If you care."

"Of course we do," Mom insisted quickly.

Dad swallowed hard, dropping his focus to his plate and slowly picking back up his flatware. He cut into his ham but studied the bite on his fork before speaking. "It takes true grit to admit we've let our loved ones down."

I waited to reply since his tone and careful word choice hinted he wasn't done.

He chewed his ham, his eyes downward. "Perhaps I haven't been the best of fathers. I'm sure I haven't lived up to my own potential or your expectation in that regard."

You think?

I held in my snort and shoved a bite of sweet potatoes into my mouth, letting him stew in whatever emotions he had going on in his chest in that moment.

"Clifford?" Mom prompted him to continue, and he heaved a heavy sigh.

"I am sorry, Charles." He finally met my gaze, the regret and pain in his eyes unexpected, hurtful, and healing all at the same time. "For speaking when I ought to have kept quiet. For not using my words to build you up rather than tear you down."

Unable to swallow or find my voice, I nodded.

Dad's lips thinned for a moment as he moved green beans around on his plate, brow still furrowed deeply as he worked through his thoughts. "You know my father was an absolute bastard."

Surprised by his language, I snuck a glance at Mom to find her watching Dad with encouragement and pride on her face.

"But my childhood is no excuse for my treatment of you," Dad continued.

"You're right." I didn't mind stating that fact for the first time in my life, but I didn't allow my hurt to lace my tone.

His lips twisted as though attempting a smile. "Perhaps someday you will be able to do what I've never been able to —forgive your father for letting you down at every turn."

My damned throat went tight again, eyes stinging.

"Well!" Mom said with breathless excitement or perhaps an overwhelming overflow of other emotions. "I believe I like this new means of communication."

"It's healthy," I agreed with a rasped voice, glancing at Dad again. "It brings healing."

He nodded agreement, his eyes a little wet too.

I filled my lungs, girding my loins for the next topic of discussion since this one had gone well. "While we're on a roll," I said, fingers crossed, "I'm pansexual. That means I like men, women, people—whatever and whoever. A person's physical makeup doesn't matter to me. I find everyone on the gender spectrum attractive."

Both parents blinked as though baffled by my announcement.

"What I'm saying is that if and when I bring someone home again they might not be female."

Dad nodded acknowledgement first, surprising the hell out of me. "Auntie Dottie's daughter is non-binary. Uncle Aubrey's son is transitioning and prefers to be called Erica instead of Eric now."

Look at Dad showing off his proper terminology.

A grin stretched my lips, one I hadn't experienced in far too long. Felt good as fuck.

I shouldn't have been surprised with how he constantly attempted to educate himself by reading books from the library and watching the news. Either the man had a learning kink or he never managed to measure up to his own father's standards and still strove to become a better man.

I hated that I could totally empathize, but I'd been dealt this hand, and I wasn't going to fold as I'd considered doing back in September.

Onward had become my new motto, one I could appreciate after having been depressed for far too long.

"So neither of you will care who I choose to date when the time comes?" I focused on Mom since she hadn't reacted in any way other than to go quiet.

"We just want you happy," Mom whispered, glancing at Dad as though seeking his agreement.

"She speaks the truth, son."

Well, fuck.

I shoveled another bite of sweet potatoes into my mouth to keep from blubbering and let the tears roll down my cheeks.

Chapter 29

Jamie

Berlin wasn't much of a city compared to Boston, but it was ten times the size of Pippen Creek, and not everyone knew their neighbors. Actual strangers existed two doors down from my apartment. Some caught up in their own little worlds, others ignorant and hateful toward those they shared the streets with.

At least the office where I worked lacked drama.

A nine-to-five was exactly what I'd expected. Drudgery and boredom, eight hours where my body began to waste away due to inactivity.

I joined a gym a couple of blocks from my place, which gave me something to do at night, but once in bed, my thoughts returned to my hometown and what I'd left behind.

The silence from Chaz was expected—I'd asked for space after all—but I missed the fuck out of him.

And Dad. Returning for a weekend to visit and accidentally bumping into Chaz would have been easy, but until he was ready, if he ever was, I had to keep my distance. The miles between us didn't lessen the ache in my bones though, the desperate longing to just see his face.

"How is he?" I asked Dad, same as I always did when he answered my call on Wednesday evening, our agreed-upon day to chat since he was off work. This was the fourth week since I'd moved out, a cold night in late January when all mankind in the far north ought to be hunkered down in their homes around fireplaces or beneath heated blankets.

A thick layer of snow lay over the city, keeping it quiet outside my bedroom's frosted-over window, but like typical New Englanders, we would go on about our business with the sunrise no matter the state of the roads or sidewalks.

"Chaz looks better every time I see him around town," Dad said.

While I was happy Chaz seemed to be getting back to life outside of being a hermit, it stung he hadn't reached out to me. Perhaps he had no intention of doing so. Maybe his shame over our affair was a line he *wouldn't* cross, like the one I'd dragged him over.

"Babs said he's gained back some weight, not that I understand how she knows that, considering everyone is an overstuffed bear in layers while walking down Main Street. He doesn't have those bags under his eyes, though. Finally got a haircut too. No more raggedy hair sticking out beneath his beanie."

"Have you spoken to him at all? Has he asked about me?" Fuck, I sounded like a whiney kid.

"Yes and no."

I huffed a curse and threw an arm over my eyes where I lay on my bed under a pile of blankets. Who knew electric bills for a mere one-bedroom apartment would be so goddamned high?

While I still had plenty of cash in the bank, it wouldn't last forever, so I'd been living frugally, just to play it safe.

Adulting like this sucked ass.

"I saw him and his dad at Dig-In the other afternoon over their lunch break," Dad said.

I whipped my arm off my face and stared at the dark ceiling. "What?"

"Clifford and Charles Henderson had lunch together at Old Man Ron's place."

"Yeah—I caught that, but what the fuck?"

I could imagine Dad's shrug. "Surprised the hell out of me too. But they weren't arguing. Didn't even appear to be angry with each other. I couldn't hear what they were saying while waiting for my takeout, but there didn't appear to be the usual animosity."

Well, fuck me sideways.

Making amends with his dad? Talking to him by choice? Eating out with the man? The fuck was going on?

"Were they drunk?" I asked, thinking maybe he'd been back in the whiskey.

"Nope. They were both clear-eyed when I said hi."

"Huh."

It sounded like Chaz was making some serious changes, but I was no longer important enough to be included in the life he'd envisioned. I rubbed over my chest and the deep ache that refused to let me breathe easy. It seemed months, *years*, since I'd been able to do so. Ever since that day I'd caught my best friend kissing Shelly.

"Jamie?"

"Yeah?" I croaked.

"Did you hear what I said?"

"Um...no. Sorry. Wool in the brain and all that shit."

"Are you liking your job any better now that you've settled in?"

I hadn't meant to complain about the work Dad had helped me find, but those first couple of weeks had been pretty shitty, I'd missed his cooking, and I was lonely as hell. "Not really?" My reply sounded more like a question than statement.

"Not a good fit, or is something else making you uncomfortable?"

"Nothing bad, just...I haven't decided yet if this is what I want long term. A desk job is too..."

"Restrictive? Boring as hell?"

"Nailed it," I said with a huff of laughter.

"You always did have trouble sitting still. There's always the police academy," Dad suggested what I'd talked about a lot as a little kid. "You love ride alongs, and I finally got the approval to hire another officer in Pippen Creek."

"You know I can't return again, Dad."

"What if your being here is exactly what Chaz needs? Seeing you all the time, reminding him he's missing out?"

"Last month you suggested the opposite." I reminded him of his push for me to move on.

"A man can't be wrong?"

An unhappy laugh barked rumbled my chest. "Are you playing matchmaker to make up for it?"

"Just trying to help my son find his way back to where I believe he belongs."

My sad smile faded. "You really think that?"

"There's a missing puzzle piece in Pippen Creek, a corner one if you ask me, and your face is on it."

I huffed a snort. "You just miss having someone praising your cooking abilities."

"Are you calling me out?" I could hear the smile in Dad's voice.

"Damned right, I am."

"I also miss having someone to take care of," Dad admitted, longing in his voice.

"There's dating apps for that," I suggested because I expected he didn't mean me.

Dad snorted. "Tried that—not interested. Too many whiney brats looking for a daddy with a heavy hand. That's not my thing."

"Ugh." I grimaced. "Dad. Seriously? I did not need that image in my head."

"Hey, you're the one who brought it up."

A smile actually lifted my lips. "So...you're considering a guy this time?"

"If I can find one willing to let me love them the way I want to without any drama or bullshit."

My lips flatlined at realizing my dad was a lonely as I was. "There's *always* drama. Gender doesn't matter. Trust me."

"That's what Dex says too," Dad said with a sigh. "Maybe I should lower my standards."

"Nope," I shot before his brain got focused on that path. "You're one of the best men I know. Don't lower shit so you have someone to stick your dick into."

"Jamie!" Dad's admonishment suggested his face had turned red.

I chuckled. "Just keeping it real, Dad."

"Shit," he muttered.

I could imagine he scrubbed a hand over his face. "Seriously, though—you want me to look into the academy?" I asked, putting our conversation on a track that wouldn't embarrass him any further.

"While some people would say to hang in there for a little while longer, you have to go with your heart, kid."

That piece of me remained back home where Dad said I belonged, but the one cradling that fragile part of me didn't seem interested in taking care of it.

"I'll think about it," I said, not sure I could until I knew one way or another where Chaz's thoughts were when it came to me.

"The May class still has openings."

I wasn't surprised in the least Dad had already checked into it for me. "Will I have any issues getting in because of my knee?"

"Nope. I'll make sure of it."

"Got connections over there too, huh?" I asked, smiling again.

"Bet your ass, I do. At least fill out the application," Dad suggested. "I'll send you the link."

Yeah, Dad had this idea brewing in his head for a while. "Not doing it tonight. Too tired."

"No rush and no pressure."

I bid Dad a good night a few minutes later, set my phone aside, and rolled onto my stomach to hug my pillow. The fluff under my head didn't smell like Chaz, no matter how much I wished it did.

Closing my eyes, I considered my future.

I'd been the one to ask for space this time around, and Chaz was too honorable a man to cross a boundary I'd set. It would be up to me to open the lines of communication, but knowing the hours he kept, ten at night was too late to call.

Maybe talking to him face-to-face would be better?

I considered that option, expecting he would take off Sunday like he always did. Maybe a couple of coffees in hand and those cranberry orange scones he loved from Kel's place would get me through his front door.

The thought he would grab hold of my shirt and yank me inside again flitted through my brain, and my dick twitched.

Four days, and it's go time. I've got this.

That positive motto faded from my mind as quickly as it had unconsciously kicked in.

No point in getting my hopes up. I'd done that too often and had ended up disappointed.

Didn't need any more of that shit in my life.

Chapter 30

Chaz

A fresh six inches of snow had fallen overnight, but typical of northern New Hampshire, the roads were cleared and salted for the so-called morning traffic. Still, there was no point in rushing south when my dinner date wasn't available until after five.

I was at the shop for most of the day, teaching Josh how to switch out a radiator on a truck older than mine and trusting him to complete that day's smaller jobs. An oil change and tail light bulb replacement, all easily finished up before the end of the workday for him.

Route 16 was pretty much empty of headlights around me as I drove, the interior of my truck as silent as my head. This sense of peace had been a long time coming. My therapist was thrilled with the results I'd sown from crossing over outside of my comfort zone.

Dad and I met up twice in the last month for lunch, discussing his past and how it had affected him throughout adulthood. Never had I ever imagined him showing such vulnerability and a desire to better himself emotionally. I'd expected to bury him as stubborn as he'd been born. He'd told me Mom had given him an ultimatum, and he loved her more than life, so I shouldn't have been surprised he'd begun to make steps toward facing his demons.

While I was no therapist, and he had no wish to meet with one, it was obvious as the nose on my face that changes were taking place inside his head and heart, and talking to me about it was good for both of us.

He even hugged me the day before after we walked out of Dig-In to head back to our office responsibilities.

Speaking of work, hiring Josh was the best thing I could have done. Besides doing exactly what I'd expected—getting more cars in and out of the shop and us seeing better profits, the boy was a whiz with numbers, just like Jamie. He had walked into the office late December to see me struggling with the shop's budget.

He offered to help out, and I'd handed that shit over, completely trusting him because the kid had integrity and had proven his work ethics.

Josh suggested software that would keep track of shit for the next calendar year, so I spent the money, and fuck me, what an investment. Hours of my time returned to me with that accounting program, and all I had to do was input some shit and let the computer do the rest to balance that month's books.

Yeah, Josh was pure gold in my opinion, and I loved seeing his and Kyle's relationship continue to thrive.

He wasn't aware why I was driving down to Berlin, that shit was a little too personal for boss/employee in my opinion, but he'd grinned when I stated I was taking off early. It was plain as hell on his face that he thought he knew why.

But Jamie wasn't my sole reason for visiting the city I

hadn't been to since Shelly's death. Didn't set the kid straight either.

I walked into the ER a few minutes later, expecting to be triggered considering what I'd seen and heard last time I'd been there. Memories flitted through my mind, but I focused on the help desk rather than allowing the lingering grief to stir up and make me emotional.

"How can I help you?" the receptionist asked, her tone and eyes kind.

"I'm looking for Tara?"

"And you are?"

"Chaz Henderson—she's expecting me."

"I'll tell her you're here."

I nodded my thanks, shoved my hands in my coat pockets to keep them from shaking, and stepped away from the desk, moving to stand in the exact spot Tara had slid to the floor with her arms wrapped around my wife's lover. While sadness filled me for both of them, the threat of tears no longer stung.

I had texted Shelly's old friend earlier in the week, asking if she would be willing to meet with me sometime. She'd suggested Thursday for dinner, and the sooner than later I'd been hoping for had me agreeing regardless of having to leave work earlier than usual.

Tara exited the Employees Only door beyond the receptionist's desk, coat and bag in hand. She eyed me a little warily but smiled. "Hi."

"Hey." I mirrored her smile even though I wasn't feeling it, trying to put her at ease. "We can eat at the cafeteria if you don't have a long break," I said, thinking she might just be halfway through her shift, but she shook her head.

"I came in at noon and took a half day since I didn't think this conversation would be a short one."

I'd expected the same but hadn't wanted to push for too much of her time.

"I heard Jackie's is where to go for a good, home-cooked meal." I suggested Mom's favorite place to eat whenever she and Dad came to Berlin.

"Sounds good to me," Tara agreed, and I motioned for her to lead the way. "Want to follow me or do you know where you're going?"

I'd already checked the vicinity out since I had plans after dinner. "I'll meet you there."

We parted ways in the parking lot, and I gripped the steering wheel tight, focused on breathing in a steady rhythm while driving across town, determined to keep from overthinking about the what-ifs.

Our discomfort was clear as we met up outside Jackie's, both of our smiles tentative. Searching.

We were shown to a booth in the front window, and we placed our orders, then peered at each other across the table once left alone.

"How have you been handling her death?" I asked, assuming they were as close as Shelly had suggested.

"Isn't that what I ought to be asking you?" Tara said, her blue eyes flitting over my face, seeking as much as her tone.

"Better than I ever expected to," I answered honestly. "You?"

She shrugged and glanced away, reaching to put a straw in her ginger ale.

"I know about her boyfriend. I saw you consoling him that night in the ER."

The blood drained from her face, and she closed her eyes, chin dipping. "It's my fault they hooked up."

"They were more than that though," I said. "He was heartbroken. Devastated by the loss."

"Yeah," she whispered, stirring her tonic. "He was a friend of a friend. We all went out for drinks in July, they hit it off, and...yeah. I'm sorry."

"It wasn't any more your fault than it was mine for ignoring her and making her needy enough she looked for love elsewhere," I said. Tara nodded but still wouldn't meet my gaze. "Would you tell me about your relationship with my wife? What she shared with you about theirs?"

Tara blew out a heavy exhale but nodded.

As expected, Shelly had complained to her friend about how she and I had grown apart, that neither of us were the same carefree kids from high school we'd been when we'd first gotten together. The hard times we'd had and resulting heartache had allowed for a wedge to slip between us rather than drawing us closer as some luckier couples tended to do.

"Shelly said over and over that she didn't know how to fix things."

"We both made mistakes." I stated the truth my therapist had helped me see, thankful to no longer feel the overwhelming guilt that had attempted to bury me a few months earlier.

"She loved you." Tara finally lifted her focus off the food she'd been attempting to eat in the half hour we'd been sitting across from each other. "Even after she met—"

"I'd rather not know his name, thanks."

Tara nodded and continued.

They had clicked. Instant chemistry, the kind that couldn't be ignored.

I understood all too well and didn't feel a single ounce of jealousy or anger over the line she'd crossed.

According to Tara, Shelly had fought the draw but continued to flirt. Messaging between the two of them continued, and the next weekend she'd visited Berlin, she'd ended up staying with him rather than Tara.

"He made her smile again," Tara said, shrugging as though unsure of what else to say.

"Were you aware she was pregnant with his child?"

Tara's face drained of color, her eyes widening. "What? No! Oh, my God." Wetness oozed over her blue irises, turning them murky. Twin tears slid over her cheeks.

"I'm sure you know a child is what she wanted more than anything."

Her stilted nod answered my unasked question.

"I couldn't give that to her, but he could. I would have gladly signed whatever divorce paperwork she'd wanted just to see her happy and finally enjoying the family she'd always dreamed about having."

Tears continued to pour down Tara's cheeks, and I struggled to keep my own sadness from welling up—but not to put on a stoic, supposed strong front as Dad would have suggested I do before our settling on walking a path of healing together. I didn't want to start crying and not be able to stop since I still had more emotional upheaval in the near future.

At least, I expected it anyway.

I reached across the table and took her hand, needing to show some sort of support. "Can I ask what happened to him?"

"He moved home." She sniffed and wiped at her cheeks with her napkin. "Washington, I think?"

I nodded, relieved over the news I probably wouldn't ever run into him again.

It was another ten minutes before we exited Jackie's. Neither of us promised to stay in touch, but we did share a brief hug outside the restaurant's entrance.

"Take care of yourself, Chaz," Tara said close to my ear. "And thanks for this—I needed the closure."

"You too, and same. I appreciate your meeting with me." I stepped back before offering to walk her to her car.

One step down, one more to go.

Chapter 31

Jamie

The chat with Dad last night had left me craving good food rather than the fast shit full of fat calories and grease.

Jackie's was only a block away from my apartment, so I got home from work, called in my order for pickup, then waited twenty minutes before heading out again. After my stomach was full, I planned to get in touch with Chaz, expecting eight would mean he'd be home and settled in for the night.

I hoped so, anyway.

My breath puffed in front of me with every exhale, and I hunkered deeper into my winter coat, telling myself the walk was good for my cold legs and frigid lungs.

I stopped before crossing the road, checking both ways, needing to wait for a car to pass. A quick glance at Jackie's on the other side kept my feet rooted on the slush-covered sidewalk.

Chaz sat in the window with a blonde woman.

Blinking a few times to clear my vision, because I had to

be seeing things, I told myself to bring whoever it really was into focus.

It was Chaz, all right, and fuck me, he looked good. A green button-down, hair freshly cut and actually styled for a change. The blonde sported a ponytail and wore a thick sweater.

A burning sensation flared in my stomach, and my breath came faster as he reached across the table and took her hand.

What the actual fuck?

He was...dating?

The urge to vomit rolled over me, making me light-headed, my mouth watering like it always did before I spewed whatever was in my stomach. I swallowed convulsively, bending at the waist, hands on my knees to keep from passing out.

Jesus fucking Christ.

I knew Chaz would be the one to kill me, but like this? Making me relive my greatest heartache all over again?

A glutton for punishment, I slunk back a ways, hiding in an empty doorway, arms wrapped around myself even though I no longer felt the cold. At least the urge to throw up had settled enough that I could see straight.

I stared as the minutes passed, watching as they finished their dinner. He paid the bill with cash. Chaz helped her with her coat, his hand on her lower back as they passed from sight behind a wall.

Breath held, I stared at Jackie's front door until it opened, and the blonde emerged, the woman from Shelly's funeral who'd handed something to Chaz.

"Shit." I swallowed against the thickness in my throat as my ex-best friend followed the woman down the steps to the sidewalk.

They stood out front in the cold, mouths moving, but I couldn't hear what was said.

Chaz held out his arms, and she stepped in willingly.

A shiver rippled through me as nausea once more stirred.

I tore my gaze off them and spun away, unable to watch him give his mouth to another woman. Couldn't fucking handle that a second time.

One block...I could make it to my apartment without losing my shit.

I didn't.

Tears coated my cheeks before I locked my door behind me, and I pulled at my hair, a whine building deep in my chest as I leaned against the wall in my entryway, coat still zipped up beneath my chin.

This could not. Be. Happening!

Pain in my throat made swallowing against sobs difficult.

I yanked at my coat's zipper, feeling as though I was choking.

"Fucking... Goddamnit!" I clenched my teeth, ripping off my coat, hands shaking while going straight for my work shirt. That landed on the floor too. Tore at the laces on my boots, jaw aching until I finished and tossed them aside.

I heaved for breath, hands fisted at my sides, no longer worried about the dinner I'd never picked up.

Numbness crept in, or perhaps my body was already shutting down, readying for what was to come. Hopefully, just an eternity of slumber rather than burning in hell for what I'd done and how I'd hurt Chaz enough he'd left the possibility of us for another woman.

My legs gave way, and I ended up on the floor, head in

my hands, knees slowly drawing up so I had something to lean against.

At least the tears had stopped.

I stared, unseeing, the only part of my body not shut down being my goddamned heart that fucking ached like never before.

Jesus.

I tipped my head back against the wall, arms falling to my sides.

Now what?

My lungs still inflated on instinct. I wasn't selfish enough to off myself—Dad would be devastated, completely alone. I had enough money saved to travel to parts of the world and see all the sights in an attempt to forget about who I wanted there with me.

But yeah, that wasn't happening.

I needed my dad. Shifting onto my knees, I crawled toward where I'd thrown my coat. My cell was in the interior pocket.

A knock sounded on the door behind me, and I cursed, head hanging. Now was *not* a good time.

"Go away!" I shouted at whoever dared to interrupt my grieving.

They knocked again.

Jaw clenched, I stood on shaky legs and stalked to the door. I yanked it open, ready to light into the asshole disturbing me—

"Jamie."

I gulped. Chaz stood in front of me, hands in his pockets, gaze wary as he looked over my face that had to be one hell of a miserable sight.

Why did he have to be so goddamned beautiful? How did he still manage to steal my breath and make my chest flutter after all the hurt between us? And where was his new woman he thought would be a better fit than the man who would give up his life for another night in his arms?

I glanced behind him and down the hallway. He was alone. "What are you doing here?" I gasped the words out past vocal cords that felt raw and ruined.

"Can I come in?"

Staring, I nodded and stepped back on autopilot, desperate to have him in my space even if minutes earlier he'd taken a knife to my heart for the second time in my life.

He peered around my entryway.

Discarded clothes and my shoes littered the tight space. I left them laying there, stepping past Chaz, because I needed to sit before my legs gave out.

My ass met the couch, and I slumped, eyeing Chaz in all his put-together gorgeousness. Freshly shaved cheeks. Perfectly mussed hair...had it been that intentional messy or had that blonde woman made it like that when he'd kissed her senseless?

"Babs gave me your address," Chaz said, walking into the living room and eyeing the other end of the couch. "Hope that's okay."

"Why are you here?" I asked, my tone wrecked. My face was probably puffy from crying.

"I know you asked for space, and I should have waited for you to reach out, but I'm ready to move on, Jamie."

Yeah, he'd made that plenty clear when he'd wrapped his arms around that woman.

"Why show up here to drop that bomb on me, huh?" I sounded pissed. Hurt. Both were so fucking true. "You could have just told me you were ready to try again with another woman. Didn't need to witness it with my own fucking *eyes*."

"Jesus—Jamie. Shit." Chaz tipped his head back and swallowed hard. "I'm going about this all wrong."

I hated that the bob of his Adam's apple made my dick swell.

"You saw me with Tara," he said.

Tara. My new, least favorite female name.

"She is—*was*—Shelly's best friend," he continued when I didn't speak. Fucking couldn't.

Memories clicked, but the burn of anger inside me didn't subside. Was he so desperate to hold onto a piece of his wife that he would hook up with her friend? How fucking sick—

"We agreed to meet for dinner for closure," Chaz said, cutting off my thoughts.

"Closure," I repeated, my tone lowering.

Chaz nodded and held my stare without flinching or hinting at needing to hide shit from me. "It was a one-time thing because I was hoping for answers. Nothing more."

"Fuck." I rubbed my hands over my face and groaned as some of the tension seeped out of me.

"From your reaction, I'm guessing you still want me?"

"I promised always," I rasped, my hands falling to my lap, refusing to let that seed of hope inside me spring to life like it was dying to do. "Fucking meant it, Chaz."

He exhaled long and quiet, once more shoving his hands into his pockets. "As much as I want to dive into you and forget about reality for a while, I have some shit to tell you first."

There was no stopping that seed from bursting into full bloom regardless of wariness over what else he had to say crept in.

"Shelly was having an affair and was pregnant with another man's child."

His blunt words knifed me like a dagger to my chest, and I whispered a few curses as he continued.

"The accident happened when she was on her way to see a lawyer to start the process of divorcing me."

"Fuck—Chaz, I'm so sorry."

Chaz shook his head, the lack of pain in his steady gaze baffling when any other man would be bent over with grief. "We hadn't...been together since last April. She met the guy in July, but I didn't know that until today."

"Tara."

"Yeah." Chaz exhaled heavily again but didn't take his focus off my face. "But I wasn't sure of the timing of their sexual involvement the night I fucked you. I'd been too caught up in my need to think straight. Afterward, the sight of my cum reminded me of how I'd failed her, but I also realized the possible consequences of going bare. I freaked the fuck out because I wasn't sure I was safe."

A tingle slid down my spine and not the pleasant sort. "It's okay," I whispered, praying like fuck that everything *was* all right.

"I should have told you right away, but I was ashamed and too caught up in my misery. I got tested the following week, and everything came back negative, so there's nothing to worry about."

Relief swept through me, causing me to sink further into the couch. I nodded, my brain and heart overloaded with what he'd shared with me. "I wish you'd told me sooner, Chaz. I could have been there for you."

"This was something I had to work through on my own," he said, a soft smile on his face even though it felt like he had more to tell me. "I couldn't have your magic dick distracting me from emotions I had to face, thoughts I needed to process, and steps I had to take. Then your admission to wanting her gone..." He swallowed hard as though my betrayal still hurt.

"I'm so fucking sorry, Chaz. I was a heartless, selfish bastard."

"I understand loving someone so desperately that moving heaven and hell to be with them oftentimes makes us wish for things we shouldn't." Chaz studied my eyes, pain radiating between us.

"I didn't mean it, Chaz, not really. I was just so goddamned jealous, and seeing the way she treated you—"

"I know you didn't really want her dead." Chaz finally removed his hands from his pockets and rubbed them down his thighs. "Forgiving *both* of us proved to be the hardest part of the grieving process so far. I never should have reacted in my anger and kicked you out that night, but I don't regret having time alone to get my priorities and heart settled on moving forward."

The wariness dissolved completely as I focused on those two final words. "So now what?"

Chaz opened his mouth then closed it again.

"What?" I pushed, hoping whatever else was on his heart didn't have the potential to re-rip scabs of healing between us.

He unzipped his coat and set it on over the end of the couch.

I sat, unable to move as he unbuttoned his green shirt and lay it atop his coat. He bent over, shoulder muscles rippling as he untied his boots. He slid them off. Unzipped his jeans and pushed them to the floor, stepping out of them, leaving himself in tight black boxer briefs and socks.

Pale, smooth skin glowed in the overhead light. Dips and swells of lean muscle flexed with every shift of his body. Thick calves and thighs made my hands greedy.

Saliva flooded my mouth, and I swallowed harshly as zaps of energy prompted me to touch and taste what he shared with me.

"Jamie."

I licked my lower lip, realizing I'd been staring in silence for who the fuck knew how long. "Come here," I ordered in a ragged whisper.

Chaz closed the distance and straddled my thighs, his hands going straight for my face, hazel eyes wary and searching. He was warmth and hardness, a perfect fit for my lap. "Will...will you fuck me?"

Jesus—not what I'd been expecting, but I wasn't about to complain or deny the man anything.

"Chaz," I croaked out his name and wrapped my arms around him, yanking him close enough that our chests crushed together. The scent of motor oil clung to him, that reminder of *home* I'd been desperate for. "I'd rather make love to you, but yes—I'll give you whatever you want."

"You, Jamie. I'm ready to live again. Make me yours."

I leaned in to lay claim to his mouth, swallowing his groan as he shuddered in my arms.

When we had kissed before, there'd been an urgency brought on by infidelity and secret lust, the knowledge we'd done wrong and could be caught. While explosive, that coming together hadn't allowed for true appreciation, and finally having the chance to love on Chaz how I'd always longed for, I wasn't going to miss the opportunity to make this special.

"Want to take my time with you," I murmured against his mouth before licking deep, stroking along his tongue.

Chaz moaned and tightened his grip on me, grinding his hard dick against mine.

I grabbed his ass and struggled to stand, his chuckle against my mouth the sweetest sound I'd ever heard.

We stumbled down the hallway in my attempts to carry him, bumping into a wall and my doorjamb. Laughter and licks over lips accompanied us. A welling of what I could only describe as helium filled my chest, making my heart buoyant, all floaty and carefree.

I laid Chaz on my bed and followed, slotting myself between his welcoming thighs. We both groaned as our lengths pressed together, and I swiveled my hips to rub over him, hissing when his fingertips dug into my back.

"Jamie."

"Yeah, baby—I've got you."

He moaned as I dragged my lips over his neck, sucking and biting with tenderness, steadily thrusting against him.

Deep hunger dictated I devour. Tear him apart and mark his skin where everyone would see that he belonged to me now. But this wasn't a claiming, nor was it a chase for release. The greatest gift sprawled on my bed, and I would savor every inch. Show him what it truly meant to be loved.

"Gonna take some time to get your virgin hole opened up for my dick," I murmured against his ear while threading my fingers through his thick hair.

"Been readying myself for a couple of weeks now."

"Shit." I shuddered and stilled atop him, eyes closed and lips against his forehead as I struggled not to come. Images of Chaz fingering his ass or using toys to stretch himself caused my dick to buck against his, and I hissed through clenched teeth.

"You like that," he murmured without a hint of question in his voice.

"Fuck yeah, I do." I lifted my head to find lust-hazed eyes on my face.

"Had my focus on being with you but needed to see to other shit first. Had to make sure my head was set straight— or not so straight." A smile curved his lips, and I traced over the smooth skin with my fingertip. "Needed some healing so I could accept the love you've always wanted to give to me. Had to recognize that I deserved it."

"Love everything about you," I whispered, my throat tight. "Always have. Always will. And I'm sorry as fuck for—"

Chaz lifted his head and shut me up with his mouth and tongue until I lost my train of thought. "You're forgiven —now fuck me before I come untouched."

Sitting on my haunches, I kept my eyes locked on his, peeling down his boxers and removing his socks. He lay naked before me like a buffet, and I planned on gorging myself until we were both sated and passed the fuck out.

I started at his toes since I had his right foot in hand, biting the big one lightly before licking up his arch.

He jerked in my hold, laughing.

A grin flashed over my face, but I moved on from that part of him for his ankles. Calves. The back of his knee.

And still, our gazes remained locked, a deep intimacy from years of unrequited love connecting us. Fulfillment finally hovered on the horizon, and I wouldn't stop until he rested in my arms, right where he was meant to be.

Chapter 32

Chaz

Jamie took his sweet ass time mapping out my body, his tongue and mouth tasting every inch of me except for where I needed him most.

Worry of what was yet left unsaid lay at the back of my mind, but I selfishly needed this from him. If he hated me afterward, I would find a way to live with the heartache. Fuck knew I'd become a goddamn pro at that shit.

Pre-cum leaked from my throbbing dick onto my belly, twitches jerking it on occasion, but I kept my hands fisted at my sides, focused on his gorgeous face as he teased the living hell out of me. He nuzzled my drawn-up balls, gently tugging them down before loving on my left leg like he had the right. At least he didn't bother with my foot. Didn't like that shit.

He bit my hip and nosed upward, ignoring my throbbing cock, humming while tonguing my navel that had a smeared mess of pre-cum all the fuck over it. His scruffy chin slid back and forth over the top half of my dick, driving me fucking *insane*.

"Jamie." I grabbed hold of his head, trying to push him

where I needed him, but he chuckled and grabbed my wrists to press them onto the mattress.

A shudder ripped through me over how he could easily dominate me if he wanted to.

"Let me," he murmured.

Fuck. Yes.

I nodded, losing myself in his dark blue eyes overblown by black pupils and lust. He'd never been more beautiful. Stunningly gorgeous, lips red and slick, cheeks flushed.

Holding my gaze, he licked up the back of my dick, and I jolted, hissing as he continued over my abs, my sternum, and detoured for my right pec. Teeth made an appearance, and I cursed as he grazed them over my nipple before suckling hard.

"Jesus—you're killing me."

"Mmm," he hummed, an agreement or his pleasure I couldn't be sure.

He returned to my mouth, tongue greedy for mine, and I wrapped my body around his, clutching at him with grasping hands and heels. He wasn't close enough. Needed more.

"Lose the pants," I ordered, desperate to have his skin on mine.

He nipped my lower lip and backed off, leaving me alone and cold, but the sight of his complete nudity sent heat rushing through me.

The man was divine. Perfectly proportioned with muscles rippling from his neck to his calves. Rippling abs. Mouthwatering V. Uncut cock flushed and hard as granite, his pelvis shaved and smooth, balls already tight against his groin.

Even though I'd yet to have him inside me, I hadn't lied about his magical dick. Wanted that part of him splitting me open and making itself right at home where it belonged.

"Give it to me," I heard myself rasp.

"Gladly." Jamie crawled between my thighs and lifted the backs of my knees as close to my chest as they would go. I grabbed hold where he did, spreading myself wide. Zero trace of embarrassment slid over me at being completely bared to him. The part of me no one had seen or touched other than myself lay directly in his line of sight.

His stare finally slid off my face, and my hole clenched as his gaze roamed over me.

I wasn't groomed like he was. Hadn't even considered taking clippers let alone a razor to my junk.

Jamie didn't seem to mind. Heat poured from his gaze, his fingertips trailing lightly over my taint. "So hot," he murmured and stretched out onto his belly. He nosed up my crack to my balls, sniffing and moaning.

"Jesus, Jamie," I gasped, on the verge of laughing and yet turned on as fuck at the same time.

"Smell so fucking good. Gonna eat you alive."

Fire raced through my veins, searing my skin.

Warm wetness slid over my hole, and I gasped, jerking from the feathered touch of what must have been his tongue.

"Easy, baby." Jamie caressed my thighs, and I lifted my head to watch him. He studied me with an intensity that made my stomach flip-flop and sent electrical currents over my body, raising the fine hairs along my arms.

"Do it again." I moaned when he gave me what I wanted, his tongue flattened and dragging from my hole to leaking slit. "Ah, fuck." My head fell back on the bed, and I panted.

Jamie licked and suckled, nibbled and caressed every

inch of my ass and groin, his saliva cooling my heated skin. He rimmed me for what seemed hours, gently poking at my hole but not breaching me before slowly making his way up over my taint and tight balls.

"Quit fucking teasing me!" I barked with a choked laugh, half-manic with the need to be filled.

"Ready to have something stuffed up your ass?" He chuckled, and butterflies lit through my stomach again.

"Fuck yes!"

"Mmm."

God, that growly hum of his did shit to me. Made me burn from the inside out. He rubbed his fingertip over my pucker, teasing as he'd done with his tongue.

I bore down, trying to fuck myself on him.

He chuckled again, moving away from me to rifle through his bedside drawer. "Someone's needy."

"Goddamn right, I am," I muttered, scowling at him as he settled once more between my spread legs, bottle of lube in hand. I licked over my lower lip as he drizzled clear liquid onto his hand. "Been waiting too long to have you—" My complaint cut out as he slid his finger fully into my ass without warning. "Fuck!" Jaw clenched, I arched at the delicious, slight sting, eyelids snapping shut. "Yes—fucking yes. Just like that. Give me more."

He crooked that single finger, rubbing...searching—

Lightning zapped through my taint and tailbone, and I shouted, my back jolting up off the bed. "Jesus!"

"Bingo." Jamie murmured and stroked over it a second time.

I panted through clenched teeth, groaning. "Don't want to come until you're inside me, goddamnit!"

The fucker chuckled *again*. "You won't. Promise." He caressed my balls, wrapped his thumb and forefinger around them, and tugged firmly until I came down, gasping over the state of my dry mouth. He stroked into me again but held my balls low.

"Oh, God."

Jamie slid another finger in, easily done since I hadn't lied about readying myself to take him over the previous couple of weeks. "You're so hot and silky inside, baby," he murmured. "Can't wait to get my dick in you."

"I'm ready—want it."

"Not yet." He stroked and stretched me. "How about a third finger though?"

"Stupid question," I muttered, bearing down with his every slick glide into my hole.

Another thick digit joined in the torturous fun, finally gifting me a sense of fullness and the real sting I'd been dying for. "Yes—*fuck*, yes."

A rotation of his hand rubbed fingertips over my prostate, and I cursed, writhing on the bed.

"Please, Jamie," I gasped, shuddering as he continued to work me open. "I—I promise I'm ready. Want you so bad."

He kissed my thigh, easing his hand from between my ass cheeks.

A snap of the cap tightened my stomach, and my hole clenched over the emptiness.

Please, please, please.

The sounds of wet fist-fucking kicked my already heightened pulse into overdrive.

Jamie lifted his gaze to my face and shifted closer, the tip of his dick gliding over my pucker.

Silence settled save for the heavy thumps in my heart. Our eyes locked, chests rising and falling in perfect rhythm.

The final moment before we came together hovered over us, tense yet blindingly beautiful at the same time.

Sunshine, sweet and warm, caressed over the cocoon wrapped around us where nothing existed but shared desire.

"I love you." I croaked the truth rising inside me, and my eyes welled at the words I'd been wanting to tell him for countless years. Relief rushed through me over finally having the freedom to be honest.

"Love you too, Chaz. Always have." Jamie knelt over me, elbows by my head, and I bore down as he pushed against my stretched ring.

He breached me, the thick head of his cock lodging inside my ass.

We both moaned, and I clutched at him, trying to draw him in closer.

Resisting, he stared at me, lips parted, eyes open and vulnerable. "You're mine."

"Always," I whispered.

A slow smile curved his lips, and I'd never seen anything so goddamned beautiful in my entire life. My cock jerked against my abs. "Give me your dick, Jamie."

He pushed in, my ready hole and generous lube easing the way. The sense of fullness with every inch made relaxing impossible, and I held my breath until he bottomed out. I squeezed around him.

"You took all of me, baby. Jesus, fuck, you're so tight. Hot."

Jamie settled atop me like a decadent heated blanket, and I clutched at him, desperate to keep him there forever.

"Don't ever leave me," I whimpered, my chest aching, body burning for him to fuck me through the mattress.

"Never." He owned my mouth with a searing kiss, and I clenched in pulses around his girth, trying to suck him in deeper.

I wanted our souls latched together. Spirits intertwined. Bodies completely wrapped up in each other until there was no telling us apart. Needed him like I did air, life-giving oxygen filling my lungs and flooding my system.

Yearning seeped through my pores, a desperate, restless craving for more, and I couldn't lay still. "Jamie," I begged although I wasn't sure what for.

"I've got you, baby." Lips hovering over mine, sweet breath caressing my mouth, he shifted his hips, dragging his slick cock out through my hole.

"Fuuuck." I groaned and choked on the word when he slowly pushed back in, stuffing me full.

"Good?"

"*God*, yes."

He licked over my lips while leaving me empty again and thrust his tongue into my mouth while filling me up. He rocked into me, loving on my body from both ends, his spine-tingling moans of enjoyment causing my balls to firm up again too damned fast. Every lush, wet glide of his girth through my ass tensed my abs.

"You're killing me with your perfect dick."

Jamie chuckled and shifted his angle. The next gentle thrust rubbed his thick head over my prostate.

A groan rumbled through my chest, and I shuddered, clutching at his shoulders.

"Bingo," he whispered against my ear and, grasping my ass to lift me higher, set to steadily pulling that noise from my lips again.

"Not g-gonna last." My vision was hazed over, so I closed my eyes and focused on the drag and push of his length through my hole, the sensation of impending euphoria waiting a breath away.

"Come on my dick, Chaz." He sounded broken like

when I'd walked in the door, and same as then, I longed to put him back together. Comfort and ease the hurt he'd experienced because of me. "Need to feel your ring clench around me before I lose it."

I lifted my hips with his every slow thrust, chasing my release. My pre-cum slickened his abs and made rubbing against him as good as any hand or mouth. "Fuck, don't stop."

A few, harsh thrusts would have sent me reeling, but Jamie kept a slower steady pace, loving rather than fucking.

"Jamie." I hovered on the verge of sobbing for relief.

He wrapped an arm beneath my leg and hefted it higher, the new angle making him grind over my prostate rather than slide against it.

"There—" I choked on a groan. "Oh my fucking God, right there."

His growl vibrated against my neck where he'd tucked his face, and I grasped his rock hard shoulders.

"C-Coming—fuck, I'm coming." I gasped, my dick on the verge of nutting.

"Give it to me, baby. Squeeze the life out of my cock."

An eruption of spunk shot up through my shaft, and I hollered, every muscle in my body tensing. I clung to Jamie as he stroked steadily through my climax, his hiss against my neck sending shivers over my skin.

Every glide of his cock over my prostate caused another spurt of cum to dribble onto my abs, and I writhed until he wrung me dry.

"Jesus." I panted, clutching at him as he lifted his head to peer down at me.

He stilled, hard dick buried, the feeling of it throbbing inside me sending another rush of butterflies through my stomach. Passion poured from his eyes, darker than any navy-blue sky.

They rolled back, and he cursed, pulling out harshly and stabbing into me.

His dick pulsed with the first wave of his release, and he cursed again, thrusting deeper.

"Fuck!" He backed out quickly and palmed his shaft, working it hard, jet after jet of his cum covering my soft balls and dick. "God*damn*...Jesus, Chaz, you're perfect—so good for me." He shuddered and collapsed, grinding his semi over my junk, smearing his spunk into my skin. "Fuck," he groaned, another tremble causing me to hold him tight again.

We both fought for breath, panted exhales bathing each other's mouths that barely brushed together.

Still, he rubbed his groin against mine, until I chuckled. "The fuck are you doing?"

"Marking you with my cum inside and out like I've been dreaming about for half of forever. Want my scent all the fuck over you so everyone knows who you belong to. Fantasized about it on your ass cheeks, but this'll do." He let out a heavy exhale, finally resting atop me.

I ran my hands along his spine, cradling his body with mine, wishing the feeling of euphoria would continue to sizzle through my extremities until we were both ready to go again.

But I'd come here with a purpose, part of my healing journey I had yet to complete.

Selfishness had overridden the need to speak first, and I'd given in to my lust. I'd needed Jamie inside me at least once just in case the secret I held onto proved as equally damaging as the one he'd shared with me.

Would it be better to rip off the Band-Aid when he couldn't escape my arms?

What kind of friend would I be if I didn't allow him at least a little space so my close proximity wouldn't affect his reaction though?

As though feeling my inner tension, he lifted onto his elbows, gaze searching. "You okay?"

"Mmm," I hummed a semi-lie.

He pressed his lips to mine in a chaste kiss and, groaning, sat on his haunches between my thighs. "Your poor hole. It's all red and puffy even though I took it easy on you." Jamie caressed my pucker, still slick with lube and cum. "So fucking hot," he murmured, pushing what leaked from me back inside my body. "Did I hurt you?"

"Not at all. It was better than I expected. Hope to do it again."

"Oh, we will." He flashed me a grin, making my stomach flip in the best way. "But I'm bottoming next time. Thirty minutes? An hour?"

I laughed at the joy in his eyes but sobered quickly.

"What's going on, Chaz?" Jamie asked, his smile slowly fading.

"I—I have to tell you one last thing."

His gaze flitted over my face as though searching for a hint of what it might be.

"I was happy you got injured and had to leave the NFL," I blurted, ready to get it over with already. "I mean, I was upset for you, of course, but...yeah. How shitty is that?" I huffed a tear-filled sarcastic laugh, pain already lancing through my heart in expectation of him ordering me to leave as I'd done to him.

Jamie scratched over his chest and exhaled loudly. "Yeah, same."

"Wh-What?" I jerked into a half-sitting position, shaky elbows keeping me upright.

Jamie shrugged. "If I hadn't torn my ACL, I wouldn't have been back home so soon. Wouldn't have been there when you needed me—which is what I live for. Wouldn't be here with you now, sated, my balls empty and cum all over your junk. Which..." He shifted down onto his stomach, sprawling between my thighs. "You look good like this, Chaz." His tongue flicked over my balls, and he groaned that same appreciative noise that made my dick twitch. "Mind if I suck on your nuts?"

I huffed a laugh, unable to believe his complete acceptance of what I'd told him and how quickly he was ready to move on—and get a little freaky.

"Gonna blow your mind, baby," he promised. "Need your dick hard again so you can fill my ass up."

"Jesus, Jamie." I laughed, but my elbows gave way as he suckled one of my balls into the wet heat of his mouth. "Oh fuck."

"Mmm."

Thirty minutes? Fuck that. Less than fifteen, and he sat on my hard shaft, showing me how washboard abs moved when he fucked himself on my dick.

Most beautiful sight I'd ever seen.

Chapter 33

Jamie

I wore Chaz out.

He sprawled half on top of me, breathing heavy, limbs all tangled with mine exactly as I'd hoped to find when I woke up. His face pressed against my pit, and thank fuck I wasn't as ticklish as he was. The man had a thing for my underarms. Whatever made him happy. I wouldn't complain as long as he continued to octopus the fuck outta me each and every day.

My clock shone five a.m. in bold red numbers, and I wondered if Chaz planned on going to work.

A huff exited my nose.

Stupid thought. Of course he did. The man was married—

Fuck that shit.

He was available for the taking, which I'd already done. Twice. While I might be a greedy son of a bitch when it came to Chaz and his body, I'd had crumbs for so goddamned long, any tiny slice of his time and presence was pure heaven in my mind. Didn't need the man with me twenty-four-seven, but I would be thankful for every minute he gifted me.

But this morning?

He was mine, and I wasn't sharing. I would chain him to my bed if he even considered leaving me for grease-stained coveralls and cars that could wait another day or three. Besides, he'd hired Josh who, according to Chaz last night, was exactly who he didn't know he'd needed to keep shit running smoothly. And Josh had just enough experience starting out that Chaz had trusted him yesterday alone in the shop after a mere month of employment.

The kid was responsible and a hard worker. Henderson Auto was in good hands.

I closed my eyes again and hugged my best friend tight, my heart set on waking up with him like this every morning from here on out. No excuses. And the best way to make that happen was to be proactive whether he was ready or not.

It's go time—I've got this.

Reaching blindly to my right, I located my cell on the bed stand. One-handed, I attempted to type out a couple of emails without too many grammatical errors. Probably should have waited until Chaz and I discussed our future, but there was no question in my mind of where I would be spending the next fifty years. We'd both lived through enough traumatic shit—nothing else could possibly come between us.

No distance, no more hellish secrets, and sure as fuck no more women.

My man was stubborn and didn't quit, so once I made him see the truth of where our path headed together, he would be on board one hundred percent. He would always be in my corner, or better yet, fighting on the front line alongside me for the future I had envisioned since middle school.

While my heart hurt for what he'd secretly endured with Shelly, her affair lessened some of my own guilt. Right, wrong, or whatever, the truth eased my own shame and made him finally being with me that much sweeter.

These choices I went with, typing with my thumb to put them into black letters across my screen, seemed to settle everything inside me once and for all. I breathed easier. Muscles relaxed. Mind rested in knowing he was mine in every way that mattered.

Dream come true.

"Whatryoudoin'?" Chaz mumbled into my armpit as I hit a final "send" on a life-changing decision.

I set my cell aside. "Stay here with me," I said, ignoring his question. "The whole weekend. From now through Monday morning."

"I gotta—"

"Don't *even*," I barked, cutting him off. I rolled into him, gathering his sleepy warmth up in my arms, throwing my leg over his so he couldn't escape me.

Chaz sighed and nuzzled my neck, snaking a lazy arm over my back to hold me just as tightly as I did him. "M'kay."

"Yeah?" I double-checked to make sure we were on the same page already.

"Yeah."

"Love this," I whispered against his hair, my heart light and every part of my body relaxed except for my morning wood pressing against his. "Waking up with you. Want to do it every day."

"Same."

I mentally raised a fist in victory that felt sweeter than

every time I had run into the end zone with a ball clutched to my chest. "So, I just gave my two weeks' notice and told my landlord I'm breaking the lease early."

"What the..." Chaz pulled away from my neck and blinked bleary hazel eyes until he could focus on my face. "Huh?"

"I'm quitting my job and moving back to Pippen Creek because I hate Berlin and sitting at a desk nine-to-five." I grinned when he stared over my spewed explanation. "How's your hole?"

"Huh?"

"Your ass." I tried again to make sense through his fuzzy brain that couldn't keep up with my wired one. "Is it sore? Or are you ready for another pounding?"

His brow furrowed slightly, gaze going glazed like his sleepy mind turned inward to check. "Uh...yeah, I think there's gonna be an exit only sign for another day at least."

"Blow jobs are always fun in the morning." I waggled my eyebrows.

Chaz huffed a laugh. "Since when are you a morning person?"

"Since opening my eyes to your fine self all up in my space and not trying to escape unnoticed like you've done when I've woken up beside you in the past."

His eye widened slightly.

"So I *was* right." I grinned, expecting I looked a bit manic but couldn't help myself. I was happy, goddamnit. "We'll be talking about that in the near future, but for now..." I grabbed hold of his ass and squeezed.

"Mmm." He rubbed his body on me, his cock the same state of granite as mine. "This *is* kinda nice."

Time to change the subject yet again because my greediness for Chaz would never be sated. "Never had a dick in your mouth, right?"

"No, but I want yours." The tiredness seemed to have faded, heat now kindling in his eyes.

"Then get this peach of an ass over here in my face and show me how easily I can make you gag." I slapped the flesh I'd been kneading.

"Wait...what? How does that—"

"Sixty-nine, baby," I whispered against his lips, foul morning breath be damned. "Think you can handle my cock down your throat?" My dick throbbed against his at the image in my head.

"Might have practiced a little for that too."

I drew back, eyes wide. "The fuck—seriously?"

Red flushed Chaz's cheeks. "I, uh, wanted to be sure I could satisfy you since I couldn't..."

"Hey." I pressed my fingers over his mouth to keep him from bring up how nothing he ever did had been good enough for the last person he'd been in a relationship with. I was not her. Didn't have any big dreams other than spending my life with him, so there was zero chance he'd ever fail. "It'll be awesome no matter what because it's you, and you're already perfect in my eyes. Always have been."

Chaz released a heavy exhale as though relieved.

I allowed my mind to wander back to his admission. "So you blew some toys?"

"Dildos."

"Fuck—dildos—while imagining it was my dick?"

His lips twitched as though he tried to hold in a smile. "Think I got decent at it too."

"Shit." My eyes rolled back inside my head, and I grabbed hold of my junk to keep from nutting untouched at the idea of Chaz sucking on something and fantasizing it was my cock. "Still got those toys in a drawer somewhere?"

"Yeah."

"Sweet. Cuz we're gonna enjoy the shit outta them once we're home."

"Home—meaning you're moving in with me?"

I studied Chaz's face, the past leaking into our newfound bubble. Did he desire that as much as I did? Was there any sacredness of the ranch house he would rather not see disturbed? Or would he prefer to stay where he felt the past and present could live in peace? "Or we can get our own house. Something new?" I suggested my own hope.

Chaz ran his hand up my spine to my nape and leaned in to give me a lingering forehead kiss that curled my toes. "That what you want?"

"A fresh start *would* be kinda nice," I gave him my honesty as I'd decided from here on out that I would always do. "A place that's all our own. No memories attached to walls or furniture."

"I can barely afford what I already have," Chaz admitted. "Won't get approved for a loan either. Don't have much equity...yeah. I'm kind of in a tight spot."

"I'm not. Well, my dick would like to be."

Chaz pinched me, and I laughed, squeezing him.

"I have a little nest egg still in the bank thanks to that partial rookie season," I explained, more than happy to be able to take care of him.

He pulled back, eyes searching. "You'd hand over your hard-earned money to make my life easier?"

"Shit." I stilled as something from the recent past rang like a bell in my head.

"What?" he asked, his brow furrowing deeply.

"Um...another secret?"

"Goddamn you, Jamie Forester. Now what?"

"I kinda already spent a decent amount of money on you," I said quietly, hating that my stomach clenched with the admission.

He stared, and I knew the second he figured it out. Wetness coated his eyes. "Was your generosity out of guilt or love?"

"Both, and I wouldn't hesitate to do it again. Anything for you." I rubbed my foot over his thigh since he didn't seem upset I'd paid all of Shelly's hospital bills.

"Thank you," he whispered. "I feared when they would start showing up."

I kissed his soft lips, and we lingered in the connection but without tongue.

Chaz seemed to come to a conclusion that required speaking because he pecked me twice before pulling away. "How about this. I ditch the shop today and tomorrow, and we fuck the hours away. Monday morning I head to work same as you, then after, you drive back to Pippen Creek. We fuck all night long, fall asleep on the new bed I bought, wake up like this—"

"Suck each other off," I interjected.

"—rinse, repeat, over and over again until we find a place to call our own. Wait. What about your job? You said you put in a two-week's notice?"

"I'll commute until my last day."

"Then what?"

"Dad said he needs to hire another officer," I told Chaz what I had already planned out in my head while he had slept. Even sent Dad a notification that I would be applying next week.

Chaz stilled, a slow grin lighting his face. "I can't fucking wait to see you in uniform."

"Gonna rip it off me and fuck me up against a wall?"

"Yes. *Fuck* yes."

I kissed him hard, ready to be done with words for a while. A slap to his ass, and I muscled him around atop me, burying my nose against his balls as his thighs came to rest on either side of my head.

"Oh fuck," he croaked, and I chuckled before suckling his soft flesh into my mouth. "Jesus, you're good at that."

I popped off. "Name's Jamie," I teased since I'd noticed he tended to use the wrong one whenever I was hell-bent on showing him pleasure.

"Asshole," he muttered.

I spread my legs wide so he had easy access. "Have at it."

He barked a laugh, jolting his body atop mine. "I've never seen you like this. So uninhibited."

"It's because I'm finally right where I'm supposed to be. Under you. And I'm happy as hell."

Chaz chuckled again. "Goddamn, do I love you."

"Love you too, baby. Now suck on my dick and see how far you can take me before you gag." I slurped him into my mouth and grinned around his girth.

Loving Chaz Henderson for the rest of my life was going to be fulfilling as fuck.

Chapter 34

Chaz

"**A**re you nervous?"

Jamie glanced over his shoulder at me from where he grilled dinner on our back deck, his bare ass sticking out from the apron he had tied around his waist. "Only of the unknown. I can handle whatever they throw at me."

I wanted to throw *myself* at him again, but I expected he was still sensitive from being thoroughly fucked a half hour earlier over the kitchen island, and my dick hadn't yet recovered. My man was a nudist enthusiast, and having the freedom of our own house with no close neighbors, I was all for it.

Easy access was fine by me. Meant more fucking because I couldn't keep my hands off his gorgeous body.

Butterflies swirled around in my stomach, and I grinned.

He narrowed his gaze. "What? Don't think I can?"

"Oh, I know you can handle the academy. You're one of the most determined people I've ever met. I wouldn't be surprised if you graduate at the top of your class."

Jamie put down the grill fork and moved to step in between my spread thighs.

I set my beer aside on the small table beside where I lounged in my Adirondack chair and grabbed hold of the backs of his legs to bring him in closer. Leaning forward, I rubbed my chin over his apron-covered bulge and looked up at him.

"Love everything about you." I kissed his dick through the cotton, running my fingertips down through his crack. "Love this hole." I worked my finger into his ass that was still sticky enough with my cum not to cause him too much discomfort. "Love when my spunk drips out of you like this too."

"Fuck." He threaded his fingers through my hair and smashed my face into his groin, rubbing all over me.

Chuckling, I turned to nip his hip through the cotton between us. "Don't overcook my steak."

"Don't fucking tease me when I'm trying to work."

"But it's my favorite thing to do."

Typical us.

When we'd bought the fixer-upper on Pippen Creek Pond, we'd taken on quite the task. The two-bedroom, three-season cabin was basically a shack in need of a total rehab. Jamie had paid cash for the property on PCP's northern side, and we'd focused hard on settling as quickly as possible. Fucking each other interrupted more often than not, but we'd managed to get shit done.

Shelly's and my old home hadn't been the best place for Jamie and I to spend the first couple of months of our relationship, but we'd made it work without too much difficulty. It'd been interesting to see the sides of him I hadn't before, being up in each other's spaces like a couple of new roommates, but we had makeup fucking to look forward to at the end of every spat.

Our arguments were nothing like I was used to because I was assured of Jamie's love and appreciation each and every day. The man's liberal spewing of positivity had done wonders for my still struggling self-esteem, and he'd never once made me feel like a failure. Quite the opposite. I'd won the goddamned lottery, and everyone we came across in town seemed to agree. Not one negative word had been spoken about me moving on too quickly or being with a man instead of another woman.

Wouldn't have really mattered if someone had.

He and I were happy together, and that was all I cared about.

"Love you," I murmured against his semi and glanced up again.

His dark blue eyes poured the same sentiment down over me like warm sunshine. "Love you too, baby."

"Steak?" I reminded him, pulling my fingers out of his hot ass and wiping them on the edge of his apron.

"Got plenty of meat right here for you."

I slapped his backside, and we both laughed.

Jamie moved away again, and I enjoyed the flexing of his ass cheeks before turning my gaze to the lake past him and the sun sinking behind the pine trees beyond. Another gorgeous May evening, not quite warm enough for nudity in my opinion, but Jamie hated clothes.

We were nestled in a cove similar to Coach Bernard's property, mere minutes from downtown and my shop. The perfect little hideaway for two lovers who didn't want to be disturbed.

Jamie was leaving for the academy tomorrow, and while I was excited for him, I'd grown accustomed to having him here at our cabin twenty-four-seven. I looked forward to getting home after work more than I'd ever imagined I could.

Who wouldn't enjoy open arms, a smile, and soft lips greeting them at the door? Never mind the muscular body clutching at mine, evidence of happiness over seeing me rock hard and needy. Jamie got on his knees more often than not, making quick work of my coveralls to get at my dick. At least we had a nice, cushiony rug in the entry, which protected his knees from the refurnished hardwood floor beneath, and he loved the fuck out of my musk. His words exactly, but I couldn't be grossed out since my nose ended up in his armpit every morning and sometimes while fucking.

While we'd hired a local contractor to do most of the rehab, Jamie had taken an active part in the lesser jobs to keep busy. While I'd logged in ten-hour days at the shop, he'd spent the previous two months ripping up carpet and sanding the oak floors beneath and repainting every single wall, trim around the newly installed windows, and base-board after the central AC and heating system was upgraded. The bathroom had been updated—with a shower big enough for the both of us—and Jamie had tackled all the tile work too.

The kitchen would have to wait. We'd run out of time since my old house had sold and we'd needed to move into our love shack, as Babs called it. Jamie also didn't want our home life in disarray while he was at the academy. We were also more than happy with grilling most of our dinners since food always tasted better if it arrived on a plate fresh off of flames anyway.

"Want to eat out here or go inside?" I asked, noting goose bumps on his arms. I'd been smart enough to wear a long-sleeved T-shirt, my favorite faded black one with the stretched neck.

"Inside."

Smirking, I stood out of my favorite chair and slid open the slider leading into our small kitchen. We had plans to tear out this exterior wall and build an addition. The open concept kitchen slash living room would double in size, and a larger deck would allow us to entertain on occasion. Not that we would host a holiday other than the Fourth of July when the outdoors and lake could be put to good use.

Maybe next year.

I made Jamie put on shorts before sitting down at the island we used as our dining room table since the space wasn't big enough for one. We nestled in, side by side, shoulders and elbows brushing as we chowed down.

"I left work early today to go see Shelly's mom," I said, bringing up the single dim spot in the new life I'd found living with Jamie.

"How's she doing?"

"Not well."

I'd gotten a voicemail that hospice had been called in, and I'd wanted to see her at least one more time even if she wouldn't be aware of my visit.

"I'm sorry," Jamie offered quietly, leaning over to kiss my temple.

"She's unconscious now. It won't be long." My throat tightened as my old friend grief weaved sadness through my heart as it did on occasion. I didn't ignore the emotion or try to distract myself, simply let it be and experienced the ache that sometimes settled in my chest.

Shelly and her mom would no longer watch sunsets over the lake or enjoy sunshine on their faces, but memories of them doing so would always be with me. That part of my life might be over, but I would always carry the best of it in my mind and remember to be thankful for what I now had.

Jamie and I didn't talk a whole lot over the rest of our meal, both of us wrapped up in our own thoughts. I expected he focused on tomorrow, then the beginning of a new career with his Dad on Pippen Creek's police force once he graduated.

My man would make a great cop since he was honest and full of integrity. Add in his kindness and empathy, the hero-type status he continued to hold in our small town, and I expected he would be adored as much as the chief.

Maybe.

That man had been deemed a hero years ago. They didn't come much better than Sutton Forester. Well, he had one hell of a kid.

The love of my life, the reason for the smile on my face every day.

"What?" Jamie asked.

I turned to find him peering at me with narrowed eyes. "What, *what?*"

"You're looking awfully damn proud of yourself."

I leaned in and pressed my mouth to his, a simple chaste kiss but full of potency and promise. "Because I landed the hottest guy in all of Pippen Creek."

Jamie made that spine-tingling hum and yanked me back in for another taste, his tongue flicking over my lips and along my waiting tongue. "I wouldn't want to be anywhere else."

"You're not missing those millions from playing on the gridiron?"

"Fuck no." He gave me one last hard kiss before returning to his steak. "I'm the richest man on the planet because I have you."

My insides melted. "I'm so going to blow you after we finish eating."

"Why wait?" he asked around a mouthful of food, a twinkle in his night-sky eyes.

He had a point, and I didn't mind kneeling on the hardwood floor for him. I slid off my stool and proved to him yet again how practice made perfect.

Epilogue

Jamie

"Welcome to Frenchie's!" Frenchie and her wife called out their usual as the bar's door closed behind us.

"The man of the hour!" Someone else hollered from the packed crowd, and a grin split my face even as heat filled it.

Once again, I felt like a sideshow freak at a party held in honor of my accomplishments, the uniform I'd kept on after graduation causing me to stand out. Chaz's pinkie was laced with mine, making me feel less alone than the last time I'd been the center of attention. It'd been over a year since my return to Pippen Creek, and so much had changed, heartache and happiness in a vicious tug-of-war that had finally relented in allowing us the joy we both deserved.

People flocked forward, offering hugs, and although I hated letting go of my man, I gave the townsfolk a few moments to congratulate me and welcome the newest member of the police force dedicated to keeping them safe.

I could feel Dad's proud gaze on me from somewhere in the vicinity, assuring me the life ahead of me was finally on course. Sure, there would be bumps and potholes in our way, same as the dirt road that led to Chaz's and my home on the lake, but the destination remained fixed in my mind at all times.

Babs threw her arms around me, Coach Bernard grinning from behind her. As promised, the man had given her a ring, they took a short jaunt to Berlin to exchange vows, and they moved in together immediately afterward. Townsfolk had been surprised, the gossip mill going, but no one judged the two got together a mere week after his return from Arizona.

Nor did they care about Chaz's and my timing.

"Proud of you, Jamie Forester," Babs murmured, squeezing me tight. "Happiness looks good on you."

"On you too," I said, unable to wipe the grin off my face.

She stepped back, still holding onto my forearms. "I knew you'd be irresistible in a uniform. All the ladies are swooning."

"Couldn't care less."

Babs laughed, her cheeks pink and eyes bright. "That young man of yours can't tear his eyes off you either."

Heat slithered through my veins as I remembered his promise to sit on my dick in celebration later tonight. Nothing more beautiful than Chaz uninhibited and riding on my cock. He fit me in every single way.

Speaking of my man, he moved in to touch my lower back, his palm warm and possessive. "Want a drink?"

"Water. Please."

Chaz kissed my temple and moved off again.

Babs sighed, hands over her heart. "You two are the sweetest. Makes my heart happy to finally see you together."

"Same."

"Congrats, Jamie." Dexter squeezed me from the side.

"Hey, Dex." I hugged him back. "Thanks." I glanced around him, expecting Christian Cole to be lingering nearby. The two were always at each other's throats, a rivalry I didn't understand the roots of. Neither did Dad. But the eventual outcome was as clear as Dex's flashing pearly whites. If they weren't already fucking, they would be. Christian couldn't keep his eyes off my dad's best friend and vice versa. It was like a magnetic force flipped its switch constantly, pulling then pushing them away from each other.

Other people stepped in to offer their congratulations, and once Chaz finally returned with my lemon water, I was parched, my facial muscles hurting from smiling. But I wasn't nearly done.

Something rested in my pocket, a titanium band, simplistic yet perfect.

Just like my man.

I glanced over at where he chatted with Kel and a guy I didn't recognize. Old Man Ron and Addy stood with them, the first time I'd seen the two socializing outside Dig-In.

Chaz glanced my way as though feeling my stare. He looked me over from head to toes and back up again, tongue flicking over his lower lip. Blood seeped into my groin, thickening my cock.

Fucking tease was lucky I had to wear briefs beneath my uniform or the entire town would see how my man affected me.

I raised an eyebrow.

He did the same.

"You're making me jealous."

I turned to find Dad at my elbow, beer in hand. "Sorry?"

"Don't be. I love seeing you happy."

"Your man will show up one of these days," I promised,

envisioning a guy Dad's age, maybe heartbroken and needing someone to hold him together. A kind soul, needy as fuck like Dad hoped for. I envisioned a peaceful, fulfilling existence for my father who deserved it more than anyone.

"Starting to think it's not going to happen," Dad muttered.

"Welcome to Frenchie's!"

I glanced toward the door to see who the latecomer was, Dad turning along with me.

"Motherfucking..." Dad's curse faded, and I blinked, taking in the sight of Elite Escort's blond twink with the big blue eyes.

"Jimmy Riley," I muttered, glancing over at Chaz to find him headed my way.

One—no, *two*—secrets I'd forgotten about. Sure, Chaz knew I wasn't a virgin when we'd gotten together but having started an OnlyFans to pay for a sex worker?

"Shit," Dad and I both whispered at the same time, my palms suddenly sweating.

I glanced at Dad, and he caught my eye before quickly turning his focus away.

"You okay?" Chaz grasped my elbow, pulling my full focus.

"Yeah, baby. Yeah." But shit wasn't. Those plans with that ring in my pocket just kicked the bucket. Yet another conversation lay ahead that had the potential to be more a crater than pothole. Definitely not something I could drop in Chaz's lap considering where we stood and all the people around us.

Smirking like a cat in a bowl of cream, Dexter sauntered over, elbowing Dad with a knowing look in his eyes.

"Fucking hell," Dad muttered and tipped back his beer,

draining the rest. "Shut up and get me another," he ordered, and Dex moved off, chuckling something about not saying a word.

"Dad, what's—"

"Why, Chief Sutton." Jimmy sauntered over, attention latched on my father with a predatory gaze if ever I'd seen one.

Oh...oh shit.

My head jerked toward Dad.

He was closed down like a sealed drum, but tension strung his shoulders tight as the skin around his eyes. "Jimmy."

"Miss me?" Jimmy winked and popped a hip out.

"Nope." Dad lied—no fucking question.

Jimmy's gaze slid to me. "I hear congratulations are in order." He stuck out his hand, and I shook it, the guy's palms and fingertips smooth as butter. And why wouldn't they be? The only hard labor he faced was a client's dick.

"Chaz." Jimmy greeted my man next, doing a double take, his groomed eyebrows arching then pulling inward. "You're a dead ringer for an old co-worker of mine. How did I not realize that before?"

"Yeah?" Chaz's voice stated he couldn't care less.

"Any chance you're related to a guy named Zack Briggs?" Jimmy asked.

My breath stalled out, and I went still as fuck.

"Don't recognize the name," Chaz said, sliding his pinkie along mine until latching.

I clung to that tiny piece of him, waiting for a bombshell to drop right there in front of the entire town. At least Chaz's parents weren't in attendance. Not that Mr. Henderson would be super judgmental. He'd chilled out quite a bit since Christmas when Chaz had finally stood up to him.

Jimmy glanced down over Chaz again. "Hmm. Could have fooled me. You two could be twins."

I waited for Jimmy to turn my way, question me, or maybe just wink.

He did none of those things, and I slowly released the pent-up air in my lungs.

Thank fuck those NDAs are effective at keeping Jimmy's loose lips shut.

Or maybe he didn't have access to Elite's clientele list. I could only hope.

My body language must have clued Chaz in on something being wrong because he bumped his shoulder against mine. "You okay?"

"Yeah," I rasped before swallowing. "Just, uh..."

Jimmy eyed the two of us, his focus settling on my face. We stared at each other.

Did he know? Was he chewing on his tongue in order to keep his big mouth shut?

Fuck.

I scratched the back of my neck, restless as fuck and ready to bolt out the door.

"I feel like I'm missing what's going on," Chaz stated, his voice low.

"I, uh..." I had to clear my throat and forced my eyes off the escort for my lover.

Chaz peered at me with a quizzical look, but zero hint of concern rested in his hazel eyes.

"Um...another secret? I mean, two?" I huffed an unsteady laugh, attempting to make light of the situation.

Chaz smirked, seemingly unfazed by possible danger ahead. "Are either damaging or life-changing?"

"No—at least, I don't think so?"

"You're cute when you worry," Chaz said, leaning in with a smile before pressing his mouth to mine. "Honesty will never make me love you less."

I squeezed his pinkie before sliding my fingers entirely through his and clasping his palm tight. Choosing to believe him, I put the unrest in the back of my mind for later.

Jimmy leaned into Dad's forearm, but whatever he intended to say got cut short by Dexter's arrival.

He offered Dad a cold beer, and Dad took the opportunity to sidestep the handsy escort. "Thanks," Dad said to Dex, ignoring Jimmy attempting to get all in his space.

What the fuck was up with that kid? Well, not a kid. Jimmy was a couple of years older than me but hadn't ever acted like it.

"So, Jimmy," Dex said, throwing his arm around Dad's shoulders. "What brings you back to Pippen Creek?"

"Personal shit." Jimmy eyed Dexter's hold on Dad, lips thinning like someone had stolen his lollipop.

Fuck.

I did *not* need that image in my head.

Dad avoided eye contact with Jimmy, taking great interest in scanning the room, but he seemed preoccupied rather than his usual observant self.

What the fuck was going on, and how long before I ended up flattening Jimmy's nose as a warning to steer clear of a man who didn't need any more drama in his life?

"Anything Chief, here, needs to worry about?"

"Oh no," Jimmy purred, his gaze heating with blatant lust.

"When are you going back to Boston?" I blurted the question, needing him to be gone already.

Jimmy tipped his head to the side, once more eyeing me. "How'd you know I've been in Boston?"

"Uh...Dex! Dexter told me."

A coy smile lifted Jimmy's lips as he glanced between Dex and Dad. "Someone's keeping tabs on me. I like it." He sauntered away, swaying that bubble butt of his as though aware we all watched him go.

Four fucking throats cleared, and we glanced around Frenchie's, an unspoken agreement not to discuss what each and every one of us had been doing.

Couldn't have been helped though. Any gay man who loved ass wouldn't be able to miss the backside Jimmy had been blessed with.

"So!" Chaz was the first to speak up. "I have a thing to take care of."

"Yeah," I agreed quickly. "That."

Dex barked out a laugh. "Have fun, boys." He grasped Dad's elbow and steered him in the opposite way of where Jimmy had gone.

Fucking hell.

It was my turn to laugh, but there wasn't anything funny about Jimmy Riley's return to Pippen Creek. I feared Dad's life was about to get a lot more interesting.

"They sell shotguns over at The Outdoor Store?" I asked, tucking Chaz against my side while heading toward the exit.

Chaz chuckled. "Yeah."

"Good. Cuz I'm gonna need to get one and sit on Dad's porch until that man gets his ass back to Boston," I muttered.

A few minutes later, we climbed into my SUV at the back of Frenchie's lot. The key rested in the ignition, but I didn't turn it to start the engine.

"Get it off your chest," Chaz said with a smile in his voice.

I clutched the steering wheel, my focus on bar's door.

"Hey." Chaz ran his hand up my thigh. "You're tense as fuck." He grabbed my junk, and I grunted, swelling automatically from his touch. "There's nothing to worry about."

"Jimmy's an escort," I stated bluntly. Might as well get this shit over with.

"And?"

I glanced over at Chaz to find his gaze as open and accepting as always. "I, uh...didn't sleep with him."

Chaz laughed. "He's more your dad's type than yours."

"Shit." I rubbed a hand over my face. "Can we please not talk about that?"

"So, I'm guessing you know this because you hooked up while in college with that co-worker Jimmy claims I'm a dead ringer for."

My eyelids slid shut, and even though his didn't sound like he cared all that much, I braced myself. "Yeah, but that's not all." I inhaled, holding it until my lungs burned. "I started up an OnlyFans to be able to afford the escort because there wasn't anything I wouldn't do to live out the fantasy of being with you."

"Was this Zack guy a good replacement?" Chaz's voice hinted at teasing.

I snorted. "Before having a taste of the real you, yeah. Now?" I shook my head, finally meeting my man's gaze.

He still smirked, completely unaffected by what I'd told him.

The tension left my shoulders, and I slumped into the driver's seat. "Nothing could compare to the man I love," I promised him.

Overwhelming love poured from Chaz's eyes as they

stayed latched on mine. "Take me home, Jamie. In case you've forgotten, we've got some celebrating to do."

Never had I ever started up a vehicle and pulled out of a parking lot so fast.

That ring burned a hole in my pocket, but first things first.

I had a man to love on and show yet again he was worth all the stars in my night sky.

THE END

About the Author

Spicy romance author Lynn Burke believes everyone deserves healing and a happily ever after. She loves writing hot, inclusive stories of various pairings or triplings and creates characters who will steal your heart.

She is a USA Today Bestselling author, a wrangler of her three spawn, and a farmer's daughter who grows organic food. To escape reality, she hides in a quiet corner with her nose in a book.

You can find more about Lynn at her website: www.authorlynnburke.com

Also By Lynn Burke

Abel's Obsession

Divulging Secrets

Healing Storms

In Between

Reluctant Lumberjack

Resisting his Mate

Billion Dollar Love Anthology

Blood Born Series

Bonds of Worship Series

Dark Leopards MC

Darkest Desires Series

Devil's Outlaws MC

Elite Escort Series

Elite Escorts MM Series

Fallen Gliders MC

Forbidden Obsession Duet

Found by Fate Series

Midnight Sun Series

Missing Link Series

Pippen Creek Series

Risso Family Series

Sandy Ridge Series

Sinful Nature Series

Vicious Vipers MC